DEAD MA

Other Brother Cadfael novels
by the same author:

ELLIS PETERS

DEAD MAN'S RANSOM

Futura

A Futura Book

ISBN 0 7088 2598 2

Printed in Great Britain by
Hazell Watson & Viney Limited,
Member of the BPCC Group,
Aylesbury, Bucks

Futura Publications
A Division of
Macdonald & Co (Publishers) Ltd
Greater London House
Hampstead Road
London NW1 7QX
A BPCC plc Company

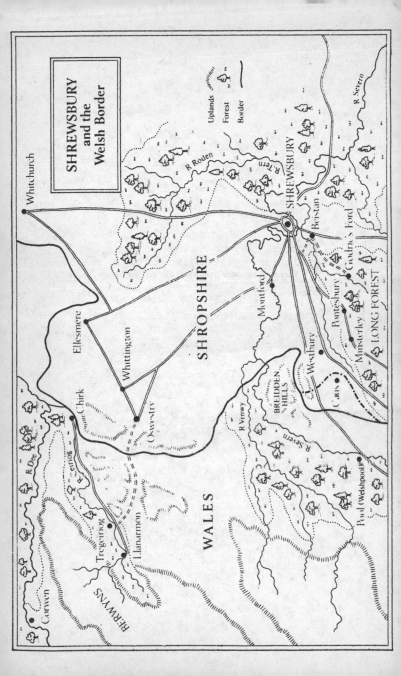

SHREWSBURY
and the Welsh Border

Uplands
Forest
Border

Whitchurch

R. Roden

R. Tern

R. Severn

SHREWSBURY

Bestan

Godric's Ford

Ellesmere

Whittington

SHROPSHIRE

Montford

Pontesbury

LONG FOREST

Minsterley

Chirk

Oswestry

Westbury

BREIDDEN
HILLS

Cluis

R. Dee

R. Ceiriog

R. Vrnwy

R. Severn

Tregeiriog

Llanarmon

Corwen

BERWYNS

WALES

Pool (Welshpool)

ONE

On that day, which was the seventh of February of the year of Our Lord 1141, they had offered special prayers at every office, not for the victory of one party or the defeat of another in the battlefields of the north, but for better counsel, for reconciliation, for the sparing of blood-letting and the respect of life between men of the same country – all desirable consummations, as Brother Cadfael sighed to himself even as he prayed, but very unlikely to be answered in this torn and fragmented land with any but a very dusty answer. Even God needs some consideration and support from his material to make reasoning and benign creatures of men.

Shrewsbury had furnished King Stephen with a creditable force to join his muster for the north, where the earls of Chester and Lincoln, ambitious half-brothers, had flouted the king's grace and moved to set up their own palatine, and with much in their favour, too. The parish part of the great church was fuller than usual even at the monastic offices, with anxious wives, mothers and grandsires fervent in praying for their menfolk. Not every man who had marched with Sheriff Gilbert Prestcote and his deputy, Hugh Beringar, would come home again unscathed to Shrewsbury. Rumours flew, but news was in very poor supply. Yet word had filtered through that Chester and Lincoln, long lurking in neutrality between rival claimants for the crown, having ambitious plans of their own in defiance of both, had made up their minds in short order when menaced by King Stephen's approach, and sent hotfoot for help from the champions of his antagonist, the Empress Maud. Thus committing themselves for the future, perhaps, so deep that they might yet live to regret it.

Cadfael came out from Vespers gloomily doubting the force, and

7

even the honesty, of his own prayers, however he had laboured to give them heart. Men drunk with ambition and power do not ground their weapons, nor stop to recognise the fellow-humanity of those they are about to slay. Not here – not yet. Stephen had gone rampaging north with his muster, a huge, gallant, simple, swayable soul roused to rage by Chester's ungrateful treachery, and drawn after him many, and many a wiser and better balanced man who could have done his reasoning for him, had he taken a little more time for thought. The issue hung in the balance and the good men of Shropshire were committed with their lord. So was Cadfael's close friend, Hugh Beringar of Maesbury, deputy sheriff of the shire, and his wife must be anxiously waiting there in the town for news. Hugh's son, a year old now, was Cadfael's godson, and he had leave to visit him whenever he wished, a godfather's duties being important and sacred. Cadfael turned his back on supper in the refectory, and made his way out of the abbey gates, along the highway between the abbey mill and mill-pond on his left, and the belt of woodland sheltering the main abbey gardens of the Gaye on his right, over the bridge that spanned the Severn, glimmering in the wintry, starlit frost, and in through the great town gate.

There were torches burning at the door of Hugh's house by Saint Mary's church and beyond, at the High Cross, it seemed to Cadfael that there were more folk abroad and stirring than was usual at this hour of a winter evening. The faintest shiver of excitement hung in the air, and as soon as his foot touched the doorstone Aline came flying to the doorway with open arms. When she knew him her face remained pleased and welcoming, but nonetheless lost in an instant its special burning brightness.

'Not Hugh!' said Cadfael ruefully, knowing for whom the door had been thus thrown wide. 'Not yet. Is there news, then? Are they homing?'

'Will Warden sent word an hour ago, before the light was quite gone. They sighted steel from the towers, a good way off then, but by now they must be in the castle foregate. The gate's open for them. Come in to the fire, Cadfael, and stay for him.' She drew him in by the hands, and closed the door resolutely on the night and her own aching impatience. 'He is there,' she said, catching in

8

Cadfael's face the reflection of her own partisan love and anxiety. 'They caught his colours. And the array in good order. Yet it cannot be quite as it went forth, that I know.'

No, never that. Those who go forth to the battle never return without holes in their ranks, like gaping wounds. Pity of all pities that those who lead never learn, and the few wise men among those who follow never quite avail to teach. But faith given and allegiance pledged are stronger than fear, thought Cadfael, and that, perhaps, is virtue, even in the teeth of death. Death, after all, is the common expectation from birth. Neither heroes nor cowards can escape it.

'He's sent no word ahead,' he asked, 'of how the day went?'

'None. But the rumour is it did not go well.' She said it firmly and freely, putting back with a small hand the pale gold hair from her forehead. A slender girl, still only twenty-one years old and mother of a year-old son and as fair as her husband was black-avised. The shy manner of her girlhood years had matured into a gentle dignity. 'This is a very wanton tide that flows and carries us all, here in England,' she said. 'It cannot always run one way, there must be an ebb.' She was brisk and practical about it, whatever that firm face cost her. 'You haven't eaten, you can't have stayed for supper,' she said, the housewife complete. 'Sit there and nurse your godson a little while, and I'll bring you meat and ale.'

The infant Giles, formidably tall for a year old when he was reared erect by holding to benches and trestles and chests to keep his balance, made his way carefully but with astonishing rapidity round the room to the stool by the fireside, and clambered unaided into Cadfael's rusty black lap. He had a flow of words, mostly of his own invention, though now and then a sound made sudden adult sense. His mother talked to him much, so did her woman Constance, his devoted slave, and this egg of the nobility listened and made voluble response. Of lordly scholars, thought Cadfael, rounding his arms to cradle the solid weight comfortably, we can never have too many. Whether he takes to the church or the sword, he'll never be the worse for a quick and ready mind. Like a pair of hound puppies nursed in the lap, Hugh's heir gave off glowing warmth, and the baked-bread scent of young and untainted flesh.

'He won't sleep,' said Aline, coming with a wooden tray to set it

9

on the chest close to the fire, 'for he knows there's something in the wind. Never ask me how, I've said no word to him, but he knows. There, give him to me now, and take your meal. We may have a long wait, for they'll see all provided at the castle before ever Hugh comes to me.'

It was more than an hour before Hugh came. By then Constance had whisked away the remains of Cadfael's supper, and carried off a drooping princeling, who could not keep his eyes open any longer for all his contrivances, but slept in sprawled abandon in her arms as she lifted him. For all Cadfael's sharp hearing, it was Aline who first pricked up her head and rose, catching the light footsteps in the doorway. Her radiant smile faltered suddenly, for the feet trod haltingly.

'He's hurt!'

'Stiff from a long ride,' said Cadfael quickly. 'His legs serve him. Go, run, whatever's amiss will mend.'

She ran, and Hugh entered into her arms. As soon as she had viewed him from head to foot, weary and weather-stained as he was, and found him whole, whatever lesser injuries he might be carrying, she became demure, brisk and calm, and would make no extravagant show of anxiety, though she watched him every moment from behind the fair shield of her wifely face. A small man, lightly built, not much taller than his wife, black-haired, black-browed. His movements lacked their usual supple ease, and no wonder after so long in the saddle, and his grin was brief and wry as he kissed his wife, drove a fist warmly into Cadfael's shoulder, and dropped with a great, hoarse sigh on to the cushioned bench beside the fire, stretching out his booted feet gingerly, the right decidedly with some pain. Cadfael kneeled, and eased off the stiff, ice-rimmed boots that dripped melting rivulets into the rushes.

'Good Christian soul!' said Hugh, leaning to clap a hand on his friend's tonsure. 'I could never have reached them myself. God, but I'm weary! No matter, that's the first need met – they're home and so am I.'

Constance came sailing in with food and a hot posset of wine, Aline with his gown and to rid him of his leather coat. He had ridden light the last stages, shedding his mail. He scrubbed with both hands at cheeks stiffened from the cold, twitched his

10

shoulders pleasurably in the warmth of the fire, and drew in a great, easing breath. They watched him eat and drink with hardly a word spoken. Even the voice stiffens and baulks after long exertion and great weariness. When he was ready the cords of his throat would soften and warm, and words find their way out without creaking.

'Your man-child held open his eyelids,' said Aline cheerfully, eyeing his every least move as he ate and warmed, 'until he could prop them up no longer, even with his fingers. He's well and grown even in this short while – Cadfael will tell you. He goes on two feet now and makes nothing of a fall or two.' She did not offer to wake and bring him; clearly there was no place here tonight for matters of childhood, however dear.

Hugh sat back from his meal, yawned hugely, smiled upwards suddenly at his wife, and drew her down to him in his arm. Constance bore away the tray and refilled the cup, and closed the door quietly on the room where the boy slept.

'Never fret for me, love,' said Hugh, clasping Aline to his side. 'I'm saddle-sore and bruised, but nothing worse. But a fall or two we have certainly taken. No easy matter to rise, neither. Oh, I've brought back most of the men we took north with us, but not all – not all! Not the chief – Gilbert Prestcote's gone. Taken, not dead, I hope and think, but whether it's Robert of Gloucester or the Welsh that hold him – I wish I knew.'

'The Welsh?' said Cadfael, pricking his ears. 'How's that? Owain Gwynedd has never put his hand in the fire for the empress? After all his careful holding off, and the gains it's brought him? He's no such fool! Why should he aid either of his enemies? He'd be more like to leave them free to cut each other's throats.'

'Spoke like a good Christian brother,' said Hugh, with a brief, grey smile, and fetched a grunt and a blush out of Cadfael to his small but welcome pleasure. 'No, Owain has judgement and sense, but alas for him, he has a brother. Cadwaladr was there with a swarm of his archers, and Madog ap Meredith of Powys with him, hot for plunder, and they've sunk their teeth into Lincoln and swept the field clear of any prisoner who promises the means of ransom, even the half-dead. And I doubt they've got Gilbert among the rest.' He shifted, easing his stiff, sore body in the

11

cushions. 'Though it's not the Welsh,' he said grimly, 'that have got the greatest prize. Robert of Gloucester is halfway to his own city this night with a prisoner worth this kingdom to deliver up to the Empress Maud. God knows what follows now, but I know what my work must be. My sheriff is out of the reckoning, and there's none now at large to name his successor. This shire is mine to keep, as best I may, and keep it I will, till fortune turns her face again. King Stephen is taken at Lincoln, and carried off prisoner to Gloucester.'

Once his tongue was loosed he had need to tell the whole of it, for his own enlightenment as much as theirs. He was the sole lord of a county now, holding and garrisoning it on the behalf of a king in eclipse, and his task was to nurse and guard it inviolate within its boundaries, until it could serve again beyond them for an effective lord.

'Ranulf of Chester slipped out of Lincoln castle and managed to get out of a hostile town before ever we got near, and off to Robert of Gloucester in a great hurry, with pledges of allegiance to the empress in exchange for help against us. And Chester's wife is Robert's daughter, when all's said, and he'd left her walled up in the castle with the earl of Lincoln and his wife, and the whole town in arms and seething round them. That was a welcome indeed, when Stephen got his muster there, the city fawned on him. Poor wretches, they've paid for it since. Howbeit, there we were, the town ours and the castle under siege, and winter on our side, any man would have said, with the distance Robert had to come, and the snow and the floods to hold him. But the man's none so easily held.'

'I never was there in the north,' said Cadfael, with a glint in his eye and a stirring in his blood that he had much ado to subdue. His days in arms were over, forsworn long since, but he could not help prickling to the sting of battle, when his friends were still venturing. 'It's a hill city, Lincoln, so they say. And the garrison penned close. It should have been easy to hold the town, Robert or no Robert. What went astray?'

'Why, granted we under-valued Robert, as always, but that need not have been fatal. The rains there'd been up there, the river round the south and west of the town was up in flood, the bridge

12

guarded, and the ford impassable. But Robert passed it, whether or no! Into the flood with him, and what could they do but come after? "A way forward, but no way back!" he says – so one of our prisoners told us. And what with the solid wall of them, they got across with barely a man swept away. Oh, surely they still had the uphill way, out of that drowned plain to our hilltop – if Stephen were not Stephen! With the mass of them camped below in the wet fields and all the omens at Mass against him – you know he half-regards such warnings – what say you he'll do? Why, with that mad chivalry of his, for which God knows I love him though I curse him, he orders his array down from the height into the plain, to meet his enemy on equal terms.'

Hugh heaved his shoulders back against the solid brace of the wall, hoisted his agile brows and grinned, torn between admiration and exasperation.

'They'd drawn up on the highest and driest bit of land they could find, in what was a half-frozen marsh. Robert had all the disinherited, Maud's liegemen who had lost lands eastward for her sake, drawn up in the first line, horsed, with nothing to lose and all to gain, and vengeance the first of all. And our knights had every man his all to lose and nothing to gain, and felt themselves far from their homes and lands, and aching to get back and strengthen their own fences. And there were these hoards of Welsh, hungry for plunder, and their own goods and gear safe as sanctuary in the west, with no man threatening. What should we look for? When the disinherited hit our horse five earls broke under the shock and ran. On the left Stephen's Flemings drove the Welshmen back: but you know their way, they went but far enough and easily enough to mass again without loss, and back they came, archers almost to a man, able to pick their ground and their prey, and when the Flemish footmen ran, so did their captains – William of Ypres and Ten Eyck and all. Stephen was left unhorsed with us, the remnant of his horse and foot, around him. They rolled over us. It was then I lost sight of Gilbert. No marvel, it was hand to hand chaos, no man saw beyond the end of his sword or dagger, whatever he had in his hand to keep his head. Stephen still had his sword then. Cadfael, I swear to you, you never saw such a man in battle once roused, for all his easy goodwill takes so much rousing. It was rather the siege of a castle than the overcoming of a man. There was a wall round him of the men he had slain, those coming had to clamber over it, and went to build it higher. Chester came after him—give him his due, there's not much can frighten Ranulf—and he might have been another stone in the rampart, but that the king's sword shattered. There was one somewhere close to him thrust a Danish axe into his hand in its place, but Chester had leaped back out of reach. And then someone clear of the mêlée grubbed a great stone out of the ground, and hurled it at Stephen from aside. It struck him down flatlings, clean out of his wits, and they swarmed over him and pinned him hand and foot while he was senseless. And I went down under another wave,' said Hugh ruefully, 'and was trampled below better men's bodies, to come to myself in the best time to make vantage of it, after they'd dragged the king away and swarmed into the town to strip it bare, and before they came back to comb the battlefield for whatever was worth picking up. So I mustered what was left of our own, more than ever I expected, and hauled them off far enough to be out of reach, while I and one or two with me looked for Gilbert. We did not find him and when they began to come back sated out of the city, scavenging, we drew off to bring back such as we had. What else could we have done?'

'Nothing to any purpose,' said Cadfael firmly. 'And thanks to God you were brought out man alive to do so much. If there's a place Stephen needs you now, it's here, keeping this shire for him.'

He was talking to himself. Hugh knew that already, or he would never have withdrawn from Lincoln. As for the slaughter there, no word was said. Better to make sure of bringing back all but a few of the solid townsfolk of Shrewsbury, his own special charge, and so he had done.

'Stephen's queen is in Kent, and mistress of Kent, with a strong army, all the south and the east she holds,' said Hugh. 'She will shift every stone between her and London, but she'll get Stephen out of captivity somehow. It is not an ending. A reverse can be reversed. A prisoner can be loosed from prison.'

'Or exchanged,' said Cadfael, but very dubiously. 'There's no great prize taken on the king's side? Though I doubt if the empress would let go of Stephen for any three of her best lords, even Robert himself, helpless as she'd be without him. No, she'll keep a fast hold of her prisoner, and make headlong for the throne. And do you see the princes of the church standing long in her way?'

'Well,' said Hugh, stretching his slight body wincingly, discovering new bruises, 'my part at least I know. It's my writ that runs here in Shropshire now as the king's writ, and I'll see to it this shire, at least, is kept for the king.'

He came down to the abbey, two days later, to attend the Mass Abbot Radulfus had decreed for the souls of all those dead at Lincoln, on both parts, and for the healing of England's raw and festering wounds. In particular there were prayers to be offered for the wretched citizens of the northern city, prey to vengeful armies and plundered of all they had, many even of their lives, and many more fled into the wilds of the winter countryside. Shropshire stood nearer to the fighting now than it had been for three years, being neighbour to an earl of Chester elated by success and greedy for still more lands. Every one of Hugh's depleted garrisons stood to arms, ready to defend its threatened security.

They were out from Mass, and Hugh had lingered in speech with the abbot in the great court, when there was sudden bustle in the arch of the gatehouse, and a small procession entered from the Foregate. Four sturdy countrymen in homespun came striding confidently, two with bows strung and slung ready for action, one shouldering a billhook, and the fourth a long-handled pikel. Between them, with two of her escort on either side, rode a plump middle-aged woman on a diminutive mule, and wearing the black habit of a Benedictine nun. The white bands of her wimple framed a rounded rosy face, well-fleshed and well-boned, and lit by a pair of bright brown eyes. She was booted like a man, and her habit kilted for riding, but she swung it loose with one motion of a broad hand as she dismounted, and stood alert and discreet, looking calmly about her in search of someone in authority.

'We have a visiting sister,' said the abbot mildly, eyeing her with interest, 'but one that I do not know.'

Brother Cadfael, crossing the court without haste towards the garden and the herbarium, had also marked the sudden brisk bustle at the gate, and checked at the sight of a well-remembered figure. He had encountered this lady once before, and found her

15

well worth remembering. And it seemed that she, also, recalled their meeting with pleasure, for the moment her eyes lit upon him the spark of recognition flashed in them, and she came at once towards him. He went to meet her gladly. Her rustic bodyguard, satisfied at having delivered her successfully where she would be, stood by the gatehouse, straddling the cobbles complacently, and by no means intimidated or impressed by their surroundings.

'I thought I should know that gait,' said the lady with satisfaction. 'You are Brother Cadfael, who came once on business to our cell. I'm glad to have found you to hand, I know no one else here. Will you make me known to your abbot?'

'Proudly,' said Cadfael, 'and he's regarding you this minute from the corner of the cloister. It's two years now . . . Am I to tell him he's honoured by a visit from Sister Avice?'

'Sister Magdalen,' she said demurely and faintly smiled; and when she smiled, however briefly and decorously, the sudden dazzling dimple he remembered flashed like a star in her weathered cheek. He had wondered then whether she had not better find some way of exorcising it in her new vocation, or whether it might not still be the most formidable weapon in her armoury. He was aware that he blinked, and that she noted it. There was always something conspiratorial in Avice of Thornbury that made every man feel he was the only one in whom she confided. 'And my errand,' she said practically, 'is really to Hugh Beringar, for I hear Gilbert Prestcote did not come back from Lincoln. They told us in the Foregate we should find him here, or we were bound up to the castle to look for him.'

'He is here,' said Cadfael, 'fresh from Mass, and talking with Abbot Radulfus. Over my shoulder you'll see them both.'

She looked, and by the expression of her face she approved. Abbot Radulfus was more than commonly tall, erect as a lance, and sinewy, with a lean hawk-face and a calmly measuring eye; and Hugh, if he stood a whole head shorter and carried but light weight, if he spoke quietly and made no move to call attention to himself, nevertheless seldom went unnoticed. Sister Magdalen studied him from head to heel with one flash of her brown eyes. She was a judge of a man, and knew one when she saw him.

'Very well so!' she said, nodding. 'Come, and I'll pay my

respects.'

Radulfus marked their first move towards him and went to meet them, with Hugh at his shoulder.

'Father Abbot,' said Cadfael, 'here is come Sister Magdalen of our order, from the cell of Polesworth which lies some miles to the south-west, in the forest at Godric's Ford. And her business is also with Hugh Beringar as sheriff of this shire.'

She made a very graceful reverence and stooped to the abbot's hand. 'Truly, what I have to tell concerns all here who have to do with order and peace, Father. Brother Cadfael here has visited our cell, and knows how we stand in these troublous times, solitary and so close to Wales. He can advise and explain, if I fall short.'

'You are welcome, sister,' said Radulfus, measuring her as shrewdly as she had measured him. 'Brother Cadfael shall be of our counsel. I trust you will be my guest for dinner. And for your guards – for I see they are devoted in attendance on you – I will give orders for their entertainment. And if you are not so far acquainted, here at my side is Hugh Beringar, whom you seek.'

Though that cheek was turned away from him, Cadfael was certain that her dimple sparkled as she turned to Hugh and made her formal acknowledgement. 'My lord, I was never so happy,' she said – and whether that was high courtesy or mischief might still be questioned – 'as to meet with you before, it was with your sheriff I once had some speech. As I have heard he did not return with you and may be prisoner, and for that I am sorry.'

'I, too,' said Hugh. 'As I hope to redeem him, if chance offers. I see from your escort, sister, that you have had cause to move with caution through the forest. I think that is also my business, now I am back.'

'Let us go into my parlour,' said the abbot, 'and hear what Sister Magdalen has to tell us. And, Brother Cadfael, will you bear word to Brother Denis that the best of our house is at the disposal of our sister's guards? And then come to join us, for your knowledge may be needed.'

She was seated a little withdrawn from the fire when Cadfael entered the abbot's parlour some minutes later, her feet drawn trimly under the hem of her habit, her back erect against the

17

panelled wall. The more closely and the longer he viewed her, the more warmly did he remember her. She had been for many years, from her beautiful youth, a baron's mistress, accepting that situation as an honest business agreement, a fair return for her body to give her escape from her poverty and cultivation for her mind. And she had held to her bargain loyally, even affectionately, as long as her lord remained alive. The loss of one profession offering scope for her considerable talents had set her looking about, with her customary resolution, for another as rewarding, at an age when such openings may be few indeed. The superior at Godric's Ford, first, and the prioress of Polesworth after, however astonished they might have been at being confronted with such a postulant, must have seen something in Avice of Thornbury well worth acquiring for the order. A woman of her word, ungrudging, to her first allegiance, she would be as good as her word now to this new attachment. Whether it could have been called a vocation in the first place might seem very doubtful, but with application and patience she would make it so.

'When this matter of Lincoln blazed up as it did in January,' she said, 'we got rumour that certain of the Welsh were ready to rise in arms. Not, I suppose, for any partisan loyalty, but for plunder to be had when these two powers collided. Prince Cadwaladr of Gwynedd was mustering a war-band, and the Welsh of Powys rose to join him, and it was said they would march to aid the earl of Chester. So before the battle we had our warning.'

It was she who had heeded it. Who else, in that small nest of holy women, could have sensed how the winds blew between claimants for the crown, between Welsh and English, between ambitious earl and greedy tribesman?

'Therefore, Father, it was no great surprise to us, some four days ago, when a lad from an assart west of us came running in haste to tell us how his father's cot and holding was laid waste, his family fled eastward, and how a Welsh raiding party was drinking its fill in what remained of his home, and boasting how it would disembowel the nunnery of Godric's Ford. Huntsmen on their way home will not despise a few stray head of game to add to their booty. We had not the news of the defeat of Lincoln then,' she said, meeting Hugh's attentive gaze, 'but we made our judgements accordingly and took heed. Cadwaladr's shortest way home with his plunder to his castle at Aberystwyth skirts Shrewsbury close. Seemingly he still feared to come too near the town, even with the garrison thinned as he knew it must be. But he felt safer with us in the forest. And with only a handful of women to deal with, it was worth his while to spend a day in sport, and strip us bare.'

'And this was four days ago?' asked Hugh, sharply intent.

'Four when the boy came. He's safe enough, and so is his sire, but their cattle are gone, driven off westward. Three days, when they reached us. We had a day to prepare.'

'This was a despicable undertaking,' said Radulfus with anger and disgust, 'to fasten like cowards upon a household of defenceless women. Great shame to the Welsh or any others who attempt such infamies. And we here knowing nothing of your need!'

'Never fear, Father, we have weathered this storm well enough. Our house yet stands, and has not been plundered, nor harm come to any of our women, and barely a scratch or two among the forest menfolk. And we were not quite defenceless. They came on the western side, and our brook runs between. Brother Cadfael knows the lie of the land there.'

'The brook would be a very frail barrier most of the year,' said Cadfael doubtfully. 'But we have had great rains this winter season. But there's both the ford and the bridge to guard.'

'True, but it takes no time there among good neighbours to raise a very fair muster. We are well thought of among the forest folk, and they are stout men.' Four of the stout men of her army were regaling themselves in the gatehouse with meat and bread and ale at this moment, proud and content, set up in their own esteem, very properly, by their own exploits. 'The brook was high in flood already, but we contrived to pit the ford, in case they should still venture it, and then John Miller opened up all his sluices to swell the waters. As for the bridge, we sawed through the wood of the piers, leaving them only the last holt, and fastened ropes from them into the bushes. You'll recall the banks are well treed both sides. We could pluck the piers loose from cover whenever we saw fit. And all the men of the forest came with bills and dung-forks and bows to line our bank, and deal with any who did get over.'

No question who had generalled that formidable reception. There she sat, solid, placid and comely, like a well-blessed village matron talking of the doings of her children and grandchildren, fond and proud of their precocious achievements, but too wise to let them see it.

'The foresters,' she said, 'are as good archers as you will find anywhere, we had them spaced among the trees, all along our bank. And the men of the other bank were drawn aside in cover, to speed the enemy's going when he ran.'

The abbot was regarding her with a warily respectful face, and brows that signalled his guarded wonder. 'I recall,' he said, 'that Mother Mariana is old and frail. This attack must have caused her great distress and fear. Happy for her that she had you, and could delegate her powers to so stout and able a deputy.'

Sister Magdalen's benign smile might, Cadfael thought, be discreet cover for her memory of Mother Mariana distracted and helpless with dread at the threat. But all she said was: 'Our superior was not well at that time, but praise be, she is now restored. We entreated her to take with her the elder sisters, and shut themselves up in the chapel, with such sacred valuables as we have, and there to pray for our safe deliverance. Which doubtless availed us above our bills and bows, for all passed without harm to us.'

'Yet their prayers did not turn the Welsh back short of the planned attempt, I doubt,' said Hugh, meeting her guileless eyes with an appreciative smile. 'I see I shall have to mend a few fences down there. What followed? You say all fell out well. You used those ropes of yours?'

'We did. They came thick and fast, we let them load the bridge almost to the near bank, and then plucked the piers loose. Their first wave went down into the flood, and a few who tried the ford lost their footing in our pits, and were swept away. And after our archers had loosed their first shafts, the Welsh turned tail. The lads we had in cover on the other side took after them and sped them on their way. John Miller has closed his sluices now. Give us a couple of dry weeks, and we'll have the bridge up again. The Welsh left three men dead, drowned in the brook, the rest they hauled out half-sodden, and dragged them away with them when they ran. All

20

but one, and he's the occasion for this journey of mine. There's a very fine young fellow,' she said, 'was washed downstream, and we pulled him out bloated with water and far gone, if we had not emptied him, and pounded him alive to tell the tale. You may send and take him off our hands whenever you please. Things being as it seems they are, you may well have a use for him.'

'For any Welsh prisoner,' said Hugh, glowing. 'Where have you stowed him?'

'John Miller has him under lock and key, and guarded. I did not venture to try and bring him to you, for good reason. He's sudden as a kingfisher and slippery as a fish, and short of tying him hand and foot I doubt if we could have held him.'

'We'll undertake to bring him away safely,' said Hugh heartily. 'What manner of man do you make of him? And has he given you a name?'

'He'll say no word but in Welsh, and I have not the knowledge of that tongue, nor has any of us. But he's young, princely provided, and lofty enough in his manner to be princely born, no common kern. He may prove valuable if it comes to an exchange.'

'I'll come and fetch him away tomorrow,' promised Hugh, 'and thank you for him heartily. By morning I'll have a company ready to ride. As well I should look to all that border, and if you can bide overnight, sister, we can escort you home in safety.'

'Indeed it would be wise,' said the abbot. 'Our guest-hall and all we have is open to you, and your neighbours who have done you such good service are equally welcome. Far better return with the assurance of numbers and arms. Who knows if there may not be marauding parties still lurking in the forest, if they're grown so bold?'

'I doubt it,' she said. 'We saw no sign of it on the way here. It was the men themselves would not let me venture alone. But I will accept your hospitality, Father, with pleasure, and be as grateful for your company, my lord,' she said, smiling thoughtfully at Hugh, 'on the way home.'

'Though, faith,' said Hugh to Cadfael, as they crossed the court together, leaving Sister Magdalen to dine as the abbot's guest, 'it would rather become me to give her the generalship of all the forest

21

than offer her any protection of mine. We should have had her at Lincoln, where our enemies crossed the floods, as hers failed to do. Riding south with her tomorrow will certainly be pleasure, it might well be profit. I'll bend a devout ear to any counsel that lady chooses to dispense.'

'You'll be giving pleasure as well as receiving it,' said Cadfael frankly. 'She may have taken vows of chastity, and what she swears she'll keep. But she has not sworn never to take delight in the looks and converse and company of a proper man. I doubt they'll ever bring her to consent to that, she'd think it a waste and a shame, so to throw God's good gifts in his teeth.'

The party mustered after Prime next morning, Sister Magdalen and her four henchmen, Hugh and his half-dozen armed guards from the castle garrison. Brother Cadfael stood to watch them gather and mount, and took a warmly appreciative leave of the lady.

'I doubt I shall be hard put to it, though,' he admitted, 'to learn to call you by your new name.'

At that her dimple dipped and flashed, and again vanished. 'Ah, that! You are thinking that I never yet repented of anything I did – and I confess I don't recall such a thing myself. No, but it was such a comfort and satisfaction to the women. They took me to their hearts so joyfully, the sweet things, a fallen sister retrieved. I couldn't forbear giving them what they wanted and thought fitting. I am their special pride, they boast of me.'

'Well they may,' said Cadfael, 'seeing you just drove back pillage, ravishment and probable murder from their nest.'

'Ah, that they feel to be somewhat unwomanly, though glad enough of the result. The doves were all aflutter – but then, I was never a dove,' said Sister Magdalen, 'and it's only the men truly admire the hawk in me.'

And she smiled, mounted her little mule and rode off homeward surrounded by men who already admired her, and men who were more than willing to offer admiration. In the court or in the cloister, Avice of Thornbury would never pass by without turning men's heads to follow her.

TWO

Before nightfall Hugh was back with his prisoner, having prospected the western fringe of the Long Forest and encountered no more raiding Welshmen and no masterless men living wild. Brother Cadfael saw them pass by the abbey gatehouse on their way up through the town to the castle, where this possibly valuable Welsh youth could be held in safe-keeping and, short of a credible parole, doubtless under lock and key in some sufficiently impenetrable cell. Hugh could not afford to lose him.

Cadfael caught but a passing glimpse of him as they rode by in the early dusk. It seemed he had given some trouble on the way, for his hands were tied, his horse on a leading rein, his feet roped into the stirrups and an archer rode suggestively close at his rear. If these precautions were meant to secure him, they had succeeded, but if to intimidate, as the young man himself appeared to suppose, they had signally failed, for he went with a high, disdainful impudence, stretching up tall and whistling as he went, and casting over his shoulder at the archer occasional volleys of Welsh, which the man might not have endured so stolidly had he been able to understand their purport as well as Cadfael did. He was, in fact, a very forward and uppish young fellow, this prisoner, though it might have been partly bravado.

He was also a very well-looking young man, middling tall for a Welshman, with the bold cheekbones and chin and the ruddy colouring of his kind, and a thick tangle of black curls that fell very becomingly about his brow and ears, blown by the south-west wind, for he wore no cap. Tethered hands and feet did not hamper him from sitting his horse like a centaur, and the voice that teased his guards in insolent Welsh was light and clear. Sister Magdalen

23

had said truly that his gear was princely, and his manner proclaimed him certainly proud and probably, thought Cadfael, spoiled to the point of ruin. Not a particularly rare condition in a well-made, personable and probably only son.

They passed, and the prisoner's loud, melodious whistle of defiance died gradually along the Foregate and over the bridge. Cadfael went back to his workshop in the herbarium, and blew up his brazier to boil a fresh elixir of horehound for the winter coughs and colds.

Hugh came down from the castle next morning with a request to borrow Brother Cadfael on his captive's behalf, for it seemed the boy had a raw gash in his thigh, ripped against a stone in the flood, and had gone to some pains to conceal it from the nuns.

'Ask me,' said Hugh, grinning, 'he'd have died rather than bare his hams for the ladies to poultice. And give him his due, though the tear is none so grave, the few miles he rode yesterday must have cost him dear in pain, and he never gave a sign. And blushed like a girl when we did notice him favouring the raw cheek, and made him strip.'

'And left his sore undressed overnight? Never tell me! So why do you need me?' asked Cadfael shrewdly.

'Because you speak good Welsh, and Welsh of the north, and he's certainly from Gwynedd, one of Cadwaladr's boys – though you may as well make the lad comfortable while you're about it. We speak English to him, and he shakes his head and answers with nothing but Welsh, but for all that, there's a saucy look in his eye that tells me he understands very well, and is having a game with us. So come and speak English to him, and trip the bold young sprig headlong when he thinks his Welsh insults can pass for civilities.'

'He'd have had short shrift from Sister Magdalen,' said Cadfael thoughtfully, 'if she'd known of his hurt. All his blushes wouldn't have saved him.' And he went off willingly enough to see Brother Oswin properly instructed as to what needed attention in the workshop, before setting out with Hugh to the castle. A fair share of curiosity, and a little over-measure, was one of the regular items in his confessions. And after all, he was a Welshman; somewhere in the tangled genealogies of his nation, this obdurate boy might be his distant kin.

They had a healthy respect for their prisoner's strength, wit and ingenuity, and had him in a windowless cell, though decently provided. Cadfael went in to him alone, and heard the door locked upon them. There was a lamp, a floating wick in a saucer of oil, sufficient for seeing, since the pale stone of the walls reflected the light from all sides. The prisoner looked askance at the Benedictine habit, unsure what this visit predicted. In answer to what was clearly a civil greeting in English, he replied as courteously in Welsh, but in answer to everything else he shook his dark head apologetically, and professed not to understand a word of it. He responded readily enough, however, when Cadfael unpacked his scrip and laid out his salves and cleansing lotions and dressings. Perhaps he had found good reason in the night to be glad of having submitted his wound to tending, for this time he stripped willingly, and let Cadfael renew the dressing. He had aggravated his hurt with riding, but rest would soon heal it. He had pure, spare flesh, lissome and firm. Under the skin the ripple of muscles was smooth as cream.

'You were foolish to bear this,' said Cadfael in casual English, 'when you could have had it healed and forgotten by now. Are you a fool? In your situation you'll have to learn discretion.'

'From the English,' said the boy in Welsh, and still shaking his head to show he understood no word of this, 'I have nothing to learn. And no, I am not a fool, or I should be as talkative as you, old shaven-head.'

'They would have given you good nursing at Godric's Ford,' went on Cadfael innocently. 'You wasted your few days there.'

'A parcel of silly women,' said the boy, brazen-faced, 'and old and ugly into the bargain.'

That was more than enough. 'A parcel of women,' said Cadfael in loud and indignant Welsh, 'who pulled you out of the flood and squeezed your lordship dry, and pummelled the breath back into you. And if you cannot find a civil word of thanks to them, in a language they'll understand, you are the most ungrateful brat who ever disgraced Wales. And that you may know it, my fine paladin, there's nothing older nor uglier than ingratitude. Nor sillier, either, seeing I'm minded to rip that dressing off you and let you burn for the graceless limb you are.'

The young man was bolt upright on his stone bench by this time, his mouth fallen open, his half-formed, comely face stricken into childishness. He stared and swallowed, and slowly flushed from breast to brow.

'Three times as Welsh as you, idiot child,' said Cadfael, cooling, 'being three times your age, as I judge. Now get your breath and speak, and speak English, for I swear if you ever speak Welsh to me again, short of extremes, I'll off and leave you to your own folly, and you'll find that cold company. Now, have we understood each other?'

The boy hovered for an instant on the brink of humiliation and rage, being unaccustomed to such falls, and then as abruptly redeemed himself by throwing back his head and bursting into a peal of laughter, both rueful for his own folly and appreciative of the trap into which he had stepped so blithely. Blessedly, he had the native good-nature that prevented his being quite spoiled.

'That's better,' said Cadfael disarmed. 'Fair enough to whistle and swagger to keep up your courage, but why pretend you knew no English? So close to the border, how long before you were bound to be smoked out?'

'Even a day or two more,' sighed the young man resignedly, 'and I might have found out what's in store for me.' His command of English was fluent enough, once he had consented to use it. 'I'm new to this. I wanted to get my bearings.'

'And the impudence was to stiffen your sinews, I suppose. Shame to miscall the holy women who saved your saucy life for you.'

'No one was meant to hear and understand,' protested the prisoner, and in the next breath owned magnanimously: 'But I'm not proud of it, either. A bird in a net, pecking every way, as much for spite as for escape. And then I didn't want to give away any word of myself until I had my captor's measure.'

'Or to admit to your value,' Cadfael hazarded shrewdly, 'for fear you should be held against a high ransom. No name, no rank, no way of putting a price on you?'

The black head nodded. He eyed Cadfael, and visibly debated within himself how much to concede, even now he was found out, and then as impulsively flung open the floodgates and let the words come hurtling out. 'To tell truth, long before ever we made that assault on the nunnery I'd grown very uneasy about the whole wild affair. Owain Gwynedd knew nothing of his brother's muster, and he'll be displeased with us all, and when Owain's displeased I mind my walking very carefully. Which is what I did *not* do when I went with Cadwaladr. I wish heartily that I had, and kept out of it. I never wanted to do harm to your ladies, but how could I draw back once I was in? And then to let myself be taken! By a handful of old women and peasants! I shall be in black displeasure at home, if not a laughing-stock.' He sounded disgusted rather than down-cast, and shrugged and grinned good-naturedly at the thought of being laughed at, but for all that, the prospect was painful. 'And if I'm to cost Owain high, there's another black stroke against me. He's not the man to take delight in paying out gold to buy back idiots.'

Certainly this young man improved upon acquaintance. He turned honestly and manfully from wanting to kick everyone else to acknowledging that he ought to be kicking himself. Cadfael warmed to him.

'Let me drop a word in your ear. The higher your value, the more welcome will you be to Hugh Beringar, who holds you here. And not for gold, either. There's a lord, the sheriff of this shire, who is most likely prisoner in Wales as you are here, and Hugh Beringar wants him back. If you can balance him, and he is found to be there alive, you may well be on your way home. At no cost to Owain Gwynedd, who never wanted to dip his fingers into that trough, and will be glad to show it by giving Gilbert Prestcote back to us.'

'You mean it?' The boy had brightened and flushed, wide-eyed. 'Then I should speak? I'm in a fair way to get my release and please both Welsh and English? That would be better deliverance than ever I expected.'

'Or deserved!' said Cadfael roundly, and watched the smooth brown neck stiffen in offence, and then suddenly relax again, as the black curls tossed and the ready grin appeared. 'Ah, well, you'll do! Tell your tale now, while I'm here, for I'm mightily curious, but tell it once. Let me fetch in Hugh Beringar, and let's all come to terms. Why lie here on stone and all but in the dark, when you could be stretching your legs about the castle wards?'

'I'm won!' said the boy, hopefully shining. 'Bring me to confession, and I'll hold nothing back.'

Once his mind was made up he spoke up cheerfully and volubly, an outward soul by nature, and very poorly given to silence. His abstention must have cost him prodigies of self-control. Hugh listened to him with an unrevealing face, but Cadfael knew by now how to read every least twitch of those lean, live brows and every glint in the black eyes.

'My name is Elis ap Cynan, my mother was cousin to Owain Gwynedd. He is my overlord, and he has over-watched me in the fosterage where he placed me when my father died. That is, with my uncle Griffith ap Meilyr, where I grew up with my cousin Eliud as brothers. Griffith's wife is also distant kin to the prince, and Griffith ranks high among his officers. Owain values us. He will not willingly leave me in captivity,' said the young man sturdily.

'Even though you hared off after his brother to a battle in which he wanted no part?' said Hugh, unsmiling but mild of voice.

'Even so,' persisted Elis firmly. 'Though if truth must out, I wish I never had, and am like to wish it even more earnestly when I must go back and face him. He'll have my hide, as like as not.' But he did not sound particularly depressed at the thought, and his sudden grin, tentative here in Hugh's untested presence, nevertheless would out for a moment. 'I was a fool. Not for the first time, and I daresay not the last. Eliud had more sense. He's grave and deep, he thinks like Owain. It was the first time we ever went different ways. I wish now I'd listened to him. I never knew him to be wrong when it came to it. But I was greedy to see action, and pig-headed, and I went.'

'And did you like the action you saw?' asked Hugh drily.

Elis gnawed a considering lip. 'The battle, that was fair fight, all in arms on both parts. You were there? Then you know yourself it was a great thing we did, crossing the river in flood, and standing to it in that frozen marsh as we were, sodden and shivering . . .' That exhilarating memory had suddenly recalled to him the second such crossing attempted, and its less heroic ending, the reverse of the dream of glory. Fished out like a drowning kitten, and hauled back to life face-down in muddy turf, hiccuping up the water he had swallowed, and being squeezed between the hands of a brawny forester. He caught Hugh's eye, and saw his own recollection reflected there, and had the grace to grin. 'Well, flood-water is on no man's side, it gulps down Welsh as readily as English. But I was not sorry then, not at Lincoln. It was a good fight. Afterwards – no – the town turned my stomach. If I'd known before, I should not have been there. But I was there, and I couldn't undo it.'

'You were sick at what was done to Lincoln,' Hugh pointed out reasonably, 'yet you went with the raiders to sack Godric's Ford.'

'What was I to do? Draw out against the lot of them, my own friends and comrades, stick my nose in the air and tell them what they intended was vile? I'm no such hero!' said Elis openly and heartily. 'Still, you'll allow I did no harm there to anyone, as it fell out. I was taken, and if it please you to say, serve me right, I'll take no offence. The end of it is, here I am and at your disposal. And I'm kin to Owain and when he knows I'm living he'll want me back.'

'Then you and I may very well come to a sensible agreement,' said Hugh, 'for I think it very likely that my sheriff, whom I want back just as certainly, is prisoner in Wales as you are here, and if that proves true, an exchange should be no great problem. I've no wish to keep you under lock and key in a cell, if you'll behave yourself seemly and wait the outcome. It's your quickest way home. Give me your parole not to attempt escape, or to go outside the wards here, and you may have the run of the castle.'

'With all my heart!' said Elis eagerly. 'I pledge you my word to attempt nothing, and set no foot outside your gates, until you have your man again, and give me leave to go.'

Cadfael paid a second visit next day, to make sure that his dressing had drawn the Welsh boy's ragged scratch together with no festering; but that healthy young flesh sprang together like the matching of lovers, and the slash would vanish with barely a scar.

He was an engaging youth, this Elis ap Cynan, readable like a book, open like a daisy at noon. Cadfael lingered to draw him out, which was easy enough, and brought a lavish and guileless harvest. All the more with nothing now to lose, and no man listening but a tolerant elder of his own race, he unfolded his leaves in garrulous innocence.

'I fell out badly with Eliud over this caper,' he said ruefully. 'He said it was poor policy for Wales, and whatever booty we might bring back with us, it would not be worth half the damage done. I should have known he'd be proved right, he always is. And yet no offence in it, that's the marvel! A man can't be angry with him – at least I can't.'

'Kin by fostering can be as close as brothers by blood, I know,' said Cadfael.

'Closer far than most brothers. Like twins, as we almost could be. Eliud had half an hour's start of me into the world, and has acted the elder ever since. He'll be half out of his wits over me now, for all he'll hear is that I was swept away in the brook. I wish we might make haste with this exchange, and let him know I'm still alive to plague him.'

'No doubt there'll be others besides your friend and cousin,' said Cadfael, 'fretting over your absence. No wife as yet?'

Elis made an urchin's grimace. 'No more than threatened. My elders betrothed me long ago as a child, but I'm in no haste. The common lot, it's what men do when they grow to maturity. There are lands and alliances to be considered.' He spoke of it as of the burden of the years, accepted but not welcomed. Quite certainly he was not in love with the lady. Probably he had known and played with her from infancy, and scarcely gave her a thought now, one way or the other.

'She may yet be a deal more troubled for you than you are for her,' said Cadfael.

'Ha!' said Elis on a sharp bark of laughter. 'Not she! If I had drowned in the brook they'd have matched her with another of suitable birth, and he would have done just as well. She never chose me, nor I her. Mind, I don't say she makes any objection, more than I do, we might both of us do very much worse.'

'Who is this fortunate lady?' Cadfael wondered drily.

'Now you grow prickly, because I am honest,' Elis reproved him airily. 'Did I ever say I was any great bargain? The girl is very well, as a matter of fact, a small, sharp, dark creature, quite handsome in her way, and if I must, then she'll do. Her father is Tudur ap Rhys, the lord of Tregeiriog in Cynllaith – a man of Powys, but close friend to Owain and thinks like him, and her mother was a woman of Gwynedd. Cristina, the girl is called. Her hand is regarded as a great prize,' said the proposed beneficiary without enthusiasm. 'So it is, but one I could have done without for a while yet.'

They were walking the outer ward to keep warm, for though the weather had turned fine it was also frosty, and the boy was loth to go indoors until he must. He went with his face turned up to the clear sky above the towers, and his step as light and springy as if he trod turf already.

'We could save you yet a while,' suggested Cadfael slyly, 'by spinning out this quest for our sheriff, and keeping you here single and snug as long as you please.'

'Oh, no!' Elis loosed a shout of laughter. 'Oh, no, not that! Better a wife in Wales than that fashion of freedom here. Though best of all Wales and no wife,' admitted the reluctant bridegroom, still laughing at himself. 'Marry or avoid, I suppose it's all one in the end. There'll still be hunting and arms and friends.'

A poor lookout, thought Cadfael, shaking his head, for that small, sharp, dark creature, Cristina daughter of Tudur, if she required more of her husband than a good-natured adolescent boy, willing to tolerate and accommodate her, but quite undisposed to love. Though many a decent marriage has started on no better ground, and burned into a glow later.

They had reached the archway into the inner ward in their circlings, and the slanting sunlight, chill and bright, shone through across their path. High in the corner tower within there, Gilbert Prestcote had made his family apartments, rather than maintain a house in the town. Between the merlons of the curtain wall the sun just reached the narrow doorway that led to the private rooms above, and the girl who emerged stepped full into the light. She was the very opposite of small, sharp and dark, being tall and slender like a silver birch, delicately oval of face, and dazzlingly fair. The sun in her uncovered, waving hair glittered as she hesitated an instant on the doorstone, and shivered lightly at the embrace of the frosty air.

Elis had seen her shimmering pallor take the light, and stood stock-still, gazing through the archway with eyes rounded and fixed, and mouth open. The girl hugged her cloak about her, closed the door at her back, and stepped out briskly across the ward towards the arch on her way out to the town. Cadfael had to pluck Elis by the sleeve to bring him out of his daze, and draw him onward out of her path, recalling him to the realisation that he was staring with embarrassing intensity, and might well give her offence if she noticed him. He moved obediently, but in a few more paces his chin went round on to his shoulder, and he checked again and stood, and could not be shifted further.

She came through the arch, half-smiling for pleasure in the fine morning, but still with something grave, anxious and sad in her countenance. Elis had not removed himself far enough to pass unobserved, she felt a presence close, and turned her head sharply. There was a brief moment when their eyes met, hers darkly blue as periwinkle flowers. The rhythm of her gait was broken, she checked at his gaze, and it almost seemed that she smiled at him hesitantly, as at someone recognised. Fine rose-colour mounted softly in her face, before she recollected herself, tore her gaze away, and went on more hurriedly towards the barbican.

Elis stood looking after her until she had passed through the gate and vanished from sight. His own face had flooded richly red.

'Who was that lady?' he asked, at once urgent and in awe.

'That lady,' said Cadfael, 'is daughter to the sheriff, that very man we're hoping to find somewhere alive in Welsh hold, and buy back with your captive person. Prestcote's wife is come to Shrewsbury on that very matter, and brought her step-daughter and her little son with her, in hopes soon to greet her lord again. This is his second lady. The girl's mother died without bringing him a son.'

'Do you know her name? The girl?'

'Her name,' said Cadfael, 'is Melicent.'

'Melicent!' the boy's lips shaped silently. Aloud he said, to the sky and the sun rather than to Cadfael: 'Did you ever see such hair, like spun silver, finer than gossamer! And her face all milk and rose . . . How old can she be?'

'Should I know? Eighteen or so by the look of her. Much the same age as your Cristina, I suppose,' said Brother Cadfael, dropping a none too gentle reminder of the reality of things. 'You'll be doing her a great service and grace if you send her father back to her. And as I know, you're just as eager to get home yourself,' he said with emphasis.

Elis removed his gaze with an effort from the corner where Melicent Prestcote had disappeared and blinked uncomprehendingly, as though he had just been startled out of a deep sleep. 'Yes,' he said uncertainly, and walked on still in a daze.

In the middle of the afternoon, while Cadfael was busy about replenishing his stock of winter cordials in his workshop in the herb-garden, Hugh came in bringing a chilly draught with him before he could close the door against the east wind. He warmed his hands over the brazier, helped himself uninvited to a beaker from Cadfael's wine-flask, and sat down on the broad bench against the wall. He was at home in this dim, timber-scented, herb-rustling miniature world where Cadfael spent so much of his time, and did his best thinking.

'I've just come from the abbot,' said Hugh, 'and borrowed you from him for a few days.'

'And he was willing to lend me?' asked Cadfael with interest, busy stoppering a still-warm jar.

'In a good cause and for a sound reason, yes. In the matter of finding and recovering Gilbert he's as earnest as I am. And the sooner we know whether such an exchange is possible, the better for all.'

Cadfael could not but agree with that. He was thinking, uneasily but not too anxiously as yet, about the morning's visitation. A vision so far from everything Welsh and familiar might well dazzle young, impressionable eyes. There was a prior pledge involved, the niceties of Welsh honour, and the more bitter consideration that Gilbert Prestcote had an old and flourishing hatred against the Welsh, which certain of that race heartily reciprocated.

'I have a border to keep and a garrison to conserve,' said Hugh, nursing his beaker in both hands to warm it, 'and neighbours across the border drunk on their own prowess, and all too likely to be running wild in search of more conquests. Getting word through to Owain Gwynedd is a risky business and we all know it. I would be dubious of letting a captain loose on that mission who lacks Welsh, for I might never see hide nor hair of him again. Even a well-armed party of five or six could vanish. You're Welsh, and have your habit for a coat of mail, and once across the border you have kin everywhere. I reckon you a far better hazard than any battle party. With a small escort, in case of masterless men, and your Welsh tongue and net of kindred to tackle any regular company that crosses you. What do you say?'

'I should be ashamed, as a Welshman,' said Cadfael comfortably, 'if I could not recite my pedigree back sixteen degrees, and some of my kin are here across the border of this shire, a fair enough start towards Gwynedd.'

'Ah, but there's word that Owain may not be so far distant as the wilds of Gwynedd. With Ranulf of Chester so set up in his gains, and greedy for more, the prince has come east to keep an eye on his own. So the rumours say. There's even a whisper he may be our side of the Berwyns, in Cynllaith or Glyn Ceiriog, keeping a close watch on Chester and Wrexham.'

'It would be like him,' agreed Cadfael. 'He thinks large and forwardly. What is the commission? Let me hear it.'

'To ask of Owain Gwynedd whether he has, or can take from his brother, the person of my sheriff, taken at Lincoln. And if he has him, or can find and possess him, whether he will exchange him for this young kinsman of his, Elis ap Cynan. You know, and can report best of any, that the boy is whole and well. Owain may have whatever safeguards he requires, since all men know that he's a man of his word, but regarding me he may not be certain of the same. He may not so much as know my name. Though he shall know me better, if he will have dealings over this. Will you go?'

'How soon?' asked Cadfael, putting his jar aside to cool, and sitting down beside his friend.

'Tomorrow, if you can delegate all here.'

'Mortal man should be able and willing to delegate at any moment,' said Cadfael soberly, 'since mortal he is. Oswin is grown wonderfully deft and exact among the herbs, more than I ever hoped for when first he came to me. And Brother Edmund is master of his own realm, and well able to do without me. If Father Abbot frees me, I'm yours. What I can, I'll do.'

'Then come up to the castle in the morning, after Prime, and you shall have a good horse under you.' He knew that would be a lure and a delight, and smiled at seeing it welcomed. 'And a few picked men for your escort. The rest is in your Welsh tongue.'

'True enough,' said Cadfael complacently, 'a fast word in Welsh is better than a shield. I'll be there. But have your terms drawn up fair on a parchment. Owain has a legal mind, he likes a bill well drawn.'

After Prime in the morning – a greyer morning than the one that went before – Cadfael donned boots and cloak, and went up through the town to the castle wards, and there were the horses of his escort already saddled, and the men waiting for him. He knew them all, even to the youngster Hugh had chosen as a possible hostage for the desired prisoner, should all go well. He spared a few moments to say farewell to Elis, and found him sleepy and mildly morose at this hour in his cell.

'Wish me well, boy, for I'm away to see what can be done about this exchange for you. With a little goodwill and a morsel of luck, you may be on your way home within a couple of weeks. You'll be mightily glad to be back in your own country and a free man.'

Elis agreed that he would, since it was obviously expected of him, but it was a very lukewarm agreement. 'But it's not yet certain, is it, that your sheriff is there to be redeemed? And even if he is, it may take some time to find him and get him out of Cadwaladr's hands.'

'In that case,' said Cadfael, 'you will have to possess your soul in patience and in captivity a while longer.'

'If I must, I can,' agreed Elis, all too cheerfully and continently for one surely not hitherto accomplished at possessing his soul in patience. 'But I do trust you may go and return safe,' he said dutifully.

'Behave yourself, while I'm about your affairs,' Cadfael advised resignedly and turned to leave him. 'I'll bear your greetings to your foster-brother Eliud, if I should encounter him, and leave him word you've come to no harm.'

Elis embraced that offer gladly enough, but crassly failed to add another name that might fittingly have been linked with the same message. And Cadfael refrained from mentioning it in his turn. He was at the door when Elis suddenly called after him: 'Brother Cadfael . . .'

'Yes?' said Cadfael, turning.

'That lady . . . the one we saw yesterday, the sheriff's daughter . . .'

'What of her?'

'Is she spoken for?'

Ah well, thought Cadfael, mounting with his mission well rehearsed in his head, and his knot of light-armed men about him, soon on, soon off, no doubt, and she has never spoken word to him and most likely never will. Once home, he'll soon forget her. If she had not been so silver-fair, so different from the trim, dark Welsh girls, he would never have noticed her.

Cadfael had answered the enquiry with careful indifference, saying he had no notion what plans the sheriff had for his daughter, and forbore from adding the blunt warning that was on the tip of his tongue. With such a springy lad as this one, to put him off would only put him on the more resolutely. With no great obstacles in the way, he might lose interest. But the girl certainly had an airy beauty, all the more appealing for being touched with innocent gravity and sadness on her father's account. Only let this mission succeed, and the sooner the better!

They left Shrewsbury by the Welsh bridge, and made good speed over the near reaches of their way, north-west towards Oswestry.

Sybilla, Lady Prestcote, was twenty years younger than her husband, a pretty, ordinary woman of good intentions towards all, and notable chiefly for one thing, that she had done what the sheriff's first wife could not do, and borne him a son. Young Gilbert was seven years old, the apple of his father's eye and the core of his mother's heart. Melicent found herself indulged but neglected, but

36

in affection to a very pretty little brother she felt no resentment. An heir is an heir; an heiress is a much less achievement.

The apartments in the castle tower, when the best had been done to make them comfortable, remained stony, draughty and cold, no place to bring a young family, and it was exceptional indeed for Sybilla and her son to come to Shrewsbury, when they had six far more pleasant manors at their disposal. Hugh would have offered the hospitality of his own town house on this anxious occasion, but the lady had too many servants to find accommodation there, and preferred the austerity of her bleak but spacious dwelling in the tower. Her husband was accustomed to occupying it alone, when his duties compelled him to remain with the garrison. Wanting him and fretting over him, she was content to be in the place which was his by right, however Spartan its appointments.

Melicent loved her little brother, and found no fault with the system which would endow him with all their father's possessions, and provide her with only a modest dowry. Indeed, she had had serious thoughts of taking the veil, and leaving the Prestcote inheritance as good as whole, having an inclination towards altars, relics and devotional candles, though she had just sense enough to know that what she felt fell far short of a vocation. It had not that quality of overwhelming revelation it should have had.

The shock of wonder, delight and curiosity, for instance, that stopped her, faltering, in her steps when she sailed through the archway into the outer ward and glanced by instinct towards the presence she felt close and intent beside her, and met the startled dark eyes of the stranger, the Welsh prisoner. It was not even his youth and comeliness, but the spellbound stare he fixed on her, that pierced her to the heart.

She had always thought of the Welsh with fear and distrust, as uncouth savages; and suddenly here was this trim and personable young man whose eyes dazzled and whose cheeks flamed at meeting her gaze. She thought of him much. She asked questions about him, careful to dissemble the intensity of her interest. And on the same day that Cadfael set out to hunt for Owain Gwynedd, she saw Elis from an upper window, half-accepted already among the young men of the garrison, stripped to the waist and trying a wrestling bout with one of the best pupils of the master-at-arms in the inner ward. He was no match for the English youth, who had the advantage in weight and reach, and he took a heavy fall that made her catch her breath in distressed sympathy, but he came to his feet laughing and blown, and thumped the victor amiably on the shoulder.

There was nothing in him, no movement, no glance, in which she did not find generosity and grace.

She took her cloak and slipped away down the stone stair, and out to the archway by which he must pass to his lodging in the outer ward. It was beginning to be dusk, they would all be putting away their work and amusement, and making ready for supper in hall. Elis came through the arch limping a little from his new bruises, and whistling, and the same quiver of awareness which had caused her to turn her head now worked the like enchantment upon him.

The tune died on his parted lips. He stood stock-still, holding his breath. Their eyes locked, and could not break free, nor did they try very hard.

'Sir,' she said, having marked the broken rhythm of his walk, 'I fear you are hurt.'

She saw the quiver that passed through him from head to foot as he breathed again. 'No,' he said, hesitant as a man in a dream, 'no, never till now. Now I am wounded to death.'

'I think,' she said, shaken and timorous, 'you do not yet know me . . .'

'I do know you,' he said. 'You are Melicent. It is your father I must buy back for you – at a price . . .'

At a price, at a disastrous price, at the price of tearing asunder this marriage of eyes that drew them closer until they touched hands, and were lost.

THREE

Cadwaladr might have had his frolics on his way back to his castle at Aberystwyth with his booty and his prisoners, but to the north of his passage Owain Gwynedd had kept a fist clamped down hard upon disorder. Cadfael and his escort had had one or two brushes with trouble, after leaving Oswestry on their right and plunging into Wales, but on the first occasion the three masterless men who had put an arrow across their path thought better of it when they saw what numbers they had challenged, and took themselves off at speed into the brush; and on the second, an unruly patrol of excitable Welsh warmed into affability at Cadfael's unruffled Welsh greeting, and ended giving them news of the prince's movements. Cadfael's numerous kinsfolk, first and second cousins and shared forebears, were warranty enough over much of Clwyd and part of Gwynedd.

Owain, they said, had come east out of his eyrie to keep a weather eye upon Ranulf of Chester, who might be so blown up with his success as to mistake the mettle of the prince of Gwynedd. He was patrolling the fringes of Chester territory, and had reached Corwen on the Dee. So said the first informants. The second, encountered near Rhiwlas, were positive that he had crossed the Berwyns and come down into Glyn Ceiriog, and might at that moment be encamped near Llanarmon, or else with his ally and friend, Tudur ap Rhys, at his maenol at Tregeiriog. Seeing it was winter, however merciful at this moment, and seeing that Owain Gwynedd was considerably saner than most Welshmen, Cadfael chose to make for Tregeiriog. Why camp, when there was a close ally at hand, with a sound roof and a well-stocked larder, in a comparatively snug valley among these bleak central hills?

Tudur ap Rhys's maenol lay in a cleft where a mountain brook came down into the river Ceiriog, and his boundaries were well but unobtrusively guarded in these shaken days, for a two-man patrol came out on the path, one on either side, before Cadfael's party were out of the scrub forest above the valley. Shrewd eyes weighed up this sedate company, and the mind behind the eyes decided that they were harmless even before Cadfael got out his Welsh greeting. That and his habit were enough warranty. The young man bade his companion run ahead and acquaint Tudur that he had visitors, and himself conducted them at leisure the rest of the way. Beyond the river, with its fringes of forest and the few stony fields and huddle of wooden cots about the maenol, the hills rose again brown and bleak below, white and bleak above, to a round snow-summit against a leaden sky.

Tudur ap Rhys came out to welcome them and exchange the civilities; a short, square man, very powerfully built, with a thick thatch of brown hair barely touched with grey, and a loud, melodious voice that ranged happily up and down the cadences of song rather than speech. A Welsh Benedictine was a novelty to him; a Welsh Benedictine sent as negotiator from England to a Welsh prince even more so, but he suppressed his curiosity courteously, and had his guest conducted to a chamber in his own house, where presently a girl came to him bearing the customary water for his feet, by the acceptance or rejection of which he would signify whether or not he intended to spend the night there.

It had not occurred to Cadfael, until she entered, that this same lord of Tregeiriog was the man of whom Elis had talked, when he poured out the tale of his boyhood betrothal to a little, sharp, dark creature who was handsome enough in her way, and who, if he must marry at all, would do. Now there she stood, with the gently steaming bowl in her hands, demure before her father's guest, by her dress and her bearing manifestly Tudur's daughter. Little she certainly was, but trimly made and carried herself proudly. Sharp? Her manner was brisk and confident, and though her approach was deferent and proper, there was an assured spark in her eyes. Dark, assuredly. Both eyes and hair fell just short of raven black by the faint, warm tint of red in them. And handsome? Not remarkably so in repose, her face was irregular in feature, tapering from wide-set eyes to pointed chin, but as soon as she spoke or moved there was such flashing life in her that she needed no beauty.

'I take your service very kindly,' said Cadfael, 'and thank you for it. And you, I think, must be Cristina, Tudur's daughter. And if you are, then I have word for you and for Owain Gwynedd that should be heartily welcome to you both.'

'I am Cristina,' she said, burning into bright animation, 'but how did a brother of Shrewsbury learn my name?'

'From a young man by the name of Elis ap Cynan, whom you may have been mourning for lost, but who is safe and well in Shrewsbury castle this moment. What may you have heard of him, since the prince's brother brought his muster and his booty home again from Lincoln?'

Her alert composure did not quiver, but her eyes widened and glowed. 'They told my father he was left behind with some that drowned near the border,' she said, 'but none of them knew how he had fared. Is it true? He is alive? And prisoner?'

'You may be easy,' said Cadfael, 'for so he is, none the worse for the battle or the brook, and can be bought free very simply, to come back to you and make you, I hope, a good husband.'

You may cast your bait, he told himself watching her face, which was at once eloquent and unreadable, as though she even thought in a strange language, but you'll catch no fish here. This one has her own secrets, and her own way of taking events into her hands. What she wills to keep to herself you're never like to get out of her. And she looked him full in the eyes and said: 'Eliud will be glad. Did he speak of him, too?' But she knew the answer.

'A certain Eliud was mentioned,' Cadfael admitted cautiously, feeling shaky ground under them. 'A cousin, I gathered, but brought up like brothers.'

'Closer than brothers,' said the girl. 'Am I permitted to tell him this news? Or should it wait until you have supped with my father and told him your errand?'

'Eliud is here?'

'Not here at this moment, but with the prince, somewhere north along the border. They'll come with the evening. They are lodged here, and Owain's companies are encamped close by.'

'Good, for my errand is to the prince, and it concerns the exchange of Elis ap Cynan for one of comparable value to us, taken, as we believe, by Prince Cadwaladr at Lincoln. If that is as good news to Eliud as it is to you, it would be a Christian act to set his mind at rest for his cousin as soon as may be.'

She kept her face bright, mute and still as she said: 'I will tell him as soon as he alights. It would be great pity to see such a comradely love blighted a moment longer than it need be.' But there was acid in the sweet, and her eyes burned. She made her courteous obeisance, and left him to his ablutions before the evening meal. He watched her go, and her head was high and her step fierce but soundless, like a hunting cat.

So that was how it went, here in this corner of Wales! A girl betrothed, and with a girl's sharp eye on her rights and privileges, while the boy went about whistling and obtuse, child to her woman, and had his arm about another youth's neck, sworn pair from infancy, oftener than he even paid a compliment to his affianced wife. And she resented with all her considerable powers of mind and heart the love that made her only a third, and barely half-welcome.

Nothing here for her to mourn, if she could but know it. A maid is a woman far before a boy is a man, leaving aside the simple maturity of arms. All she need do was wait a little, and use her own arts, and she would no longer be the neglected third. But she was proud and fierce and not minded to wait.

Cadfael made himself presentable, and went to the lavish but simple table of Tudur ap Rhys. In the dusk torches flared at the hall door and up the valley from the north, from the direction of Llansantffraid, came a brisk bustle of horsemen back from their patrol. Within the hall the tables were spread and the central fire burned bright, sending up fragrant wood-smoke into the blackened roof, as Owain Gwynedd, lord of North Wales and much country beside, came content and hungry to his place at the high table.

Cadfael had seen him once before, a few years past, and he was not a man to be easily forgotten, for all he made very little ado about state and ceremony, barring the obvious royalty he bore about in his own person. He was barely thirty-seven years old, in his vigorous prime; very tall for a Welshman, and fair, after his grandmother Ragnhild of the Danish kingdom of Dublin, and his mother Angharad, known for her flaxen hair among the dark women of the south. His young men, reflecting his solid self-confidence, did it with a swagger of which their prince had no need. Cadfael wondered which of all these boisterous boys was Eliud ap Griffith, and whether Cristina had yet told him of his cousin's survival, and in what terms, and with what jealous bitterness at being still a barely-regarded hanger-on in this sworn union.

'And here is Brother Cadfael of the Shrewsbury Benedictines,' said Tudur heartily, placing Cadfael close at the high table, 'with an embassage to you, my lord, from that town and shire.'

Owain weighed and measured the stocky figure and weathered countenance with a shrewd blue gaze, and stroked his close-trimmed golden beard. 'Brother Cadfael is welcome, and so is any motion of amity from that quarter, where I can do with an assured peace.'

'Some of your countrymen and mine,' said Cadfael bluntly, 'paid a visit recently to Shropshire's borders with very little amity in mind, and left our peace a good deal less assured, even, than it could be said to be after Lincoln. You may have heard of it. Your princely brother did not come raiding himself, it may even be that he never sanctioned the frolic. But he left a few drowned men in one of our brooks in flood whom we have buried decently. And one,' he said, 'whom the good sisters took out of the water living, and whom your lordship may wish to redeem, for by his own tale he's of your kinship.'

'Do you tell me!' The blue eyes had widened and brightened. 'I have not been so busy about fencing out the earl of Chester that I have failed to go into matters with my brother. There was more than one such frolic on the way home from Lincoln, and every one a folly that will cost me some pains to repair. Give your prisoner a name.'

'His name,' said Cadfael, 'is Elis ap Cynan.'

'Ah!' said Owain on a long, satisfied breath, and set down his cup ringing on the board. 'So the fool boy's alive yet to tell the tale, is he? I'm glad indeed to hear it, and thank God for the deliverance and you, brother, for the news. There was not a man of my

43

brother's company could swear to how he was lost or what befell him.'

'They were running too fast to look over their shoulders,' said Cadfael mildly.

'From a man of our own blood,' said Owain grinning, 'I'll take that as it's meant. So Elis is live and prisoner! Has he come to much harm?'

'Barely a scratch. And he may have come by a measure of sense into the bargain. Sound as a well-cast bell, I promise you, and my mission is to offer an exchange with you, if by any chance your brother has taken among his prisoners one as valuable to us as Elis is to you. I am sent,' said Cadfael, 'by Hugh Beringar of Maesbury, speaking for Shropshire, to ask of you the return of his chief and sheriff, Gilbert Prestcote. With all proper greetings and compliments to your lordship, and full assurance of our intent to maintain the peace with you as hitherto.'

'The time's ripe for it,' acknowledged Owain drily, 'and it's to the vantage of both of us, things being as they are. Where is Elis now?'

'In Shrewsbury castle, and has the run of the wards on his parole.'

'And you want him off your hands?'

'No haste for that,' said Cadfael. 'We think well enough of him to keep him yet a while. But we do want the sheriff, if he lives, and if you have him. For Hugh looked for him after the battle, and found no trace, and it was your brother's Welsh who overran the place where he fought.'

'Bide here a night or two,' said the prince, 'and I will send to Cadwaladr, and find out if he holds your man. And if so, you shall have him.'

There was harping after supper, and singing, and drinking of good wine long after the prince's messenger had ridden out on the first stage of his long journey to Aberystwyth. There was also a certain amount of good-natured wrestling and horse-play between Owain's young cockerels and the men of Cadfael's escort, though Hugh had taken care to choose some who had Welsh kin to recommend them, no very hard task in Shrewsbury at any time.

'Which of all these,' asked Cadfael, surveying the hall, smoky now from the fire and the torches, and loud with voices, 'is Eliud ap Griffith?'

'I see Elis has chattered to you as freely as ever,' said Owain smiling, 'prisoner or no. His cousin and foster-brother is hovering this moment at the end of the near table, and eyeing you hard, waiting his chance to have speech with you as soon as I withdraw. The long lad in the blue coat.'

No mistaking him, once noticed, though he could not have been more different from his cousin: such a pair of eyes fixed upon Cadfael's face in implacable determination and eagerness and such a still, braced body waiting for the least encouragement to fly to respond. Owain, humouring him, lifted a beckoning finger, and he came like a lance launched, quivering. A long lad he was, and thin and intense, with bright hazel eyes in a grave oval face, featured finely enough for a woman, but with good lean bones in it, too. There was a quality of devotional anxiety about him that must be for Elis ap Cynan at this moment, but at another might be for Wales, for his prince, some day, no doubt, for a woman, but whatever its object it would always be there. This one would never be quite at rest.

He bent the knee eagerly to Owain, and Owain clouted him amiably on the shoulder and said: 'Sit down here with Brother Cadfael, and have out of him everything you want to know. Though the best you know already. Your other self is alive and can be bought back for you at a price.' And with that he left them together and went to confer with Tudur.

Eliud sat down willingly and spread his elbows on the board to lean ardently close. 'Brother, it *is* true, what Cristina told me? You have Elis safe in Shrewsbury? They came back without him . . . I sent to know, but there was no one could tell me where he went astray or how. I have been hunting and asking everywhere and so has the prince, for all he makes a light thing of it. He is my father's fostering—you're Welsh yourself, so you know. We grew up together from babes, and there are no more brothers, either side . . .'

'I do know,' agreed Cadfael, 'and I say again, as Cristina said to you, he is safe enough, man alive and as good as new.'

45

'You've seen him? Talked to him? You're sure it's Elis and no other? A well-looking man of his company,' explained Eliud apologetically, 'if he found himself prisoner, might award himself a name that would stead him better than his own . . .'

Cadfael patiently described his man, and told over the whole tale of the rescue from the flooded brook and Elis's obstinate withdrawal into the Welsh tongue until a Welshman challenged him. Eliud listened, his lips parted and his eyes intent, and was visibly eased into conviction.

'And was he so uncivil to those ladies who saved him? Oh, now I do know him for Elis, he'd be so shamed, to come back to life in such hands – like a babe being thumped into breathing!' No mistake, the solemn youth could laugh, and laughter lit up his grave face and made his eyes sparkle. It was no blind love he had for his twin who was no twin, he knew him through and through, scolded, criticised, fought with him, and loved him none the less. The girl Cristina had a hard fight on her hands. 'And so you got him from the nuns. And had he no hurts at all, once he was wrung dry?'

'Nothing worse than a gash in his hinder end, got from a sharp rock in the brook, while he was drowning. And that's salved and healed. His worst trouble was that you would be mourning him for dead, but my journey here eases him of that anxiety, as it does you of yours. No need to fret about Elis ap Cynan. Even in an English castle he is soon and easily at home.'

'So he would be,' agreed Eliud in the soft, musing voice of tolerant affection. 'So he always was and always will be. He has the gift. But so *free* with it, sometimes I fret for him indeed!'

Always, rather than sometimes, thought Cadfael, after the young man had left him, and the hall was settling down for the night round the turfed and quiet fire. Even now, assured of his friend's safety and well-being, and past question or measure glad of that, even now he goes with locked brows and inward-gazing eyes. He had a troubled vision of those three young creatures bound together in inescapable strife, the two boys linked together from childhood, locked even more securely by the one's gravity and the other's innocent rashness, and the girl betrothed in infancy to half of an inseparable pair. Of the three the prisoner in

46

Shrewsbury seemed to him the happiest by far, since he lived in the day, warming in its sunlight, taking cover from its storms, in every case finding by instinct the pleasant corner and the gratifying entertainment. The other two burned like candles, eating their own substance and giving an angry and vulnerable light.

He said prayers for all three before he slept, and awoke in the night to the uneasy reflection that somewhere, shadowy as yet, there might be a fourth to be considered and prayed for.

The next day was clear and bright, with light frost that lost its powdery sparkle as soon as the sun came up; and it was pleasure to have a whole day to spend in his own Welsh countryside with a good conscience and in good company. Owain Gwynedd again rode out eastward upon another patrol with a half-dozen of his young men, and again came back in the evening well content. It seemed that Ranulf of Chester was lying low for the moment, digesting his gains.

As for Cadfael, since word could hardly be expected to come back from Aberystwyth until the following day, he gladly accepted the prince's invitation to ride with them, and see for himself the state of readiness of the border villages that kept watch on England. They returned to the courtyard of Tudur's maenol in the early dusk, and beyond the flurry and bustle of activity among the grooms and the servants, the hall door hung open, and sharp and dark against the glow of the fire and the torches within stood the small, erect figure of Cristina, looking out for the guests returning, in order to set all forward for the evening meal. She vanished within for a few moments only, and then came forth to watch them dismount, her father at her side.

It was not the prince Cristina watched. Cadfael passed close by her as he went within, and saw by the falling light of the torches how her face was set, her lips taut and unsmiling, and her eyes fixed insatiably upon Eliud as he alighted and handed over his mount to the waiting groom. The glint of dark red that burned in the blackness of hair and eyes seemed by this light to have brightened into a deep core of anger and resentment.

What was no less noticeable, when Cadfael looked back in sheer human curiosity, was the manner in which Eliud, approaching the doorway, passed by her with an unsmiling face and a brief word, and went on his way with averted eyes. For was not she as sharp a thorn in his side as he in hers?

The sooner the marriage, the less the mischief, and the better prospect of healing it again, thought Cadfael, departing to his Vesper office; and instantly began to wonder whether he was not making far too simple a matter of this turmoil between three people, of whom only one was simple at all.

The prince's messenger came back late in the afternoon of the following day, and made report to his master, who called in Cadfael at once to hear the result of the quest.

'My man reports that Gilbert Prestcote is indeed in my brother's hands, and can and shall be offered in exchange for Elis. There may be a little delay, for it seems he was badly wounded in the fighting at Lincoln, and is recovering only slowly. But if you will deal directly with me, I will secure him as soon as he is fit to be moved, and have him brought by easy stages to Shrewsbury. We'll lodge him at Montford on the last night, where Welsh princes and English earls used to meet for parley, send Hugh Beringar word ahead, and bring him to the town. There your garrison may hand over Elis in exchange.'

'Content, indeed!' said Cadfael heartily, 'And so will Hugh Beringar be.'

'I shall require safeguards,' said Owain, 'and am willing to give them.'

'As for your good faith, nowhere in this land of Wales or my foster-land of England is it in question. But *my* lord you do not know, and he is content to leave with you a hostage, to be his guarantee until you have Elis safe in your hands again. From you he requires none. Send him Gilbert Prestcote, and you may have Elis ap Cynan, and send back the guarantor at your pleasure.'

'No,' said Owain firmly. 'If I ask warranty of a man, I also give it. Leave me your man here and now, if you will, and if he has his orders and is ready and willing, and when my men bring Gilbert Prestcote home I will send Eliud with him to remain with you as surety for his cousin's honour and mine until we again exchange hostages halfway – on the border dyke by Oswestry, shall we say, if

I am still in these parts? – and conclude the bargain. There is virtue, sometimes, in observing the forms. And besides, I should like to meet your Hugh Beringar, for he and I have a common need to be on our guard against others you wot of.'

'The same thought has been much in Hugh's mind,' agreed Cadfael fervently, 'and trust me, he will take pleasure in coming to meet you wherever may be most suited to the time. He shall bring you Eliud again, and you shall restore him a young man who is his cousin on his mother's side, John Marchmain. You noted him this morning, the tallest among us. John came with me ready and willing to remain if things went well.'

'He shall be well entertained,' said Owain.

'Faith, he's been looking forward to it, though his knowledge of Welsh is small. And since we are agreed,' said Cadfael, 'I'll see him instructed in his duty tonight, and make an early start back to Shrewsbury in the morning with the rest of my company.'

Before sleeping that night he went out from the smoke and warmth of the hall to take a look at the weather. The air was on the softer edge of frost, no wind stirring. The sky was clear and full of stars, but they had not the blaze and bite of extreme cold. A beautiful night, and even without his cloak he was tempted to go as far as the edge of the maenol, where a copse of bushes and trees sheltered the gate. He drew in deep, chill breaths, scented with timber, night and the mysterious sweetness of turf and leaf sleeping but not dead, and blew the smokiness of withindoors out of his nose.

He was about to turn back and compose his mind for the night prayers when the luminous darkness quickened around him, and two people came up from the shadowy buildings of the stables towards the hall, softly and swiftly, but with abrupt pauses that shook the air more than their motion. They were talking as they came, just above the betraying sibilance of whispers, and their conference had an edge and an urgency that made him freeze where he stood, covered by the bulk and darkness of the trees. By the time he was aware of them they were between him and his rest, and when they drew close enough he could not choose but hear. But man being what he is, it cannot be avowed that he would so have chosen, even if he could.

'– mean me no harm!' breathed the one, bitter and soft. 'And do you not harm me, do you not rob me of what's mine by right, with every breath you draw? And now you will be off to him, as soon as this English lord can be moved . . .'

'Have I a choice,' protested the other, 'when the prince sends me? And he is my foster-brother, can you change that? Why can you not let well alone?'

'It is *not* well, it is very ill! Sent, indeed!' hissed the girl's voice viciously. 'Ha! And you would murder any who took the errand from you, and well you know it. And I to sit here! While you will be together again, his arm around your neck, and never a thought for me!'

The two shadows glared in the muted gleam from the dying fire within, black in the doorway. Eliud's voice rose perilously. The taller shadow, head and shoulders taller, wrenched itself away.

'For God's love, woman, will you not hush, and let me be!'

He was gone, casting her off roughly, and vanishing into the populous murmur and hush of the hall. Cristina plucked her skirts about her with angry hands, and followed slowly, withdrawing to her own retiring place.

And so did Cadfael, as soon as he was sure there was none to be discomposed by his going. There went two losers in this submerged battle. If there was a winner, he slept with a child's abandon, as seemed to be his wont, in a stone cell that was no prison, in Shrewsbury castle. One that would always fall on his feet. Two that probably made a practice of falling over theirs, from too intense peering ahead, and too little watching where they trod.

Nevertheless, he did not pray for them that night. He lay long in thought instead, pondering how so complex a knot might be disentangled.

In the early morning he and his remaining force mounted and rode. It did not surprise him that the devoted cousin and foster-brother should be there to see him go, and send by him all manner of messages to his captive friend, to sustain him until his release. Most fitting that the one who was older and wiser should stand proxy to rescue the younger and more foolish. If folly can be measured so?

'I was not clever,' owned Eliud ruefully, holding Cadfael's stirrup as he mounted, and leaning on his horse's warm shoulder when he was up. 'I made too much of it that he should not go with Cadwaladr. I doubt I drove him the more firmly into it. But I *knew* it was mad!'

'You must grant him one grand folly,' said Cadfael comfortably. 'Now he's lived through it, and knows it was folly as surely as you do. He'll not be so hot after action again. And then,' he said, eyeing the grave oval countenance close, 'I understand he'll have other causes for growing into wisdom when he comes home. He's to be married, is he not?'

Eliud faced him a moment with great hazel eyes shining like lanterns. Then: 'Yes!' he said very shortly and forbiddingly, and turned his head away.

FOUR

The news went round in Shrewsbury – abbey, castle and town – almost before Cadfael had rendered account of his stewardship to Abbot Radulfus, and reported his success to Hugh. The sheriff was alive, and his return imminent, in exchange for the Welshman taken at Godric's Ford. In her high apartments in the castle, Lady Prestcote brightened and grew buoyant with relief. Hugh rejoiced not only in having found and recovered his chief, but also in the prospect of a closer alliance with Owain Gwynedd, whose help in the north of the shire, if ever Ranulf of Chester did decide to attack, might very well turn the tide. The provost and guildsmen of the town, in general, were well pleased. Prestcote was a man who did not encourage close friendships, but Shrewsbury had found him a just and well-intentioned officer of the crown, if heavy-handed at times, and was well aware that it might have fared very much worse. Not everyone, however, felt the same simple pleasure. Even just men make enemies.

Cadfael returned to his proper duties well content, and having reviewed Brother Oswin's stewardship in the herbarium and found everything in good order, his next charge was to visit the infirmary and replenish the medicine-cupboard there.

'No new invalids since I left?'

'None. And two have gone out, back to the dortoir, Brother Adam and Brother Everard. Strong constitutions they have, both, in spite of age, and it was no worse than a chest cold, and has cleared up well. Come and see how they all progress. If only we could send out Brother Maurice with the same satisfaction as those two,' said Edmund sadly. 'He's eight years younger, strong and able, and barely sixty. If only he was as sound in mind as in body!

52

But I doubt we'll never dare let him loose. It's the bent his madness has taken. Shame that after a blameless life of devotion he now remembers only his grudges, and seems to have no love for any man. Great age is no blessing, Cadfael, when the body's strength outlives the mind.'

'How do his neighbours bear with him?' asked Cadfael with sympathy.

'With Christian patience! And they need it. He fancies now that every man is plotting some harm against him. And says so, outright, besides any real and ancient wrongs he's kept in mind all too clearly.'

They came into the big, bare room where the beds were laid, handy to the private chapel where the infirm might repair for the offices. Those who could rise to enjoy the brighter part of the day sat by a large log fire, warming their ancient bones and talking by fits and starts, as they waited for the next meal, the next office or the next diversion. Only Brother Rhys was confined to his bed, though most of those within here were aged, and spent much time there. A generation of brothers admitted in the splendid enthusiasm of an abbey's founding also comes to senility together, yielding place to the younger postulants admitted by ones and twos after the engendering wave. Never again, thought Cadfael, moving among them, would a whole chapter of the abbey's history remove thus into retirement and decay. From this time on they would come one by one, and be afforded each a death-bed reverently attended, single and in solitary dignity. Here were four or five who would depart almost together, leaving even their attendant brothers very weary, and the world indifferent.

Brother Maurice sat installed by the fire, a tall, gaunt, waxen-white old man of elongated patrician face and irascible manner. He came of a noble house, an oblate since his youth, and had been removed here some two years previously, when after a trivial dispute he had suddenly called out Prior Robert in a duel to the death, and utterly refused to be distracted or reconciled. In his more placid moments he was gracious, accommodating and courteous, but touch him in his pride of family and honour and he was an implacable enemy. Here in his old age he called up from the past, vivid as when they happened, every affront to his line, every lawsuit waged against them, back to his own birth and beyond, and brooded over every one that had gone unrevenged.

It was a mistake, perhaps, to ask him how he did, but his enthroned hauteur seemed to demand it. He raised his narrow hawk-nose, and tightened his bluish lips. 'None the better for what I hear, if it be true. They're saying that Gilbert Prestcote is alive and will soon be returning here. Is that truth?'

'It is,' said Cadfael. 'Owain Gwynedd is sending him home in exchange for the Welshman captured in the Long Forest a while since. And why should you be none the better for good news of a decent Christian man?'

'I had thought justice had been done,' said Maurice loftily, 'after all too long a time. But however long, divine justice should not fail in the end. Yet once again it has glanced aside and spared the malefactor.' The glitter of his eyes was grey as steel.

'You'd best leave divine justice to its own business,' said Cadfael mildly, 'for it needs no help from us. And I asked you how *you* did, my friend, so never put me off with others. How is it with that chest of yours, this wintry weather? Shall I bring you a cordial to warm you?'

It was no great labour to distract him, for though he was no complainer as to his health, he was open to the flattery of concerned attention and enjoyed being cosseted. They left him soothed and complacent, and went out to the porch very thoughtful.

'I knew he had these hooks in him,' said Cadfael when the door was closed between, 'but not that he had such a barb from the Prestcote family. What is it he holds against the sheriff?'

Edmund shrugged, and drew resigned breath. 'It was in his father's time, Maurice was scarcely born! There was a lawsuit over a piece of land and long arguments either side, and it went Prestcote's way. For all I know, as sound a judgement as ever was made, and Maurice was in his cradle, and Gilbert's father, good God, was barely a man, but here the poor ancient has dredged it up as a mortal wrong. And it is but one among a dozen he keeps burnished in his memory, and wants blood for them all. Will you believe it, he has never set eyes on the sheriff? Can you hate a man you've never seen or spoken to, because his grandsire beat your father at a suit at law? Why should old age lose everything but the all-present evil?'

A hard question. And yet sometimes it went the opposite way, kept the good, and let all the malice and spite be washed away. And why one old man should be visited by such grace, and another by so heavy a curse, Cadfael could not fathom. Surely a balance must be restored elsewhere.

'Not everyone, I know,' said Cadfael ruefully, 'loves Gilbert Prestcote. Good men can make as devoted enemies as bad men. And his handling of law has not always been light or merciful, though it never was corrupt or cruel.'

'There's one here has somewhat better cause than Maurice to bear him a grudge,' said Edmund. 'I am sure you know Anion's history as well as I do. He's on crutches, as you'll have seen before you left us on this journey, and getting on well, and we like him to go forth when there's no frost and the ground's firm and dry, but he's still bedded with us, within there. He says nothing, while Maurice says too much, but you're Welsh, and you know how a Welshman keeps his counsel. And one like Anion, half-Welsh, half-English, how do you read such a one?'

'As best you can,' agreed Cadfael, 'bearing in mind both are humankind.'

He knew the man Anion, though he had never been brought close to him, since Anion was a lay servant among the livestock, and had been brought into the infirmary in late autumn from one of the abbey granges, with a broken leg that was slow to knit. He was no novelty in the district about Shrewsbury, offspring of a brief union between a Welsh wool-trader and an English maid-servant. And like many another of his kind, he had kept touch with his kin across the border, where his father had a proper wife, and had given her a legitimate son no long time after Anion was conceived.

'I do remember now,' said Cadfael, enlightened. 'There were two young fellows came to sell their fleeces that time, and drank too deep and got into a brawl, and one of the gate-keepers on the bridge was killed. Prestcote hanged them for it. I did hear tell at the time the one had a half-brother this side the border.'

'Griffri ap Griffri, that was the young man's name. Anion had got to know him, the times he came into town, they were on good

55

terms. He was away among the sheep in the north when it happened or he might well have got his brother to bed without mischief. A good worker and honest, Anion, but a surly fellow and silent, and never forgets a benefit nor an injury.'

Cadfael sighed, having seen in his time a long line of decent men wiped out in alternate savageries as the result of just such a death. The blood-feud could be a sacred duty in Wales.

'Ah, well, it's to be hoped the English half of him can temper his memories. That must be two years ago now. No man can bear a grudge for ever.'

In the narrow, stone-cold chapel of the castle by the meagre light of the altar lamp, Elis waited in the gloom of the early evening, huddled into his cloak in the darkest corner, biting frost without and gnawing fire within. It was a safe place for two to meet who could otherwise never be alone together. The sheriff's chaplain was devout, but within limits, and preferred the warmth of the hall and the comforts of the table, once Vespers was disposed of, to this cold and draughty place.

Melicent's step on the threshold was barely audible, but Elis caught it, and turned eagerly to draw her in by both hands, and swing the heavy door closed to shut out the rest of the world.

'You've heard?' she said, hasty and low. 'They've found him, they're bringing him back. Owain Gwynedd has promised it . . .'

'I know!' said Elis, and drew her close, folding the cloak about them both, as much to assert their unity as to shield her from the chill and the trespassing wind. For all that, he felt her slipping away like a wraith of mist out of his hold. 'I'm glad you'll have your father back safely.' But he could not sound glad, no matter how manfully he lied. 'We knew it must be so if he lived . . .' His voice baulked there, trying not to sound as if he wished her father dead, one obstacle out of the way from between them, and himself still a prisoner, unransomed. Her prisoner, for as long as might be, long enough to work the needful miracle, break one tie and make another possible, which looked all too far out of reach now.

'When he comes back,' she said, her cold brow against his cheek, 'then you will have to go. How shall we bear it!'

'Don't I know it! I think of nothing else. It will all be vain, and I shall never see you again. I won't, I can't accept that. There *must* be a way . . .'

'If you go,' she said, 'I shall die.'

'But I must go, we both know it. How else can I even do this one thing for you, to buy your father back?' But neither could he bear the pain of it. If he let her go now he was for ever lost, there would be no other to take her place. The little dark creature in Wales, so faded from his mind he could hardly recall her face, she was nothing, she had no claim on him. Rather a hermit's life, if he could not have Melicent. 'Do you not *want* him back?'

'Yes!' she said vehemently, torn and shivering, and at once took it back again: '*No!* Not if I must lose you! Oh, God, do I know what I want? I want both you and him – *but you most!* I do love my father, but as a father. I must love him, love is due between us, but . . . Oh, Elis, I hardly know him, he never came near enough to be loved. Always duty and affairs taking him away, and my mother and I lonely, and then my mother dead . . . He was never unkind, always careful of me, but always a long way off. It is a kind of love, but not like this . . . not as I love you! It's no fair exchange . . .'

She did not say: 'Now if he had died . . .' but it was there stark at the back of her mind, horrifying her. If they had failed to find him, or found him dead, she would have wept for him, yes, but her stepmother would not have cared too much where she chose to marry. What would have mattered most to Sybilla was that her son should inherit all, and her husband's daughter be content with a modest dowry. And so she would have been content, yes, with none.

'But it must not be an end!' vowed Elis fiercely. 'Why should we submit to it? I won't give you up, I can't, I won't part from you.'

'Oh, foolish!' she said, her tears gushing against his cheek, 'The escort that brings him home will take you away. There's a bargain struck, and no choice but to keep it. You must go, and I must stay, and that will be the end. Oh, if he need never reach here . . .' Her own voice uttering such things terrified her, she buried her lips in the hollow of his shoulder to smother the unforgivable words.

'No, but listen to me, my heart, my dear! Why should I not go to him and offer for you? Why should he not give me fair hearing? I'm born princely, I have lands, I'm his equal, why should he refuse to let me have you? I can endow you well, and there's no man could ever love you more.'

He had never told her, as he had so light-heartedly told Brother Cadfael, of the girl in Wales, betrothed to him from childhood. But that agreement had been made over their heads, by consent of others, and with patience and goodwill it could be honourably dissolved by the consent of all. Such a reversal might be a rarity in Gwynedd, but it was not unheard of. He had done no wrong to Cristina, it was not too late to withdraw.

'Sweet fool innocent!' she said, between laughter and rage. 'You do not know him! Every manor he holds is a border manor, he has had to sweat and fight for them many a time. Can you not see that after the empress, his enemy is Wales? And he as good a hater as ever was born! He would as soon marry his daughter to a blind leper in St Giles as to a Welshman, if he were the prince of Gwynedd himself. Never go near him, you will but harden him, and he'll rend you. Oh, trust me, there's no hope there.'

'Yet I will not let you go,' vowed Elis into the cloud of her pale hair, that stirred and stroked against his face with a life of its own, in nervous, feathery caresses. 'Somehow, somehow, I swear I'll keep you, no matter what I must do to hold you, no matter how many I must fight to clear the way to you. I'll kill whoever comes between us, my love, my dear . . .'

'Oh, hush!' she said. 'Don't talk so. That's not for you. There must, there must be some way for us . . .'

But she could see none. They were caught in an inexorable process that would bring Gilbert Prestcote home, and sweep Elis ap Cynan away.

'We have still a little time,' she whispered, taking heart as best she could. 'They said he is not well, he had wounds barely healed. They'll be a week or two yet.'

'And you'll still come? You *will* come? Every day? How should I bear it if I could no longer see you?'

'I'll come,' she said, 'these moments are my life, too. Who knows, something may yet happen to save us.'

'Oh, God, if we could but stop time! If we could hold back the days, make him take for ever on the journey, and never, never reach Shrewsbury!'

*　　*　　*

It was ten days before the next word came from Owain Gwynedd. A runner came in on foot, armed with due authorisation from Einon ab Ithel, who ranked second only to Owain's own *penteulu*, the captain of his personal guard. The messenger was brought to Hugh in the castle guardroom early in the afternoon; a border man, with some business dealings into England, and well acquainted with the language.

'My lord, I bring greetings from Owain Gwynedd through the mouth of his captain, Einon ab Ithel. I am to tell you that the party lies tonight at Montford, and tomorrow we shall bring you our charge, the lord Gilbert Prestcote. But there is more. The lord Gilbert is still very weak from his wounds and hardships, and for most of the way we have carried him in a litter. All went well enough until this morning, when we had hoped to reach the town and discharge our task in one day. Because of that, the lord Gilbert would ride the last miles, and not be carried like a sick man into his own town.'

The Welsh would understand and approve that, and not presume to deter him. A man's face is half his armour, and Prestcote would venture any discomfort or danger to enter Shrewsbury erect in the saddle, a man master of himself even in captivity.

'It was like him and worthy of him,' said Hugh, but scenting what must follow. 'And he tried himself too far. What has happened?'

'Before we had gone a mile he swooned and fell. Not a heavy fall, but a healed wound in his side has started open again, and he lost some blood. It may be that there was some manner of fit or seizure, more than the mere exertion, for when we took him up and tended him he was very pale and cold. We wrapped him well – Einon ab Ithel swathed him further in his own cloak – and laid him again in the litter, and have carried him back to Montford.'

'Has he his senses? Has he spoken?' asked Hugh anxiously.

'As sound in his wits as any man, once he opened his eyes, and speaks clearly, my lord. We would keep him at Montford longer, if need be, but he is set to reach Shrewsbury now, being so near. He may take more harm, being vexed, than if we carry him here as he wishes, tomorrow.'

So Hugh thought, too, and gnawed his knuckles a while pondering what was best. 'Do you think this setback may be dangerous to him? Even mortal?'

The man shook his head decidedly. 'My lord, though you'll find him a sick man and much fallen and aged, I think he needs only rest and time and good care to be his own man again. But it will not be a quick or an easy return.'

'Then it had better be here, where he desires to be,' Hugh decided, 'but hardly in these cold, harsh chambers. I would take him to my own house, gladly, but the best nursing will surely be at the abbey, and there you can just as well bear him, and he may be spared being carried helpless through the town. I will bespeak a bed for him in the infirmary there, and see his wife and children into the guest-hall to be near him. Go back now to Einon ab Ithel with my greetings and thanks, and ask him to bring his charge straight to the abbey. I will see Brother Edmund and Brother Cadfael prepared to receive him, and all ready for his rest. At what hour may we expect your arrival? Abbot Radulfus will wish to have your captains be his guests before they leave again.'

'Before noon,' said the messenger, 'we should reach the abbey.'

'Good! Then there shall be places at table for all, for the midday meal, before you set forth with Elis ap Cynan in exchange for my sheriff.'

Hugh carried the news to the tower apartments, to Lady Prestcote, who received them with relief and joy, though tempered with some uneasiness when she heard of her husband's collapse. She made haste to collect her son and her maid, and make ready to move to the greater comfort of the abbey guest-hall, ready for her lord's coming, and Hugh conducted them there and went to confer with the abbot about the morrow's visit. And if he noted that one of the party went with them mute and pale, brilliant-eyed as much with tears as with eagerness, he thought little of it then. The daughter of the first wife, displaced by the son of the second, might well be the one who missed her father most, and had worn her courage so threadbare with the grief of waiting that she could not yet translate her exhaustion into joy.

Meantime, there was hum and bustle about the great court.

Abbot Radulfus issued orders, and took measures to furnish his own table for the entertainment of the representatives of the prince of Gwynedd. Prior Robert took counsel with the cooks concerning properly lavish provision for the remainder of the escort, and room enough in the stables to rest and tend their horses. Brother Edmund made ready the quietest enclosed chamber in the infirmary, and had warm, light covers brought, and a brazier to temper the air, while Brother Cadfael reviewed the contents of his workshop with the broken wound in mind, and the suggestion of something more than a swoon. The abbey had sometimes entertained much larger parties, even royalty, but this was the return of a man of their own, and the Welsh who had been courteous and punctilious in providing him his release and his safe-conduct must be honoured like princes, as they stood for a prince.

In his cell in the castle Elis ap Cynan lay face-down on his pallet, the heart in his breast as oppressive as a hot and heavy stone. He had watched her go, but from hiding, unwilling to cause her the same suffering and despair he felt. Better she should go without a last reminder, able at least to try to turn all her thoughts towards her father, and leave her lover out of mind. He had strained his eyes after her to the last, until she vanished down the ramp from the gatehouse, the silver-gold of her coiled hair the only brightness in a dull day. She was gone, and the stone that had taken the place of his heart told him that the most he could hope for now was a fleeting glimpse of her on the morrow, when they released him from the castle wards and conducted him down to the abbey, to be handed over to Einon ab Ithel; for after the morrow, unless a miracle happened, he might never see her again.

FIVE

Brother Cadfael was ready with Brother Edmund in the porch of the infirmary to see them ride in, as they did in the middle of the morning, just after High Mass was ended. Owain's trusted captain in the lead with Eliud ap Griffith, very solemn of face, close behind him as body-squire and two older officers following, and then the litter, carefully slung between two strong hill ponies, with attendants on foot walking alongside to steady the ride. The long form in the litter was so cushioned and swathed that it looked bulky, but the ponies moved smoothly and easily, as if the weight was very light.

Einon ab Ithel was a big, muscular man in his forties, bearded, with long moustaches and a mane of brown hair. His clothing and the harness of the fine horse under him spoke his wealth and importance. Eliud leaped down to take his lord's bridle, and walked the horse aside as Hugh Beringar came to greet the arrivals and after him, with welcoming dignity, Abbot Radulfus himself. There would be a leisurely and ceremonious meal in the abbot's lodging for Einon and the elder officers of his party, together with Lady Prestcote and her daughter and Hugh himself, as was due when two powers came together in civilised agreement. But the most urgent business fell to Brother Edmund and his helpers.

The litter was unharnessed, and carried at once into the infirmary, to the room already prepared and warmed for the sick man's reception. Edmund closed the door even against Lady Prestcote, who was blessedly delayed by the civilities, until they should have unwrapped, unclothed and installed the invalid, and had some idea of his state.

They unfastened from the high, close-drawn collar of the clipped sheepskin cloak that was his outer wrapping, a long pin with a large, chased gold head, secured by a thin gold chain. Everyone knew there was gold worked in Gwynedd, probably this came from Einon's own land, for certainly this must be his cloak, added to pillow and protect his sacred charge. Edmund laid it aside, folded, on a low chest beside the bed, the great pin showing clearly, for fear someone should run his hand on to the point if it were hidden. Between them they unwound Gilbert Prestcote from the layers in which he was swathed, and as they handled him his eyes opened languidly, and his long, gaunt body made some feeble moves to help them. He was much fallen in flesh, and bore several scars, healed but angry, besides the moist wound in his flank which had gaped again with his fall. Carefully Cadfael dressed and covered the place. Even being handled exhausted the sick man. By the time they had lifted him into the warmed bed and covered him his eyes were again closed. As yet he had not tried to speak.

A marvel how he had ever ridden even a mile before foundering, thought Cadfael, looking down at the figure stretched beneath the covers, and the lean, livid face, all sunken blue hollows and staring, blanched bones. The dark hair of his head and beard was thickly sown with grey, and lay lank and lifeless. Only his iron spirit, intolerant of any weakness, most of all his own, had held him up in the saddle, and when even that failed he was lost indeed.

But he drew breath, he had moved to assert his rights in his own body, however weakly, and again he opened the dulled and sunken eyes and stared up into Cadfael's face. His grey lips formed, just audibly: 'My son?' Not: 'My wife?' Nor yet: 'My daughter?' Cadfael thought with rueful sympathy, and stooped to assure him: 'Young Gilbert is here, safe and well.' He glanced at Edmund, who signalled back agreement. 'I'll bring him to you.'

Small boys are very resilient, but for all that Cadfael said some words, both of caution and reassurance, as much for the mother as the child, before he brought them in and drew aside into a corner to leave them the freedom of the bedside. Hugh came in with them. Prestcote's first thought was naturally for his son, the second, no less naturally, would be for his shire. And his shire, considering all things, was in very good case to encourage him to live, mend and mind it again.

Sybilla wept, but quietly. The little boy stared in some wonder at a father hardly recognised, but let himself be drawn close by a gaunt, cold hand, and stared at hungrily by eyes like firelit caverns. His mother leaned and whispered to him, and obediently he stooped his rosy, round face and kissed a bony cheek. He was an accommodating child, puzzled but willing, and not at all afraid. Prestcote's eyes ranged beyond, and found Hugh Beringar.

'Rest content,' said Hugh, leaning close and answering what need not be asked, 'your borders are whole and guarded. The only breach has provided you your ransom, and even there the victory was ours. And Owain Gwynedd is our ally. What is yours to keep is in good order.'

The dulling glance faded beneath drooping lids, and never reached the girl standing stark and still in the shadows near the door. Cadfael had observed her, from his own retired place, and watched the light from brazier and lamp glitter in the tears flowing freely and mutely down her cheeks. She made no sound at all, she hardly drew breath. Her wide eyes were fixed on her father's changed, aged face, in the most grievous and desperate stare.

The sheriff had understood and accepted what Hugh said. Brow and chin moved slightly in a satisfied nod. His lips stirred to utter almost clearly: 'Good!' And to the boy, awed but curious, hanging over him: 'Good boy! Take care . . . of your mother . . .'

He heaved a shallow sigh, and his eyes drooped closed. They held still for some time, watching and listening to the heave and fall of the covers over his sunken breast and the short, harsh in and out of his breath, before Brother Edmund stepped softly forward and said in a cautious whisper: 'He's sleeping. Leave him so, in quiet. There is nothing better or more needed any man can do for him.'

Hugh touched Sybilla's arm, and she rose obediently and drew her son up beside her. 'You see him well cared for,' said Hugh gently. 'Come to dinner, and let him sleep.'

The girl's eyes were quite dry, her cheeks pale but calm, when she followed them out to the great court, and down the length of it to the abbot's lodging, to be properly gracious and grateful to the Welsh guests, before they left again for Montford and Oswestry.

Over their midday meal, which was served before the brothers ate in the refectory, the inhabitants of the infirmary laid their ageing but inquisitive heads together to make out what was causing the unwonted stir about their retired domain. The discipline of silence need not be rigorously observed among the old and sick, and just as well, since they tend to be incorrigibly garrulous, from want of other active occupation.

Brother Rhys, who was bedridden and very old indeed, but sharp enough in mind and hearing even if his sight was filmed over, had a bed next to the corridor, and across from the retired room where some newcomer had been brought during the morning, with unusual to-do and ceremony. He took pleasure in being the member who knew what was going on. Among so few pleasures left to him, this was the chief, and not to be lightly spent. He lay and listened. Those who sat at the table, as once in the refectory, and could move around the infirmary and sometimes the great court if the weather was right, nevertheless were often obliged to come to him for knowledge.

'Who should it be,' said Brother Rhys loftily, 'but the sheriff himself, brought back from being a prisoner in Wales.'

'Prescote?' said Brother Maurice, rearing his head on its stringy neck like a gander giving notice of battle. 'Here? In our infirmary? Why should they bring him here?'

'Because he's a sick man, what else? He was wounded in the battle, and in no shape to shift for himself yet, or trouble any other man. I heard their voices in there – Edmund, Cadfael and Hugh Beringar – and the lady, too, and the child. It's Gilbert Prestcote, take my word.'

'There is justice,' said Maurice with sage satisfaction, and the gleam of vengeance in his eye, 'though it be too long delayed. So Prestcote is brought low, neighbour to the unfortunate. The wrong done to my line finds a balance at last, I repent that ever I doubted.'

They humoured him, being long used to his obsessions. They murmured variously, most saying reasonably enough that the shire had not fared badly in Prestcote's hands, though some had old grumbles to vent and reservations about sheriffs in general, even if this one of theirs was not by any means the worst of his kind. On the whole they wished him well. But Brother Maurice was not to be reconciled.

'There was a wrong done,' he said implacably, 'which even now is not fully set right. Let the false pleader pay for his offence, I say, to the bitter end.'

The stockman Anion, at the end of the table, said never a word, but kept his eyes lowered to his trencher, his hip pressed against the crutch he was almost ready to discard, as though he needed a firm contact with the reality of his situation, and the reassurance of a weapon to hand in the sudden presence of his enemy. Young Griffri had killed, yes, but in drink, in hot blood, and in fair fight man against man. He had died a worse death, turned off more casually than wringing a chicken's neck. And the man who had made away with him so lightly lay now barely twenty yards away, and at the very sound of his name every drop of blood in Anion ran Welsh, and cried out to him of the sacred duty of *galanas*, the blood-feud for his brother.

Eliud led Einon's horse and his own down the great court into the stable-yard, and the men of the escort followed with their own mounts, and the shaggy hill ponies that had carried the litter. An easy journey those two would have on the way back to Montford. Einon ab Ithel, when representing his prince on a ceremonial occasion, required a squire in attendance, and Eliud undertook the grooming of the tall bay himself. Very soon now he would be changing places with Elis, and left to chafe here while his cousin rode back to his freedom in Wales. In silence he hoisted off the heavy saddle, lifted aside the elaborate harness, and draped the saddle-cloth over his arm. The bay tossed his head with pleasure in his freedom, and blew great misty breaths. Eliud caressed him absently; his mind was not wholly on what he was doing, and his companions had found him unusually silent and withdrawn all that day. They eyed him cautiously and let him alone. It was no great surprise when he suddenly turned and tramped away out of the stable-yard, back to the open court.

'Gone to see whether there's any sign of his cousin yet,' said his neighbour tolerantly, rubbing down one of the shaggy ponies. 'He's been like a man maimed and out of balance ever since the other one went off to Lincoln. He can hardly believe it yet that he'll turn up here without a scratch on him.'

'He should know his Elis better than that,' grunted the man beside him. 'Never yet did that one fall anywhere but on his feet.'

Eliud was away perhaps ten minutes, long enough to have been all the way to the gatehouse and peered anxiously along the Foregate towards the town, but he came back in dour silence, laid aside the saddle-cloth he was still carrying, and went to work without a word or a look aside.

'Not come yet?' asked his neighbour with careful sympathy.

'No,' said Eliud shortly, and continued working vigorously on the bright bay hide.

'The castle's the far side of the town, they'll have kept him there until they were sure of our man. They'll bring him. He'll be at dinner with us.'

Eliud said nothing. At this hour the monks themselves were at their meal in the refectory, and the abbot's guests with him at his own table in his lodging. It was the quietest hour of the day; even the comings and goings about the guest-hall were few at this time of year, though with the spring the countryside would soon be on the move again.

'Never show him so glum a face,' said the Welshman, grinning, 'even if you must be left here in his place. Ten days or so, and Owain and this young sheriff will be clasping hands on the border, and you on your way home to join him.'

Eliud muttered a vague agreement, and turned a forbidding shoulder on further talk. He had Einon's horse stalled and glossy and watered by the time Brother Denis the hospitaller came to bid them to the refectory, newly laid and decked for them after the brothers had ended their repast, and dispersed to enjoy their brief rest before the afternoon's work began. The resources of the house were at their disposal, warmed water brought to the lavatorium for their hands, towels laid out and their table, when they entered the refectory, graced with more dishes than the brothers had enjoyed. And there waiting, somewhat in the manner of a nervous host, was Elis ap Cynan, freshly brushed and spruced for the occasion, and on his most formal behaviour.

The awe of the exchange, himself the unwise cause of it and to some extent already under censure for his unwisdom, or something

67

else of like weight, had had its effect upon Elis, for he came with stiff bearing and very sombre face, who was known rather for his hearty cheerfulness in and out of season. Certainly his eyes shone at the sight of Eliud entering, and he came with open arms to embrace him, but thereafter shoved free again. The grip of his hand had some unaccountable tension about it, and though he sat down to table beside his cousin, the talk over that meal was general and restrained. It caused some mild wonder among their companions. There were these two inseparables, together again after long and anxious separation, and both as mute as blocks, and as pale and grave of face as men arraigned for their lives.

It was very different when the meal was over, the grace said, and they were free to go forth into the court. Elis caught his cousin by the arm and hauled him away into the cloister, where they could take refuge in one of the carrels where no monk was working or studying, and go to earth there like hunted foxes, shoulder warm for comfort against shoulder, as when they were children and fled into sanctuary from some detected misdeed. And now Eliud could recognise his foster-brother as he had always been, as he always would be, and marvelled fondly what misdemeanour or misfortune he could have to pour out here, where he had been so loftily on his dignity.

'Oh, Eliud!' blurted Elis, hugging him afresh in arms which had certainly lost none of their heedless strength. 'For God's sake, what am I to do? How shall I tell you! I can't go back! If I do, I've lost all. Oh, Eliud, I must have her! If I lose her I shall die! You haven't seen her? Prestcote's daughter?'

'His daughter?' whispered Eliud, utterly dazed. 'There was a lady, with a grown girl and a young boy . . . I hardly noticed.'

'For God's sake, man, how could you *not* notice her? Ivory and roses, and her hair all pale, like spun silver . . . I love her!' proclaimed Elis in high fever. 'And she is just as fain, I swear it, and we've pledged ourselves. Oh, Eliud, if I go now I shall never have her. If I leave her now, I'm lost. And he's an enemy, she warned me, he hates the Welsh. Never go near him, she said . . .'

Eliud, who had sat stunned and astray, roused himself to take his friend by the shoulders and shake him furiously until he fell silent for want of breath, staring astonished.

68

'*What* are you telling me? You have a girl here? You *love* her? You no longer want to make any claim on Cristina? Is *that* what you're saying?'

'Were you not listening? Haven't I told you?' Elis, unsubdued and unchastened, heaved himself free and grappled in his turn. 'Listen, let me tell you how it fell. What pledge did I myself ever give Cristina? Is it her fault or mine if we're tied like tethered cattle? She cares no more for me than I for her. I'd brother the girl and dance at her wedding, and kiss her and wish her well heartily. But this . . . this is another matter! Oh, Eliud, hush and hear me!'

It poured forth like music, the whole story from his first glimpse of her, the silver maiden at the door, blue-eyed, magical. Plenty of bards had issued from the stock to which Elis belonged, he had both the gift of words and the eloquent tune. Eliud sat stricken mute, gaping at him in blanched astonishment and strange dismay, his hands gripped and wrung in Elis's persuading hands.

'And I was frantic for you!' he said softly and slowly, almost to himself. 'If I had but known . . .'

'But Eliud, he's here!' Elis held him by the arms, peering eagerly into his face. 'He *is* here? You brought him, you must know. She says, don't go, but how can I lose this chance? I'm noble, I pledge the girl my whole heart, all my goods and lands, where will he find a better match? And she is not spoken for. I can, I must win him, he must listen to me . . . why should he not?' He flashed one sweeping glance about the almost vacant court. 'They're not yet ready, they haven't called us. Eliud, you know where he's laid. I'm going to him! I must, I will! Show me the place!'

'He's in the infirmary.' Eliud was staring at him with open mouth and wide, shocked eyes. 'But you can't, you mustn't . . . He's sick and weary, you can't trouble him now.'

'I'll be gentle, humble, I'll kneel to him, I'll put my life in his hands. The infirmary—which is it? I never was inside these walls until now. Which door?' He caught Eliud by the arm and dragged him to the archway that looked out on the court. 'Show me, quickly!'

'*No!* Don't go! Leave him be! For shame, to rush in on his rest . . .'

'*Which door?*' Elis shook him fiercely. 'You brought him, you

69

saw!'

'There! The building drawn back to the precinct wall, to the right from the gatehouse. But don't do it! Surely the girl knows her father best. Wait, don't harry him now—an old, sick man!'

'You think I'd offer any hardihood to *her father*? All I want is to tell him my heart, and that I have her favour. If he curses me, I'll bear it. But I must put it to the test. What chance shall I ever have again?' He made to pull clear, and Eliud held him convulsively, then as suddenly heaved a great sigh and loosed his hold.

'Go, then, try your fortune! I can't keep you.'

Elis was away, without the least caution or dissembling, out into the court and straight as an arrow across it to the door of the infirmary. Eliud stood in shadow to watch him vanish within, and leaned his forehead against the stone and waited with eyes closed some while before he looked again.

The abbot's guests were just emerging from the doorway of his lodging. The young man who was now virtually sheriff set off with the lady and her daughter, to conduct them again to the porch of the guest-hall. Einon ab Ithel lingered in talk with the abbot, his two companions, having less English, waited civilly a pace aside. Very soon he would be ordering the saddling of the horses, and the ceremonious leave-taking.

From the doorway of the infirmary two figures emerged, Elis first, stiffly erect, and after him one of the brothers. At the head of the few stone steps the monk halted, and stood to watch Elis stalk away across the great court, taut with offence, quenched in despair, like our first forefather expelled from Eden.

'He's sleeping,' he said, coming in crestfallen. 'I couldn't speak with him, the infirmarer turned me away.'

Barely half an hour now, and they would be on their way back to Montford, there to spend the first night of their journey into Wales. In the stables Eliud led out Einon's tall bay, and saddled and bridled him, before turning his attention to the horse he himself had ridden, which now Elis must ride in his place, while he lingered here.

The brothers had roused themselves after their customary rest, and were astir about the court again, on their way to their allotted labours. Some days into March, there was already work to be done in field and garden, besides the craftsmen who had their workshops in cloister and scriptorium. Brother Cadfael, crossing at leisure towards the garden and the herbarium, was accosted suddenly by an Eliud evidently looking about him for a guide, and pleased to recognise a face he knew.

'Brother, if I may trouble you – I've been neglecting my duty, there's something I had forgotten. My lord Einon left his cloak wrapping the lord Gilbert in the litter, for an extra covering. Of sheared sheepskins – you'll have seen it? I must reclaim it, but I don't want to disturb the lord Gilbert. If you will show me the place, and hand it forth to me . . .'

'Very willingly,' said Cadfael, and led the way briskly. He eyed the young man covertly as they walked together. That passionate, intense face was closed and sealed, but trouble showed in his eyes. He would always be carrying half the weight of that easy foster-brother of his who went so light through the world. And a fresh parting imminent, after so brief a reunion; and that marriage waiting to make parting inevitable and lifelong. 'You'll know the place,' said Cadfael, 'though not the room. He was deep asleep when we all left him. I hope he is still. Sleep in his own town, with his family by and his charge in good heart, is all he needs.'

'There was no mortal harm, then?' asked Eliud, low-voiced.

'None that time should not cure. And here we are. Come in with me. I remember the cloak. I saw Brother Edmund fold it aside on the chest.'

The door of the narrow chamber had been left ajar, to avoid the noise of the iron latch, but it creaked on being opened far enough to admit entrance. Cadfael slipped through the opening sidewise, and paused to look attentively at the long, still figure in the bed, but it remained motionless and oblivious. The brazier made a small, smokeless eye of gold in the dimness within. Reassured, Cadfael crossed to the chest on which the clothes lay folded and gathered up the sheepskin cloak. Unquestionably it was the one Eliud sought, and yet even at this moment Cadfael was oddly aware that it did not answer exactly to his recollection of it, though he did not stop to try and identify what was changed about it. He had turned back to the door, where Eliud hovered half-in, half-out, peering anxiously, when the young man made a step aside to let him go first into the passage, and knocked over the stool that stood in the corner. It fell with a loud wooden clap and rolled. Eliud bent to arrest its flight and snatch it up from the tiled floor and Cadfael, waving a hand furiously at him for silence, whirled round to see if the noise had startled the sleeper awake.

Not a movement, not a sharp breath, not a sigh. The long body, scarcely lifting the bedclothes, lay still as before. Too still. Cadfael went close, and laid a hand to draw down the brychan that covered the grizzled beard and hid the mouth. The bluish eyelids in their sunken hollows stared up like carven eyes in a tomb sculpture. The lips were parted and drawn a little back from clenched teeth, as if in some constant and customary pain. The gaunt breast did not move at all. No noise could ever again disturb Gilbert Prestcote's sleep.

'What is it?' whispered Eliud, creeping close to gaze.

'Take this,' ordered Cadfael, thrusting the folded cloak into the boy's hands. 'Come with me to your lord and Hugh Beringar, and God grant the women are safe indoors.'

He need not have been in immediate anxiety for the women, he saw as he emerged into the open court with Eliud mute and quivering at his heels. It was chilly out there, and this was men's business now the civilities were properly attended to, and Lady Prestcote had made her farewells and withdrawn with Melicent into the guest-hall. The Welsh party were waiting with Hugh in an easy group near the gatehouse, ready to mount and ride, the horses saddled and tramping the cobbles with small, ringing sounds. Elis stood docile and dutiful at Einon's stirrup, though he did not look overjoyed at being on his way home. His face was overcast like the sky. At the sound of Cadfael's rapid steps approaching, and the sight of his face, every eye turned to fasten on him.

'I bring black news,' said Cadfael bluntly. 'My lord, your labour has been wasted, and I doubt your departure must wait yet a while. We are just come from the infirmary. Gilbert Prestcote is dead.'

SIX

They went with him, Hugh Beringar and Einon ab Ithel, jointly responsible here for this exchange of prisoners which had suddenly slithered away out of their control. They stood beside the bed in the dim, quiet room, the little lamp a mild yellow eye on one side, the brazier a clear red one on the other. They gazed and touched, and held a bright, smooth blade to the mouth and nose, and got no trace of breath. The body was warm and pliable, no long time dead; but dead indeed.

'Wounded and weak, and exhausted with travelling,' said Hugh wretchedly. 'No blame to you, my lord, if he had sunk too far to climb back again.'

'Nevertheless, I had a mission,' said Einon. 'My charge was to bring you one man, and take another back from you in exchange. This matter is void, and cannot be completed.'

'So you did bring him, living, and living you delivered him over. It is in our hands his death came. There is no bar but you should take your man and go, according to the agreement. Your part was done, and done well.'

'Not well enough. The man is dead. My prince does not countenance the exchange of a dead man for one living,' said Einon haughtily. 'I split no hairs, and will have none split in my favour. Nor will Owain Gwynedd. We have brought you, however innocently, a dead man. I will not take a live one for him. This exchange cannot go forward. It is null and void.'

Brother Cadfael, though with one ear pricked and aware of these meticulous exchanges, which were no more than he had foreseen, had taken up the small lamp, shielding it from draughts with his free hand, and held it close over the dead face. No very arduous or

73

harsh departure. The man had been deeply asleep, and very much enfeebled, to slip over a threshold would be all too easy. Not, however, unless the threshold were greased or had too shaky a doorstone. This mute and motionless face, growing greyer as he gazed, was a face familiar to him for some years, fallen and aged though it might be. He searched it closely, moving the lamp to illumine every plane and every cavernous hollow. The pitted places had their bluish shadows, but the full lips, drawn back a little, should not have shown the same livid tint, nor the pattern of the large, strong teeth within, and the staring nostrils should not have gaped so wide and shown the same faint bruising.

'You will do what seems to you right,' said Hugh at his back, 'but I, for my part, make plain that you are free to depart in company as you came, and take both your young men with you. Send back mine, and I consider the terms will have been faithfully observed. Or if Owain Gwynedd still wants a meeting, so much the better, I will go to him on the border, wherever he may appoint, and take my hostage from him there.'

'Owain will speak his own mind,' said Einon, 'when I have told him what has happened. But without his word I must leave Elis ap Cynan unredeemed, and take Eliud back with me. The price due for Elis has not been paid, not to my satisfaction. He stays here.'

'I am afraid,' said Cadfael, turning abruptly from the bed, 'Elis will not be the only one constrained to remain here.' And as they fixed him with two blank and questioning stares: 'There is more here than you know. Hugh said well, there was no mortal harm to him, all he needed was time, rest and peace of mind, and he would have come back to himself. An older self before his time, perhaps, but he would have come. This man did not simply drown in his own weakness and weariness. There was a hand that held him under.'

'You are saying,' said Hugh, after a bleak silence of dismay and doubt, 'that this was murder?'

'I am saying so. There are the signs on him clear.'

'Show us,' said Hugh.

He showed them, one intent face stooped on either side to follow the tracing of his finger. 'It would not take much pressure, there would not be anything to be called a struggle. But see what signs

74

there are. These marks round nose and mouth, faint though they are, are bruises he had not when we bedded him. His lips are plainly bruised, and if you look closely you will see the shaping of his teeth in the marks on the upper lip. A hand was clamped over his face to cut off breath. I doubt if he awoke, in his deep sleep and low state it would not take long.'

Einon looked at the furnishings of the bed, and asked, low-voiced: 'What was used to muffle nose and mouth, then? These covers?'

'There's no knowing yet. I need better light and time enough. But as sure as God sees us, the man was murdered.'

Neither of them raised a word to question further. Einon had experience of many kinds of dying, and Hugh had implicit trust by now in Brother Cadfael's judgement. They looked wordlessly at each other for a long, thinking while.

'The brother here is right,' said Einon then, 'I cannot take away any of my men who may by the very furthest cast have any part in this killing. Not until truth is shown openly can they return home.'

'Of all your party,' said Hugh, 'you, my lord, and your two captains are absolutely clear of any slur. You never entered the infirmary until now, they have not entered it at all, and all three have been in my company and in the abbot's company every minute of this visit, besides the witness of the women. There is no one can keep you, and it is well you should return to Owain Gwynedd, and let him know what has happened here. In the hope that truth may out very soon, and set all the guiltless free.'

'I will so return, and they with me. But for the rest . . .' They were both considering that, recalling how the party had separated to its several destinations, the abbot's guests with him to his lodging, the rest to the stables to tend their horses, and after that to wander where they would and talk to whom they would until they were called to the refectory for their dinner. And that half-hour before the meal saw the court almost empty.

'There is not one other among us,' said Einon, 'who could not have entered here. Six men of my own, and Eliud. Unless some of them were in company with men of this household, or within sight of such, throughout. That I doubt, but it can be examined.'

'There are also all within here to be considered. Of all of us, surely your Welshmen had the least cause to wish him dead, having carried and cared for him all this way. It is madness to think it. Here are the brothers, such wayfarers as they have within the precinct, the lay servants, myself, though I have been with you the whole while, my men who brought Elis from the castle . . . Elis himself . . .'

'He was taken straight to the refectory,' said Einon. 'However, he above all stays here. We had best be about sifting out any of mine who can be vouched for throughout, and if there are such I will have them away with me, for the sooner Owain Gwynedd knows of this, the better.'

'And I,' said Hugh ruefully, 'must go break the news to his widow and daughter, and make report to the lord abbot, and a sorry errand that will be. Murder in his own enclave!'

Abbot Radulfus came, grimly composed, looked long and grievously at the dead face, heard what Cadfael had to tell, and covered the stark visage with a linen cloth. Prior Robert came, jolted out of his aristocratic calm, shaking his silver head over the iniquity of the world and the defilement of holy premises. There would have to be ceremonies of re-consecration to make all pure again, and that could not be done until truth was out and justice vindicated. Brother Edmund came, distressed beyond all measure at such a happening in his province and under his devoted and careful rule, as though the guilt of it fouled his own hands and set a great black stain against his soul. It was hard to comfort him. Over and over he lamented that he had not placed a constant watch by the sheriff's bed, but how could any man have known that there would be need? Twice he had looked in, and found all quiet and still, and left it so. Quietness and stillness, time and rest, these were what the sick man most required. The door had been left ajar, any brother passing by could have heard if the sleeper had awakened and wanted for any small service.

'Hush you, now!' said Cadfael sighing. 'Take to yourself no more than your due, and that's small enough. There's no man takes better care of his fellows, as well you know. Keep your balance, for you and I will have to question all those within here, if they heard or saw anything amiss.'

Einon ab Ithel was gone by then, with only his two captains to bear him company, his hill ponies on a leading rein, back to Montford for the night, and then as fast as might be to wherever Owain Gwynedd now kept his border watch in the north. There was not one of his men could fill up every moment of his time within here, and bring witnesses to prove it. Here or in the closer ward of the castle they must stay, until Prestcote's murderer was found and named.

Hugh, wisely enough, had gone first to the abbot, and only after speeding the departing Welsh did he go to perform the worst errand of all.

Edmund and Cadfael withdrew from the bedside when the two women came in haste and tears from the guest-hall, Sybilla stumbling blindly on Hugh's arm. The little boy they had managed to leave in happy ignorance with Sybilla's maid. There would be a better time than this to tell him he was fatherless.

Behind him, as he drew the door quietly to, Cadfael heard the widow break into hard and painful weeping, as quickly muffled in the coverings of her husband's bed. From the girl not a sound. She had walked into the room stiffly, with blanched, icy face and eyes fallen empty with shock.

In the great court the little knot of Welshmen hung uneasily together, with Hugh's guards unobtrusive but watchful on all sides, and in particular between them and the closed wicket in the gate. Elis and Eliud, struck silent and helpless in this disaster, stood a little apart, not touching, not looking at each other. Now for the first time Cadfael could see a family resemblance in them, so tenuous that in normal times it would never be noticed, while the one went solemn and thoughtful, and the other as blithe and untroubled as a bird. Now they both wore the same shocked visage, the one as lost as the other, and they could almost have been twin brothers.

They were still standing there waiting to be disposed of, and shifting miserably from foot to foot in silence, when Hugh came back across the court with the two women. Sybilla had regained a bleak but practical control over her tears, and showed more stiffening in her backbone than Cadfael, for one, had expected. Most likely she had already turned a part of her mind and energy

77

to the consideration of her new situation, and what it meant for her son, who was now the lord of six valuable manors, but all of them in this vulnerable border region. He would need either a very able steward or a strong and well-disposed step-father. Her lord was dead, his overlord the king a prisoner; there was no one to force her into an unwelcome match. She was many years younger than her lost husband, and had a dower of her own, and good enough looks to make her a fair bargain. She would live, and do well enough.

The girl was another matter. Within her frosty calm a faint fire had begun to burn again, deep sparks lurked in the quenched eyes. She turned one unreadable glance upon Elis, and then looked straight before her.

Hugh checked for a moment to commit the Welshmen of the escort to his sergeants, and have them led away to the security of the castle, with due civility, since all of them might be entirely innocent of wrong, but into close and vigilant guard. He would have passed on, to see the women into their apartments before attempting any further probing, but Melicent suddenly laid a hand upon his arm.

'My lord, since Brother Edmund is here, may I ask him a question, before we leave this in your hands?' She was very still, but the fire in her was beginning to burn through, and her pallor to show sharp edges of steel. 'Brother Edmund, you best know your own domain, and I know you watch over it well. There is no blame falls upon you. But tell us, who, if anyone, entered my father's chamber after he was left there asleep?'

'I was not constantly by,' said Edmund unhappily. 'God forgive me, I never dreamed there could be any need. Anyone could have gone in to him.'

'But you know of one who certainly did go in?'

Sybilla had plucked her step-daughter by the sleeve, distressed and reproving, but Melicent shook her off without a glance. 'And only one?' she said sharply.

'To my knowledge, yes,' agreed Edmund uncomprehendingly, 'but surely no harm. It was shortly before you all returned from the abbot's lodging. I had time then to make a round, and I saw the sheriff's door opened, and found a young man beside the bed, as though he meant to disturb his sleep. I could not have that, so I took him by the shoulder and turned him about, and pointed him out of the room. And he went obediently and made no protest. There was no word spoken,' said Edmund simply, 'and no harm done. The patient had not awakened.'

'No,' said Melicent, her voice shaken at last out of its wintry calm, 'nor never did again, nor never will. Name him, this *one.*'

And Edmund did not even know the boy's name, so little had he had to do with him. He indicated Elis with a hesitant hand. 'It was our Welsh prisoner.'

Melicent let out a strange, grievous sound of anger, guilt and pain, and whirled upon Elis. Her marble whiteness had become incandescent, and the blue of her eyes was like the blinding fire sunlight strikes from ice. 'Yes, *you*! None but you! None but you went in there. Oh, God, what have you and I done between us! And I, fool, fool, I never believed you could mean it, when you told me, many times over, you'd kill for me, kill whoever stood between us. Oh, God, and I *loved* you! I may even have invited you, urged you to the deed. I never understood. Anything, you said, to keep us together a while longer, anything to prevent your being sent away, back to Wales. *Anything!* You said you would kill, and now you have killed, and God forgive me, I am guilty along with you.'

Elis stood facing her, the poor lucky lad suddenly most unlucky and defenceless as a babe. He stared with dropped jaw and startled, puzzled, terrified face, struck clean out of words and wits, open to any stab. He shook his head violently from side to side, as if he could shake away a nightmare, after the fashion of those clever dreamers who use their fingers to prise open eyelids beset by unbearable dreams. He could not get out a word or a sound.

'I take back every evidence of love,' raged Melicent, her voice like a cry of pain. 'I hate you, I loathe you . . . I hate myself for ever loving you. You have so mistaken me, you have killed my father.'

He wrenched himself out of his stupor then, and made a wild move towards her. 'Melicent! For God's sake, what are you saying?'

She drew back violently out of his reach. 'No, don't touch me, don't come near me. Murderer!'

'This shall end,' said Hugh, and took her by the shoulders and put her into Sybilla's arms. 'Madam, I had thought to spare you

79

any further distress today, but you see this will not wait. Bring her! And sergeant, have these two into the gatehouse, where we may be private. Edmund and Cadfael, go with us, we may well need you.'

'Now,' said Hugh, when he had herded them all, accused, accuser and witnesses, into the anteroom of the gatehouse out of the cold and out of the public eye, 'now let us get to the heart of this. Brother Edmund, you say you found this man in the sheriff's chamber, standing beside his bed. How did you read it? Did you think, by appearances, he had been long in there? Or that he had but newly come?'

'I thought he had but just crept in,' said Edmund. 'He was close to the foot of the bed, a little stooped, looking down as though he wondered whether he dared wake the sleeper.'

'Yet he could have been there longer? He could have been standing over a man he had smothered, to assure himself it was thoroughly done?'

'It might be interpretable so,' agreed Edmund very dubiously, 'but the thought did not enter my mind. If there had been anything so sinister in him, would it not have shown? It's true he started when I touched him, and looked guilty – but I mean as a boy caught in mischief, nothing that caused me an ill thought. And he went, when I ordered him, as biddably as a child.'

'Did you look again at the bed, after he was gone? Can you say if the sheriff was still breathing then? And the coverings of the bed, were they disarranged?'

'All was smooth and quiet as when we left him sleeping. But I did not look more closely,' said Edmund sadly. 'I wish to God I had.'

'You knew of no cause, and his best cure was to be let alone to sleep. One more thing – had Elis anything in his hands?'

'No, nothing. Nor had he on the cloak he has on his arm now.' It was of a dark red cloth, smooth-surfaced and close-woven.

'Very well. And you have no knowledge of any other who may have made his way into the room?'

'No knowledge, no. But at any time entry was possible. There may well have been others.'

Melicent said with deadly bitterness: 'One was enough! And

80

that one we do know.' She shook Sybilla's hand from her arm, refusing any restraint but her own. 'My lord Beringar, hear me speak. I say again, he has killed my father. I will not go back from that.'

'Have your say,' said Hugh shortly.

'My lord, you must know that this Elis and I learned to know each other in your castle where he was prisoner, but with the run of the wards on his parole, and I was with my mother and brother in my father's apartments waiting for news of him. We came to see and touch – my bitter regret that I am forced to say it, we loved. It was not our fault, it happened to us, we had no choice. We came to extreme dread that when my father came home we must be parted, for then Elis must leave in his place. And you, my lord, who best knew my father, know that he would never countenance a match with a Welshman. Many a time we talked of it, many a time we despaired. And he said – I swear he said so, he dare not deny it! – he said he would kill for me if need be, kill any man who stood between us. Anything, he said, to hold us together, even murder. In love men say wild things. I never thought of harm, and yet I am to blame, for I was as desperate for love as he. And now he has done what he threatened, for he has surely killed my father.'

Elis got his breath, coming out of his stunned wretchedness with a heave that almost lifted him out of his boots. 'I did not! I swear to you I never laid hand on him, never spoke word to him. I would not for any gain have hurt your father, even though he barred you from me. I would have reached you somehow, there would have been a way . . . You do me terrible wrong!'

'But you did go to the room where he lay?' Hugh reminded him equably. 'Why?'

'To make myself known to him, to plead my cause with him, what else? It was the only present hope I had; I could not let it slip through my fingers. I wanted to tell him that I love Melicent, that I am a man of lands and honour, and desire nothing better than to serve her with all my goods and gear. He might have listened! I knew, she had told me, that he was sworn enemy to the Welsh, I knew it was a poor hope, but it was all the hope I had. But I never got the chance to speak. He was deep asleep, and before I ventured to disturb him the good brother came and banished me. This is the truth, and I will swear to it on the altar.'

'It *is* truth!' Eliud spoke up vehemently for his friend. He stood close, since Elis had refused a seat, his shoulder against Elis's shoulder for comfort and assurance. He was as pale as if the accusation had been made against him, and his voice was husky and low. 'He was with me in the cloister, he told me of his love, and said he would go to the lord Gilbert and speak to him man to man. I thought it unwise, but he would go. It was not many minutes before I saw him come forth, and Brother Infirmarer making sure he departed. And there was no manner of stealth in his dealings,' insisted Eliud stoutly, 'for he crossed the court straight and fast, not caring who might see him go in.'

'That may well be true,' agreed Hugh thoughtfully, 'but for all that, even if he went in with no ill intent, and no great hope, once he stood there by the bedside it might come into his mind how easy, and how final, to remove the obstacle – a man sleeping and already very low.'

'He never would!' cried Eliud. 'His is no such mind.'

'I did not,' said Elis, and looked helplessly at Melicent, who stared back at him stonily and gave him no aid. 'For God's sake, believe me! I think I could not have touched or roused him, even if there had been no one to send me away. To see a fine, strong man so – quite defenceless . . .'

'Yet no one entered there but you,' she said mercilessly.

'That cannot be proved!' flashed Eliud. 'Brother Infirmarer has said that the way was open, anyone might have gone in.'

'Nor can it be proved that anyone did,' she said with aching bitterness.

'But I think it can,' said Brother Cadfael.

He had all eyes on him in an instant. All this time some morsel of his memory had been worrying at the flaw he could not quite identify. He had picked up the folded sheepskin cloak from the chest, where he had watched Edmund lay it, and there had been something different about it, though he could not think what it could be. And then the encounter with death had driven the matter to the back of his mind, but it had lodged there ever since, like chaff in the throat after eating porridge. And suddenly he had it. The cloak was gone now, gone with Einon ab Ithel back to Wales, but

Edmund was there to confirm what he had to say. And so was Eliud, who would know his lord's belongings.

'When we disrobed and bedded Gilbert Prestcote,' he said, 'the cloak that wrapped him, which belonged to Einon ab Ithel, was folded and laid by – Brother Edmund will remember it – in such case as to leave plain to be seen in the collar a great gold pin that fastened it. When Eliud, here, came to ask me to show him the room and hand out his lord's cloak to him and I did so, the cloak was folded as before, but the pin was gone. Small wonder if we forgot the matter, seeing what else we found. But I knew there was something I should have noted, and now I have recalled what it was.'

'It is truth!' cried Eliud, his face brightening eagerly. 'I never thought! And I have let my lord go without it, never a word said. I fastened the collar of the cloak with it myself, when we laid him in the litter, for the wind blew cold. But with this upset, I never thought to look for it again. Here is Elis and has never been out of men's sight since he came from the infirmary – ask all here! If he took it, he has it on him still. And if he has it not, then someone else has been in there before him and taken it. My foster-brother is no thief and no murderer – but if you doubt, you have your remedy.'

'What Cadfael says is truth,' said Edmund. 'The pin was there plain to be seen. If it is gone, then someone went in and took it.'

Elis had caught the fierce glow of hope, in spite of the unchanging bitterness and grief of Melicent's face. 'Strip me!' he demanded, glittering. 'Search my body! I won't endure to be thought thief and murderer both.'

In justice to him, rather than having any real doubts in the matter, Hugh took him at his word, but allowed only Cadfael and Edmund to be witnesses with him in the borrowed cell where Elis, with sweeping, arrogant, hurt gestures, tore off his clothes and let them fall about him, until he stood naked with braced feet astride and arms outspread, and dragged disdainful fingers painfully through his thick thatch of curls and shook his head violently to show there was nothing made away there. Now that he was safe from the broken, embittered stare of Melicent's eyes the tears he had defied came treacherously into his own, and he blinked and shook them

83

proudly away.

Hugh let him cool gradually and in considerate silence.

'Are you content?' the boy demanded stiffly, when he had his voice well in rein.

'Are *you*?' said Hugh, and smiled.

There was a brief, almost consoling silence. Then Hugh said mildly: 'Cover yourself, then. Take your time.' And while Elis was dressing, with hands that shook now in reaction: 'You do understand that I must hold you in close guard, you and your foster-brother and the others alike. As at this moment, you are no more in suspicion than many who belong here within the pale, and will not be let out of it until I know to the last moment where they spent this morn and noon. This is no more than a beginning, and you but one of many.'

'I do understand,' said Elis and wavered, hesitant to ask a favour. 'Need I be separated from Eliud?'

'You shall have Eliud,' said Hugh.

When they went out again to those who still waited in the anteroom the two women were on their feet, and plainly longing to withdraw. Sybilla had but half her mind here in support of her step-daughter, the better half was with her son; and if she had been a faithful and dutiful wife to her older husband and mourned him truly now after her fashion, love was much too large a word for what she had felt for him and barely large enough for what she felt for the boy he had given her. Sybilla's thoughts were with the future, not the past.

'My lord,' she said, 'you know where we may be found for the days to come. Let me take my daughter away now, we have things which must be done.'

'At your pleasure, madam,' said Hugh. 'You shall not be troubled more than is needful.' And he added only: 'But you should know that the matter of this missing pin remains. There has been more than one intruder into your husband's privacy. Bear it in mind.'

'Very gladly I leave it all in your hands,' said Sybilla fervently. And forth she went, her hand imperative at Melicent's elbow. They passed close by Elis in the doorway, and his starving stare fastened on the girl's face. She passed him by without a glance, she even drew aside her skirts for fear they should brush him in departing. He was too young, too open, too simple to understand that more than half the hatred and revulsion she felt for him belonged rather to herself, and her dread that she had gone far towards desiring the death she now so desperately repented.

SEVEN

In the death-chamber, with the door closed fast, Hugh Beringar and Brother Cadfael stood beside Gilbert Prestcote's body and turned back the brychan and sheet to the sunken breast. They had brought in lamps to set close where they would burn steadily and cast a strong light on the dead face. Cadfael took the small saucer lamp in his hand and moved it slowly across the bruised mouth and nostrils and the grizzled beard, to catch every angle of vision and pick out every mote of dust or thread.

'No matter how feeble, no matter how deep asleep, a man will fight as best as he can for his breath, and whatever is clamped over his face, unless so hard and smooth it lacks any surface pile, he will inhale. And so did this one.' The dilated nostrils had fine hairs within, a trap for tiny particles of thread. 'Do you see colour there?'

In an almost imperceptible current of air a gossamer wisp quivered, taking the light. 'Blue,' said Hugh, peering close, and his breath caused the cobweb strand to dance. 'Blue is a difficult and expensive dye. And there's no such tint in these brychans.'

'Let's have it forth,' said Cadfael, and advanced his small tweezers, used for extracting thorns and splinters from unwary labouring fingers, to capture a filament almost too delicate to be seen. There was more of it, however, when it emerged, two or three fine strands that had the springy life of wool.

'Hold your breath,' said Cadfael, 'till I have this safe under a lid from being blown away.' He had brought one of the containers in which he stored his tablets and lozenges when he had moulded and dried them, a little polished wooden box, almost black in colour, and against the glossy dark surface the shred of wool shone brightly, a full, clear blue. He shut the lid upon it carefully, and probed again with the tweezers. Hugh shifted the lamp to cast its light at a new angle, and there was a brief gleam of red, the soft, pale red of late summer roses past their prime. It winked and vanished. Hugh moved the light to find it again. Barely two frail, curling filaments of the many that must have made up this wool that had woven the cloth, but wool carries colour bravely.

'Blue and rose. Both precious colours, not for the furnishings of a bed.' Cadfael captured the elusive thing after two or three casts, and imprisoned it with the blue. The light, carefully deployed, found no more such traces in the stretched nostrils. 'Well, he also wore a beard. Let us see!'

There was a clear thread of the blue fluttering in the greying beard. Cadfael extracted it, and carefully combed the grizzled strands out into order to search for more. When he shook and stroked out the dust and hairs from the comb into his box, two or three points of light glimmered and vanished, like motes of dust lit by the sun. He tilted the box from side to side to recover them, for they were invisible once dimmed, and one single gold spark rewarded him. He found what he sought caught between the clenched teeth. One strand had frayed from age or use, and the spasm of death had bitten and held it. He drew it forth and held it to the light in his tweezers. A first finger-joint long, brittle and bright, glinting in the lamplight, the gold thread that had shed those invisible, scintillating particles.

'Expensive indeed!' said Cadfael, shutting it carefully into his box. 'A princely death, to be smothered under cloth of fine wool embroidered with thread of gold. Tapestry? Altar-cloth? A lady's brocaded gown? A piece from a worn vestment? Certainly nothing here within the infirmary, Hugh. Whatever it may have been, some man brought it with him.'

'So it would seem,' agreed Hugh, brooding.

They found nothing more, but what they had found was puzzling enough.

'So where is the cloth that smothered him?' wondered Cadfael, fretting. 'And where is the gold pin that fastened Einon ab Ithel's cloak?'

'Search for the cloth,' said Hugh, 'since it has a richness that could well be found somewhere within the abbey walls. And I will search for the pin. I have six Welshmen of the escort and Eliud yet to question and strip, and if that fails, we'll burrow our way through the entire enclave as best we can. If they are here, we'll find them.'

They searched, Cadfael for a cloth, any cloth which could show the rich colours and the gold thread he was seeking, Hugh for the gold pin. With the abbot's leave and the assistance of Prior Robert, who had the most comprehensive knowledge of the riches of the house and demonstrated its treasures with pride, Cadfael examined every hanging, tapestry and altar-cloth the abbey possessed, but none of them matched the quivering fragments he brought to the comparison. Shades of colour are exact and consistent. This rose and this blue had no companions here.

Hugh, for his part, thoroughly searched the clothing and harness of all the Welshmen made prisoners by this death, and Prior Robert, though with disapproval, sanctioned the extension of the search into the cells of the brothers and novices, and even the possessions of the boys, for children may be tempted by a bright thing, without realising the gravity of what they do. But nowhere did they find any trace of the old and massive pin that had held the collar of Einon's cloak close to keep the cold away from Gilbert Prestcote on his journey.

The day was spent by then and the evening coming on, but after Vespers and supper Cadfael returned to the quest. The inhabitants of the infirmary were quite willing to talk; they had not often so meaty a subject on which to debate. Yet neither Cadfael nor Edmund got much information out of them. Whatever had happened had happened during the half-hour or more when the brothers were at dinner in the refectory, and at that time the infirmary, already fed, was habitually asleep. There was one, however, who, being bedridden, slept a great deal at odd times, and was well able to remain wakeful if something more interesting than usual was going on.

'As for seeing,' said Brother Rhys ruefully, 'I'm as little profit to you, brother, as I am to myself. I know if another inmate passes by me and I know which of them it is, and I know light from dark, but little more. But my ears, I dare swear, have grown sharper as my eyes have grown dimmer. I heard the door of the chamber opposite, where the sheriff lay, open twice, now you ask me to cudgel my memory. You know it creaks, opening. Closing, it's silent.'

'So someone entered there or at least opened the door. What more did you hear? Did anyone speak?'

'No, but I heard a stick tapping – very lightly – and then the door creaked. I reckoned it must be Brother Wilfred, who helps here when he's needed, for he's the only brother who walks with a stick, being lame from a young man.'

'Did he go in?'

'That you may better ask him, for I can't tell you. All was quiet a while, and then I heard him tap away along the passage to the outer door. He may only have pushed the door open to look and listen if all was well in there.'

'He must have drawn the door to again after him,' said Cadfael, 'or you would not have heard it creak again the second time. When was it Brother Wilfred paid his visit?'

But Rhys was vague about time. He shook his head and pondered. 'I did drowse for a while after my dinner. How should I know for how long? But they must have been still in the refectory some time after that, for it wasn't until later that Brother Edmund came back.'

'And the second time?'

'That must have been some while later, it might be as much as a quarter-hour. The door creaked again. He had a light step, whoever came, I just caught the fall of his foot on the threshold, and then nothing. The door making no sound, drawn to, I don't know how long he was within there, but I fancy he did go in. Brother Wilfred might have a proper call to peer inside to see all was well, but this other one had none.'

'How long was he within there? How long *could* he have been? Did you hear him leave?'

'I was in a doze again,' admitted Rhys regretfully. 'I can't tell you. And he did tread very soft, a young man's tread.'

So the second could have been Elis, for there had been no word spoken when Edmund followed him in and expelled him, and Edmund from long sojourning among the sick trod as silently as a

89

cat. Or it might have been someone else, someone unknown, coming and going undisturbed and deadly, before ever Elis intruded with his avowedly harmless errand.

Meantime, he could at least find out if Brother Wilfred had indeed been left here to keep watch, for Cadfael had not numbered the brothers in the refectory at dinner, or noticed who was present and who absent. He had another thought.

'Did anyone from within here leave this room during all that time? Brother Maurice, for one, seldom sleeps much during the day, and when others are sleeping he may well be restless, wanting company.'

'None of them passed by me to the door while I was waking,' said Rhys positively. 'And I was not so deep asleep but I think I should have awakened if they had.'

Which might very well be true, yet could not be taken for granted. But of what he had heard he was quite certain. Twice the door had creaked open wide enough to let somebody in.

Brother Maurice had spoken up for himself without even being asked, as soon as the sheriff's death was mentioned, as daily it would be now until the truth was known and the sensation allowed to fade away into oblivion. Brother Edmund reported it to Cadfael after Compline, in the half-hour of repose before bed.

'I had prayers said for his soul, and told them tomorrow we should say a Mass for him – an honourable officer who died here among us and had been a good patron of our house. Up stands Maurice and says outright that he will faithfully put up prayers for the man's salvation, for now at last his debts are fully paid, and divine justice has been done. I asked him by whose hand, seeing he knew so much,' said Edmund with uncharacteristic bitterness, but even more resignation, 'and he reproved me for doubting that the hand was God's. Sometimes I question whether his ailment of the mind is misfortune or cunning. But try to pin him down and he'll slip through your fingers every time. He is certainly very content with this death. God forgive us all our backslidings and namely those into which we fall unwitting.'

'Amen!' said Cadfael fervently. 'And he's a strong, able man, and always in the right, even if it came to murder. But where would he lay hands on such a cloth as I have in mind?' He remembered to

90

ask: 'Did you leave Brother Wilfred to keep a close eye on things here, when you went to dinner in the refectory?'

'I wish I had,' owned Edmund sadly. 'There might have been no such evil then. No, Wilfred was at dinner with us, did you never see him? I wish I had set a watch, with all my heart. But that's hindsight. Who was ever to suppose that murder would walk in and let loose chaos on us? There was nothing to give me warning.'

'Nothing,' agreed Cadfael and brooded, considering. 'So Wilfred is out of the reckoning. Who else among us walks with a stick? None that I know of.'

'There's Anion is still on a crutch,' said Edmund, 'though he's about ready to discard it. He rather flies with it now than hobbles, but for the moment it's grown a habit with him, after so stubborn a break. Why, are you looking for a man with a prop?'

Now there, thought Cadfael, going wearily to his bed at last, is a strange thing. Brother Rhys, hearing a stick tapping, looks for the source of it only among the brothers; and I, making my way round the infirmary, never give a thought to any but those who are brothers, and am likely to be blind and deaf to what any other may be up to even in my presence. For it had only now dawned on him that when he and Brother Edmund entered the long room, already settling for the evening, one younger and more active soul had risen from the corner where he sat and gone quietly out by the door to the chapel, the leather-shod tip of his crutch so light upon the stones that it seemed he hardly needed it, and could only have taken it away with him, as Edmund said, out of habit or in order to remove it from notice.

Well, Anion would have to wait until tomorrow. It was too late to trouble the repose of the ageing sick tonight.

In a cell of the castle, behind a locked door, Elis and Eliud shared a bed no harder than many they had shared before and slept like twin babes, without a care in the world. They had care enough now. Elis lay on his face, sure that his life was ended, that he would never love again, that nothing was left to him, even if he escaped this coil alive, but to go on Crusade or take the tonsure or undergo some barefoot pilgrimage to the Holy Land from which he would certainly never return. And Eliud lay patient and agonising at his back, with an arm wreathed over the rigid, rejecting shoulders, fetching up comfort from where he himself had none. This cousin-brother of his was far too vehemently alive to die for love, or to succumb for grief because he was accused of an infamy he had not committed. But his pain, however curable, was extreme while it lasted.

'She never loved me,' lamented Elis, tense and quivering under the embracing arm. 'If she had, she would have trusted me, she would have known me better. If ever she'd loved me, how could she believe I would do murder?' As indignantly as if he had never in his transports sworn that he would! That or *anything*.

'She's shocked to the heart for her father,' pleaded Eliud stoutly. 'How can you ask her to be fair to you? Only wait, give her time. If she loved you, then still she does. Poor girl, she can't choose. It's for her you should be sorry. She takes this death to her own account – have you not told me? You've done no wrong and so it will be proved.'

'No, I've lost her, she'll never let me near her again, never believe a word I say.'

'She will, for it will be proven you're blameless. I swear to you it will! Truth will come out, it must, it will.'

'If I don't win her back,' Elis vowed, muffled in his cradling arms, 'I shall die!'

'You won't die, you won't fail to win her back,' promised Eliud in desperation. 'Hush, hush and sleep!' He reached out a hand and snuffed out the failing flame of their tiny lamp. He knew the tensions and releases of this body he had slept beside from childhood, and knew that sleep was already a weight on Elis's smarting eyelids. There are those who come brand-new into the new day and have to rediscover their griefs. Eliud was no such person. He nursed his griefs, unsleeping, into the small hours, with the chief of them fathoms deep under his protecting arm.

EIGHT

Anion the cattle-man, for want of calf or lamb to keep his hand in within the abbey enclave, had taken to spending much of his time in the stables, where at least there was horseflesh to be tended and enjoyed. Very soon now he would be fit to be sent back to the grange where he served, but he could not go until Brother Edmund discharged him. He had a gifted hand with animals, and the grooms were on familiar and friendly terms with him.

Brother Cadfael approached him somewhat sidelong, unwilling to startle or dismay him too soon. It was not difficult. Horses and mules had their sicknesses and injuries, as surely as men, and called frequently for remedies from Cadfael's store. One of the ponies the lay servants used as pack-horses had fallen lame and was in need of Cadfael's rubbing oils to treat the strain, and he brought the flask himself to the stable-yard, as good as certain he would find Anion there. It was easy enough to entice the practised stockman into taking over the massage, and to linger to watch and admire as he worked his thick but agile fingers into the painful muscles. The pony stood like a statue for him, utterly trusting. That in itself had something eloquent to say.

'You spend less and less time in the infirmary now,' said Cadfael, studying the dour, dark profile under the fall of straight black hair. 'Very soon we shall be losing you at this rate. You're as fast on a crutch as many of us are with two sturdy legs that never suffered a break. I fancy you could throw the prop away anytime you pleased.'

'I'm told to wait,' said Anion shortly. 'Here I do what I'm told. It's some men's fate in life, brother, to take orders.'

'Then you'll be glad to be back with your cattle again, where

93

they do obedience to you for a change.'

'I tend and care for them and mean them well,' said Anion, 'and they know it.'

'So does Edmund to you, and you know it.' Cadfael sat down on a saddle beside the stooping man, to come down to his level and view him on equal terms. Anion made no demur, it might even have been the faint shadow of a smile that touched his firmly-closed mouth. Not at all an ill-looking man, and surely no more than twenty-seven or twenty-eight years old. 'You know the thing that happened there in the infirmary,' said Cadfael. 'You may well have been the most active man in there that dinner time. Though I doubt if you stayed long after you'd eaten. You're over-young to be shut in there with the ailing old. I've asked them all, did they hear or see any man go in there, by stealth or any other way, but they slept after they'd eaten. That's for the aged, not for you. You'd be up and about while they drowsed.'

'I left them snoring,' said Anion, turning the full stare of his deep-set eyes on Cadfael. He reached for a rag to wipe his hands, and rose nimbly enough, the still troublesome leg drawn up after him.

'Before we were all out of the refectory? And the Welsh lads led in to their repast?'

'While it was all quiet. I reckon you brothers were in the middle of your meal. Why?' demanded Anion pointblank.

'Because you might be a good witness, what else? Do you know of anyone who made his way into the infirmary about that time that you left it? Did you see or hear aught to give you pause? Any man lurking who should not have been there? The sheriff had his enemies,' said Cadfael firmly, 'like the rest of us mortals, and one of them deadly. Whatever he owed is paid now, or shortly to pay. God send none of us may take with him a worse account.'

'Amen!' said Anion. 'When I came forth from the infirmary, brother, I met no man, I saw no man, friend or enemy, anywhere near that door.'

'Where were you bound? Down here to view the Welsh horses? If so,' explained Cadfael easily, warding off the sharp glance Anion gave him, 'you'd be a witness if any of those lads went off and left his fellows about that time.'

94

Anion shrugged that off disdainfully. 'I never came near the stables, not then. I went through the garden and down to the brook. With a west wind it smells of the hills down there,' said Anion. 'I grow sick of the shut-in smell of tired old men, and their talk that goes round and round.'

'Like mine!' said Cadfael tolerantly, and rose from the saddle. His eye lingered upon the crutch that was laid carelessly aside against the open door of a stall, a good fifty paces from where its owner was working. 'Yes, I see you're about ready to throw it away. You were still using it yesterday, though, unless Brother Rhys was mistaken. He heard you tap your way out for your walk in the garden, or thought he did.'

'He well might,' said Anion, and shook back his shaggy black mane from his round brown forehead. 'It's habit with me, after so long, even after the need's gone. But when there's a beast to see to, I forget, and leave it behind me in corners.'

He turned deliberately, laid an arm over the pony's neck, and led him slowly round on the cobbles, to mark his gait. And that was the end of the colloquy.

Brother Cadfael was fully occupied with his proper duties all that day, but that did not prevent him from giving a great deal of thought to the matter of Gilbert Prestcote's death. The sheriff had long ago requested space for his tomb in the abbey church of which he had been a steady patron and benefactor, and the next day was to see him laid to rest there. But the manner of his death would not allow any rest to those who were left behind him. From his distracted family to the unlucky Welsh suspects and prisoners in the castle, there was no one who did not find his own life disrupted and changed by this death.

The news was surely making its way about the countryside by this time, from village to village and assart to manor round the shire, and no doubt men and women in the streets of Shrewsbury were busily allotting the blame to this one and that one, with Elis ap Cynan their favourite villain. But they had not seen the minute, bright fragments Cadfael nursed in his little box, or hunted in vain through the precinct for any cloth that could show the identical tints and the twisted gold thread. They knew nothing about the massive gold pin that had vanished from Gilbert's death-chamber and could not be found within the pale.

Cadfael had caught glimpses of Lady Prestcote about the court, moving between the guest-hall and the church, where her husband lay in the mortuary chapel, swathed for his burial. But the girl had not once shown her face. Gilbert the younger, a little bewildered but oblivious of misfortune, played with the child oblates and the two young pupils, and was tenderly shepherded by Brother Paul, the master of the children. At seven years old he viewed with untroubled tolerance the eccentricities of grown-up people, and could make himself at home wherever his mother unaccountably conveyed him. As soon as his father was buried she would certainly take him away from here, to her favourite among her husband's manors, where his life would resume its placid progress untroubled by bereavement.

A few close acquaintances of the sheriff had begun to arrive and take up residence ready for the morrow. Cadfael lingered to watch them, and fit noble names to the sombre faces. He was thus occupied, on his way to the herbarium, when he observed one unexpected but welcome face entering. Sister Magdalen, on foot and alone, stepped briskly through the wicket, and looked about her for the nearest known face. To judge by her brightening eye and prompt advance, she was pleased that it should be Cadfael's.

'Well, well!' said Cadfael, going to meet her with equal pleasure. 'We had no thought of seeing you again so soon. Is all well in your forest? No more raiders?'

'Not so far,' said Sister Magdalen cautiously, 'but I would not say they might not try again, if ever they see Hugh Beringar looking the other way. It must have gone much against the grain with Madog ap Meredith to be bested by a handful of foresters and cottars, he may well want his revenge when he feels it safe to bid for it. But the forest men are keeping a good watch. It's not we who are in turmoil now, it seems. What's this I've been hearing in the town? Gilbert Prestcote dead, and that Welsh youngster I sent you blamed for the deed?'

'You've been in the town, then? And no stout escort with you this time?'

'Two,' she said, 'but I've left them up in the Wyle, where we

96

shall lie overnight. If it's true the sheriff is to be buried tomorrow I must stay to do him honour among the rest. I'd no thought of such a thing when we set out this morning. I came on quite different business. There's a great-niece of Mother Mariana, daughter to a cloth-merchant here in Shrewsbury, who's coming to take the veil among us. A plain child, none too bright, but willing, and knows she has small hopes of a pleasing marriage. Better with us than sold off like an unpromising heifer to the first that makes a grudging offer for her. I've left my men and horses in their yard, where I heard tell of what had happened here. Better to get the tale straight – there are any number of versions up there in the streets.'

'If you have an hour to spare,' said Cadfael heartily, 'come and share a flask of wine of my own making in the herb-garden, and I'll tell you the whole truth of it, so far as any man knows what's truth. Who knows, you may find a pattern in it that I have failed to find.'

In the wood-scented dimness of the workshop in the herbarium he told her, at leisure and in detail, everything he knew or had gathered concerning the death of Gilbert Prestcote, everything he had observed or thought concerning Elis ap Cynan. She listened, seated with spread knees and erect back on the bench against the wall, with her cup nursed in both hands to warm it, for the wine was red and full. She no longer exerted herself to be graceful, if ever she had, but her composed heaviness had its own impressive grace.

'I would not say but that boy *might* kill,' she said at the end of it. 'They act before they think and regret only too late. But I don't think he would kill his girl's father. Very easy, you say, and I believe it, to ease the man out of the world, so that even one not given to murder might do it before ever he realised. Yes, but those a man kills easily are commonly strangers to him. Hardly people at all. But this one would be armoured in identity – her father, no less, the man that begot her. And yet,' she owned, shaking her head, 'I may be wrong about him. He may be the one of his kind who does what his kind does not do. There is always one.'

'The girl believes absolutely that he is guilty,' said Cadfael thoughtfully, 'perhaps because she is all too well aware of what she feels to be her own guilt. The sire returns and the lovers are to be torn apart – no great step to dream of his failure to return, and only

97

one more leap to see death as the final and total cause of that failure. But dreams they surely were, never truly even wished. The boy is on firmer ground when he swears he went to try and win her father to look kindly on his suit. For if ever I saw a lad sunlit and buoyed up with hope by nature, Elis is the one.'

'And this girl?' wondered Sister Magdalen, twirling her wine-cup between nursing palms. 'If they're of an age, then she must be the more mature by some years. So it goes! Is it anyway possible that she. . . ?'

'No,' said Cadfael with certainty. 'She was with the lady, and Hugh, and the Welsh princelings, throughout. I know she left her father living, and never came near him again until he was dead, and then in Hugh's company. No, she torments herself vainly. If you had her in your hands,' said Cadfael with conviction, 'you would soon find her out for the simple, green child she is.'

Sister Magdalen was in the act of saying philosophically: 'I'm hardly likely to get the chance,' when the tap on the door came. So light and tentative a sound, and yet so staunchly repeated, they fell silent and still to make sure of it.

Cadfael rose to open it and peer out through the narrowest possible chink, convinced there was no one there; and there she stood, her hand raised to knock again, pallid, wretched and resolute, half a head taller than he, the simple, green child of his description, with a steely core of Norman nobility forcing her to transcend herself. Hastily he flung the door wide. 'Come within from the cold. How can I serve you?'

'The porter told me,' said Melicent, 'that the sister from Godric's Ford came a while ago, and might be here wanting remedies from your store. I should like to speak with her.'

'Sister Magdalen is here,' said Cadfael. 'Come, sit with her by the brazier, and I'll leave you to talk with her in private.'

She came in half afraid, as though this small, unfamiliar place held daunting secrets. She stepped with fastidious delicacy, almost inch by inch, and yet with that determination in her that would not let her turn back. She looked at Sister Magdalen eye to eye, fascinated, doubtless having heard her history both ancient and recent, and found some difficulty in reconciling the two.

'Sister,' said Melicent, going arrow-straight to the point, 'when you go back to Godric's Ford, will you take me with you?'

Cadfael, as good as his word, withdrew softly and with alacrity, drawing the door to after him, but not so quickly that he did not hear Sister Magdalen reply simply and practically: 'Why?'

She never did or said quite what was expected of her, and it was a good question. It left Melicent in the delusion that this formidable woman knew little or nothing about her, and necessitated the entire re-telling of the disastrous story, and in the re-telling it might fall into truer proportion, and allow the girl to reconsider her situation with somewhat less desperate urgency. So, at any rate, Brother Cadfael hoped, as he trotted away through the garden to go and spend a pleasant half-hour with Brother Anselm, the precentor, in his carrel in the cloister, where he would certainly be compiling the sequence of music for the burial of Gilbert Prestcote.

'I intend,' said Melicent, rather grandly because of the jolt the blunt question had given her, 'to take the veil, and I would like it to be among the Benedictine sisters of Polesworth.'

'Sit down here beside me,' said Sister Magdalen comfortably, 'and tell me what has turned you to this withdrawal, and whether your family are in your confidence and approve your choice. You are very young, and have the world before you . . .'

'I am done with the world,' said Melicent.

'Child, as long as you live and breathe you will not have done with this world. We within the pale live in the same world as all poor souls without. Come, you have your reasons for wishing to enter the conventual life. Sit and tell me, let me hear them. You are young and fair and nobly born, and you wish to abandon marriage, children, position, honours, all . . . Why?'

Melicent, yielding, sank beside her on the bench, hugged her slenderness in the warmth of the brazier, and let fall the barriers of her bitterness to loose the flood. What she had vouchsafed to the preoccupied ears of Sybilla was no more than the thread on which this confession was strung. All that heady dream of minstrels' love-tales poured out of her.

'Even if you are right in rejecting one man,' said Magdalen mildly, 'you may be most unjust in rejecting all. Let alone the possibility that you mistake even this Elis ap Cynan. For until it is proved he lies, you must bear in mind he *may* be telling truth.'

'He said he would kill for me,' said Melicent, relentless, 'he went to where my father lay, and my father is dead. There was no other known to have gone near. As for me, I have no doubts. I wish I had never seen his face, and I pray I never may again.'

'And you will not wait to make your peace with one betrayal, and still show your countenance to others who do not betray?'

'At least I do know,' said Melicent bitterly, 'that God does not betray. And I am done with men.'

'Child,' said Sister Magdalen, sighing, 'not until the day of your death will you have done with men. Bishops, abbots, priests, confessors, all are men, blood-brothers to the commonest of sinful mankind. While you live, there is no way of escape from your part in humanity.'

'I have finished, then, with love,' said Melicent, all the more vehemently because a morsel of her heart cried out to her that she lied.

'Oh, my dear soul, love is the one thing with which you must never dispense. Without it, what use are you to us or to any? Granted there are ways and ways of loving,' said the nun come late to her celibacy, recalling what at the time she had hardly recognised as deserving the title, but knew now for one aspect of love, 'yet for all there is a warmth needed, and if that fire goes out it cannot be rekindled. Well,' she said, considering, 'if your stepmother approve your going with me, then you may come, and welcome. Come and be quiet with us for a while, and we shall see.'

'Will you come with me to my mother, then, and hear me ask her leave?'

'I will,' said Sister Magdalen, and rose and plucked her habit about her ready to set forth.

She told Brother Cadfael the gist of it when she stayed to attend Vespers before going back to the cloth-merchant's house in the town.

'She'll be better out of here, away from the lad, but left with the image of him she already carries about with her. Time and truth are what the pair of them most need, and I'll see she takes no vows

100

until this whole matter is resolved. The boy is better left to you, if you can keep an eye on him now and then.'

'You don't believe,' said Cadfael with certainty, 'that he ever did violence to her father.'

'Do I know? Is there man or woman who might not kill, given the driving need? A proper, upstanding, impudent, open-hearted lad, though,' said Sister Magdalen, who had never repented anything she did, 'one that I might have fancied, when my fancying days were.'

Cadfael went to supper in the refectory, and then to Collations in the chapter-house, which he often missed if he had vulnerable preparations brewing in his workshop. In thinking over such slight gains as he had made in his quest for the truth, he had got nowhere, and it was good to put all that aside and listen with good heart to the lives of saints who had shrugged off the cares of the world to let in the promises of a world beyond, and viewed earthly justice as no more than a futile shadow-play obscuring the absolute justice of heaven, for which no man need wait longer than the life-span of mortality.

They were past St Gregory and approaching St Edward the Confessor and St Benedict himself – the middle days of March, and the blessed works of spring beginning, with everything hopeful and striving ahead. A good time. Cadfael had spent the hours before Sister Magdalen came digging and clearing the fresh half of his mint-bed, to give it space to proliferate new and young and green, rid of the old and debilitated. He emerged from the chapter-house feeling renewed, and it came at first as no more than a mild surprise when Brother Edmund came seeking him before Compline, looking almost episcopal as he brandished in one hand what at first sight might have been a crozier, but when lowered to the ground reached no higher than his armpit, and was manifestly a crutch.

'I found it lying in a corner of the stable-yard. Anion's! Cadfael, he did not come for his supper tonight and he is nowhere in the infirmary – neither in the common room, nor in his bed, nor in the chapel. Have you seen him anywhere this day?'

'Not since morning,' said Cadfael, thinking back with something of an effort from the peace of the chapter-house. 'He came to dinner at midday?'

'So he did, but I find no man who has seen him since. I've looked for him everywhere, asked every man, and found nothing more of him than this, discarded. Anion is gone! Oh, Cadfael, I doubt he has fled his mortal guilt. Why else should he run from us?'

It was well past Compline when Hugh Beringar entered his own hall, empty-handed and discontented from his enquiries among the Welshmen, and found Brother Cadfael sitting by the fireside with Aline, waiting for him with a clouded brow.

'What brings you here so late?' wondered Hugh. 'Out without leave again?' It had been known to happen, and the recollection of one such expedition, before the austere days of Abbot Radulfus, was an old and private joke between them.

'That I am not,' said Cadfael firmly. 'There's a piece of unexpected news even Prior Robert thought had better come to your ears as soon as possible. We had in our infirmary, with a broken leg mending and all but ready to leave us, a fellow named Anion. I doubt if the name means much to you, it was not you had to do with his brother. But do you remember a brawl in the town, two years ago now, when a gate-keeper on the bridge was knifed? Prestcote hanged the Welshman that did it – well, whether he did it or not, and naturally he'd say he didn't, but he was blind drunk at the time and probably never knew the truth of it himself. However it was, he was hanged for it. A young fellow who used to trade in fleeces to the town market from somewhere in Mechain. Well, this Anion is his brother born the wrong side of the brychan, when the father was doing the trading, and there was no bad blood between the two. They got to know each other and there was a fondness.'

'If ever I knew of this,' said Hugh, drawing up to the fire with him, 'I had forgot it.'

'So had not Anion. He's said little, but it's known he's nursed his grudge, and there's enough Welsh in him to make him look upon revenge as a duty, if ever the chance came his way.'

'And what of him now?' Hugh was studying his friend's face intently, foreseeing what was to come. 'Are you telling me this fellow was within the pale now, when the sheriff was brought there helpless?'

'He was, and only a door ajar between him and his enemy – if so he held him, as rumour says he did. Not the only one with a grudge, either, so that's no proof of anything more than this, that the opportunity was there. But tonight there's another mark against him. The man's gone. He did not come for his supper, he's not in his bed, and no man has seen him since dinner. Edmund missed him at the meal and has been looking for him ever since, but never a sign. And the crutch he was still using, though more from habit than need, was lying in the stable-yard. Anion has taken to his heels. And the blame, if blame there is,' said Cadfael honestly, 'is mine. Edmund and I have been asking every man in the infirmary if he saw or heard anything of note about the sheriff's chamber, any traffic in or out. It was but the same asking with Anion, indeed I was more cautious with him than with any when I spoke with him this morning in the stables. But for all that, no question, I've frightened him away.'

'Not necessarily a proof of guilt, to take fright and run,' said Hugh reasonably. 'Men without privilege are apt to suppose they'll be blamed for whatever's done amiss. Is it certain he's gone? A man just healed of a broken leg? Has he taken horse or mule? Nothing stolen?'

'Nothing. But there's more to tell. Brother Rhys, whose bed is by the door, across the passage from where the sheriff lay, heard the door creak twice and the first time he says someone entered, or at least pushed the door open, who walked with a stick. The second time came later, and may have been the time the Welsh boy went in there. Rhys is hazy about time, and slept before and after, but both visitors came while the court was quiet – he says, while we of the house were in the refectory. With that, and now he's run – even Edmund is taking it for granted Anion is your murderer. They'll be crying his guilt in the town by morning.'

'But you are not so sure,' said Hugh, eyeing him steadily.

'Something he had on his mind, surely, something he saw as guilt, or knew others would call guilt, or he would not have run. But murderer. . . ? Hugh, I have in that pill-box of mine certain proof of dyed wools and gold thread in whatever cloth was used to kill. *Certain* – whereas flight is uncertain proof of anything worse than fear. You know as I know that there was no such woven cloth anywhere in that room, or in the infirmary, or in the entire pale so far as we can discover. Whoever used it brought it with him. Where would Anion get hold of any such rich material? He can never have handled anything better than drab homespun and unbleached flax in his life. It casts great doubt on his guilt, though it does not utterly rule it out. It's why I did not press him too far – or thought I had not!' he added ruefully.

Hugh nodded guarded agreement, and put the point away in his mind. 'But for all that, tomorrow at dawn I must send out search parties between here and Wales, for surely that's the way he'll go. A border between him and his fear will be his first thought. If I can take him, I must and will. Then we may get out of him whatever it is he does know. A lame man cannot yet have got very far.'

'But remember the cloth. For those threads do not lie, though a mortal man may, guilty or innocent. The instrument of death is what we have to find.'

The hunt went forth at dawn, in small parties filtering through the woods by all the paths that led most directly to Wales; but they came back with the dark, empty-handed. Lame or no, Anion had contrived to vanish within half a day.

The tale had gone forth through the town and the Foregate by then, every shop had it and every customer, the ale-houses discussed it avidly, and the general agreement was that neither Hugh Beringar nor any other man need look further for the sheriff's murderer. The dour cattle-man with a grudge had been heard going into and leaving the death-chamber, and on being questioned had fled. Nothing could be simpler.

And that was the day when they buried Gilbert Prestcote, in the tomb he had had made for himself in a transept of the abbey church. Half the nobility of the shire was there to do him honour, and Hugh Beringar with an escort of his officers, and the provost of Shrewsbury, Geoffrey Corviser, with his son Philip and his son's wife Emma, and all the solid merchants of the town guild. The sheriff's widow came in deep mourning, with her small son round-eyed and awed at the end of her arm. Music and ceremony, and the immensity of the vault, and the candles and the torches, all charmed and fascinated him; he was good as gold throughout the service.

And whatever personal enemies Gilbert Prestcote might have had, he had been a fair and trusted sheriff to this county in general, and the merchant princes were well aware of the relative security and justice they had enjoyed under him, where much of England suffered a far worse fate.

So in his passing Gilbert had his due, and his people's weighty and deserved intercession for him with his God.

'No,' said Hugh, waiting for Cadfael as the brothers came out from Vespers that evening, 'nothing as yet. Crippled or not, it seems your Anion has got clean away. I've set a watch along the border, in case he's lying in covert this side till the hunt is called off, but I doubt he's already over the dyke. And whether to be glad or sorry for it, that's more than I know. I have Welsh in my own manor, Cadfael, I know what drives them, and the law that vindicates them where ours condemns. I've been a frontiersman all my life, tugged two ways.'

'You must pursue it,' said Cadfael with sympathy. 'You have no choice.'

'No, none. Gilbert was my chief,' said Hugh, 'and had my loyalty. Very little we two had in common, I don't know that I even liked him overmuch. But respect—yes, that we had. His wife is taking her son back to the castle tonight, with what little she brought here. I'm waiting now to conduct her.' Her step-daughter was already departed with Sister Magdalen and the cloth-merchant's daughter, to the solitude of Godric's Ford. 'He'll miss his sister,' said Hugh, diverted into sympathy for the little boy.

'So will another,' said Cadfael, 'when he hears of her going. And the news of Anion's flight could not change her mind?'

'No, she's marble, she's damned him. Scold if you will,' said Hugh, wryly smiling, 'but I've let fall the word in his ear already that she's off to study the nun's life. Let him stew for a while—he owes us that, at least. And I've accepted his parole, his and the other lad's, Eliud. Either one of them has gone bail for himself *and* his cousin, not to stir a foot beyond the barbican, not to attempt escape, if I let them have the run of the wards. They've pledged their necks, each for the other. Not that I want to wring either neck, they suit very well as they are, untwisted, but no harm in accepting their pledges.'

'And I make no doubt,' said Cadfael, eyeing him closely, 'that you have a very sharp watch posted on your gates, and a very alert watchman on your walls, to see whether either of the two, or which of the two, breaks and runs for it.'

'I should be ashamed of my stewardship,' said Hugh candidly, 'if I had not.'

'And do they know, by this time, that a bastard Welsh cowman in the abbey's service has cast his crutch and run for his life?'

'They know it. And what do they say? They say with one voice, Cadfael, that such a humble soul and Welsh into the bargain, without kin or privilege here in England, would run as soon as eyes were cast on him, sure of being blamed unless he could show he was a mile from the matter at the fatal time. And can you find fault with that? It's what I said myself when you brought me the same news.'

'No fault,' said Cadfael thoughtfully. 'Yet matter for consideration, would you not say? From the threatened to the threatened, that's large grace.'

NINE

Owain Gwynedd sent back his response to the events at
Shrewsbury on the day after Anion's flight, by the mouth of young
John Marchmain, who had remained in Wales to stand surety for
Gilbert Prestcote in the exchange of prisoners. The half-dozen
Welsh who had escorted him home came only as far as the gates of
the town, and there saluted and withdrew again to their own
country.

John, son to Hugh's mother's younger sister, a gangling youth of
nineteen, rode into the castle stiff with the dignity of the embassage
with which he was entrusted, and reported himself ceremoniously
to Hugh.

'Owain Gwynedd bids me say that in the matter of a death so
brought about, his own honour is at stake, and he orders his men
here to bear themselves in patience and give all possible aid until
the truth is known, the murderer uncovered, and they vindicated
and free to return. He sends me back as freed by fate. He says he
has no other prisoner to exchange for Elis ap Cynan, nor will he lift
a finger to deliver him until both guilty and innocent are known.'

Hugh, who had known him from infancy, hoisted impressed
eyebrows into his dark hair, whistled and laughed. 'You may stoop
now, you're flying too high for me.'

'I speak for a high-flying hawk,' said John, blowing out a great
breath and relaxing into a grin as he leaned back against the
guard-room wall. 'Well, you've understood him. That's the
elevated tenor of it. He says hold them and find your man. But
there's more. How recent is the news you have from the south? I
fancy Owain has his eyes and ears alert up and down the borders,
where your writ can hardly go. He says that the empress is likely to

win her way and be crowned queen, for Bishop Henry has let her into Winchester cathedral, where the crown and the treasure are guarded, and the archbishop of Canterbury is dilly-dallying, putting her off with – he can't well acknowledge her until he's spoken with the king. And by God, so he has, for he's been to Bristol and taken a covey of bishops with him, and been let in to speak with Stephen in his prison.'

'And what says King Stephen?' wondered Hugh.

'He told them, in that large way of his, that they kept their own consciences, that they must do, of course, what seemed to them best. And so they will, says Owain, what seems to them best for their own skins! They'll bend their necks and go with the victor. But here's what counts and what Owain has in mind. Ranulf of Chester is well aware of all this, and knows by now that Gilbert Prestcote is dead and this shire, he thinks, is in confusion, and the upshot is he's probing south, towards Shropshire and over into Wales, pouring men into his forward garrisons and feeling his way ahead by easy stages.'

'And what does Owain ask of us?' questioned Hugh, with kindling brightness.

'He says, if you will come north with a fair force, show your hand all along the Cheshire border, and reinforce Oswestry and Whitchurch and every other fortress up there, you will be helping both yourself and him, and he will do as much for you against the common enemy. And he says he'll come to the border at Rhyd-y-Croesau by Oswestry two days from now, about sunset, if you're minded to come and speak with him there.'

'Very firmly so minded!' said Hugh heartily, and rose to embrace his glowing cousin round the shoulders, and haul him out about the business of meeting Owain's challenge and invitation, with the strongest force possible from a beleaguered shire.

That Owain had given them only two and a half days in which to muster, provide cover for the town and castle with a depleted garrison, and get their host into the north of the shire in time for the meeting on the border, was rather an earnest of the ease and speed with which Owain could move about his own mountainous land than a measure of the urgency of their mutual watch. Hugh spent the rest of that day making his dispositions in Shrewsbury and sending out his call for men to those who owed service. At dawn the next day his advance party would leave, and he himself with the main body by noon. There was much to be done in a matter of hours.

Lady Prestcote was also marshalling her servants and possessions in her high, bleak apartments, ready to leave next morning for the most easterly and peaceful of her manors. She had already sent off one string of pack-ponies with three of her men-servants. But while she was in town it was sensible to purchase such items as she knew to be in short supply where she was bound, and among other commodities she had requested a number of dried herbs from Cadfael's store. Her lord might be dead and in his tomb, but she had still an honour to administer, and for her son's sake had every intention of proving herself good at it. Men might die, but the meats necessary to the living would still require preservatives, salts and spices to keep them good and palatable. The boy was given, also, to a childish cough in spring, and she wanted a jar of Cadfael's herbal rub for his chest. Between them, Gilbert Prestcote the younger and domestic cares would soon fill up the gap, already closing, where Gilbert Prestcote the elder had been.

There was no real need for Cadfael to deliver the herbs and medicines in person, but he took advantage of the opportunity as much to satisfy his curiosity as to enjoy the walk and the fresh air on a fine, if blustery, March day. Along the Foregate, over the bridge spanning a Severn muddied and turgid from the thaw in the mountains, in through the town gate, up the long, steep curve of the Wyle, and gently downhill from the High Cross to the castle gatehouse, he went with eyes and ears alert, stopping many times to exchange greetings and pass the time of day. And everywhere men were talking of Anion's flight, and debating whether he would get clean away or be hauled back before night in a halter.

Hugh's muster was not yet common gossip in the town, though by nightfall it surely would be. But as soon as Cadfael entered the castle wards it was plain, by the purposeful bustle everywhere, that something of importance was in hand. The smith and the fletchers were hard at work, so were the grooms, and store-wagons were being loaded to follow stolidly after the faster horse- and foot-men.

Cadfael delivered his herbs to the maid who came down to receive them, and went looking for Hugh. He found him directing the stalling of commandeered horses in the stables.

'You're moving, then? Northward?' said Cadfael, watching without surprise. 'And making quite a show, I see.'

'With luck, it need be only a show,' said Hugh, breaking his concentration to give his friend a warm sidelong smile.

'Is it Chester feeling his oats?'

Hugh laughed and told him. 'With Owain one side of the border and me the other, he should think twice. He's no more than trying his arm. He knows Gilbert is gone, but me he does not know. Not yet!'

'High time he should know Owain,' observed Cadfael. 'Men of sense have measured and valued him some while since, I fancy. And Ranulf is no fool, though I wouldn't say he's not capable of folly, blown up by success as he is. The wisest man in his cups may step too large and fall on his face.' And he asked, alert to all the sounds about him, and all the shadows that patterned the cobbles: 'Do your Welsh pair know where you're bound, and why, and who sent you word?'

He had lowered his voice to ask it, and Hugh, without need of a reason, did the same. 'Not from me. I've had no time to spare for civilities. But they're at large. Why?' He did not turn his head; he had noted where Cadfael was looking.

'Because they're bearing down on us, the pair in harness. And in anxiety.'

Hugh made their approach easier, waving into the groom's hands the thickset grey he had been watching about the cobbles, and turning naturally to withdraw from the stables as from a job finished for the present. And there they were, Elis and Eliud, shoulders together as though they had been born in one linked birth, moving in on him with drawn brows and troubled eyes.

'My lord Beringar . . .' It was Eliud who spoke for them, the quiet, the solemn, the earnest one. 'You're moving to the border? There's threat of war? Is it with Wales?'

'To the border, yes,' said Hugh easily, 'there to meet with the prince of Gwynedd. The same that bade you and all your company here bear your souls in patience and work with me for justice concerning the matter you know of. No, never fret! Owain Gwynedd lets me know that both he and I have a common interest in the north of this shire, and a common enemy trying his luck there. Wales is in no danger from me and my shire, I believe, in no danger from Wales. At least,' he added, reconsidering briskly, 'not from Gwynedd.'

The cousins looked along wide, straight shoulders at each other, measuring thoughts. Elis said abruptly: 'My lord, but keep an eye to Powys. They . . . we,' he corrected in a gasp of disgust, '*we* went to Lincoln under the banner of Chester. If it's Chester now, they'll know in Caus as soon as you move north. They may think it time . . . think it safe . . . The ladies there at Godric's Ford . . .'

'A parcel of silly women,' said Cadfael musingly into his cowl, but audibly, 'and old and ugly into the bargain.'

The round, ingenuous face under the tangle of black curls flamed from neck to brow, but did not lower its eyes or lose its fixed intensity. 'I'm confessed and shriven of all manner of follies,' said Elis sturdily, 'that among them. Only do keep a watch on them! I mean it! That failure will rankle, they may still venture.'

'I had thought of it,' said Hugh patiently. 'I have no mind to strip this border utterly of men.'

The boy's blush faded and flamed anew. 'Pardon!' he said. 'It is your field. Only I do know . . . It will have gone deep, that rebuff.'

Eliud plucked at his cousin's arm, drawing him back. They withdrew some paces without withdrawing their twin, troubled gaze. At the gate of the stables they turned, still with one last glance over their shoulders, and went away still linked, as one disconsolate creature.

'Christ!' said Hugh on a blown breath, looking after them. 'And I with less men than I should like, if truth be told, and that green child to warn me! As if I do not know I take chances now with every breath I draw and every archer I move. Should I ask him how a man spreads half a company across three times a company's span?'

'Ah, but he would have your whole force drawn up between Godric's Ford and his own countrymen,' said Cadfael tolerantly. 'The girl he fancies is there. I doubt if he cares so much what happens to Oswestry or Whitchurch, provided the Long Forest is left undisturbed. They've neither of them given you any trouble?'

'Good as gold! Not a step even into the shadow of the gate.' It was said with casual certainty. Cadfael drew his own conclusions. Hugh had someone commissioned to watch every move the two prisoners made, and knew all that they did, if not all that they said, from dawn to dark, and if ever one of them did advance a foot over the threshold, his toes would be promptly and efficiently trampled on. Unless, of course, it was more important to follow, and find out with what intent he broke his parole. But when Hugh was in the north, who was to say his deputy would maintain the same unobtrusive watch?

'Who is it you're leaving in charge here?'

'Young Alan Herbard. But Will Warden will have a hand on his shoulder. Why, do you expect a bolt for it as soon as my back's turned?' By the tone of his voice Hugh was in no great anxiety on that score. 'There's no absolute certainty in any man, when it comes to it, but those two have been schooled under Owain, and measure themselves by him, and by and large I'd take their word.'

So thought Cadfael, too. Yet it's truth that to any man may come the one extreme moment when he turns his back on his own nature and goes the contrary way. Cadfael caught one more glimpse of the cousins as he turned for home and passed through the outer ward. They were up on the guard-walk of the curtain wall, leaning together in one of the wide embrasures between the merlons, and gazing clean across the busy wards of the castle into the hazy distance beyond the town, on the road to Wales. Eliud's arm was about Elis's shoulders, to settle them comfortably into the space, and the two faces were close together and equally intent and reticent. Cadfael went back through the town with that dual likeness before his mind's eye, curiously memorable and deeply disturbing. More than ever they looked to him like mirror images, where left and right were interchangeable, the bright side and the dark side of the same being.

Sybilla Prestcote departed, her son on his stout brown pony at her elbow, her train of servants and pack-horses stirring the March mire which the recent east winds were drying into fine dust. Hugh's advance party had left at dawn, he and his main body of archers and men-at-arms followed at noon, and the commissariat

112

wagons creaked along the northern road between the two groups, soon overhauled and left behind on the way to Oswestry. In the castle a somewhat nervous Alan Herbard, son of a knight and eager for office, mounted scrupulous guard and made every round of his responsibilities twice, for fear he had missed something the first time. He was athletic, fairly skilled in arms, but of small experience as yet, and well aware that any one of the sergeants Hugh had left behind was better equipped for the task in hand than he. They knew it, too, but spared him the too obvious demonstration of it.

A curious quiet descended on town and abbey with the departure of half the garrison, as though nothing could now happen here. The Welsh prisoners were condemned to boredom in captivity, the quest for Gilbert's murderer was at a standstill, there was nothing to be done but go on with the daily routine of work and leisure and worship, and wait.

And think, since action was suspended. Cadfael found himself thinking all the more steadily and deeply about the two missing pieces that held the whole puzzle together, Einon ab Ithel's gold pin, which he remembered very clearly, and that mysterious cloth which he had never seen, but which had stifled a man and urged him out of the world.

But was it so certain that he had never seen it? Never consciously, yet it had been here, here within the enclave, within the infirmary, within that room. It had been here, and now was not. And the search for it had been begun the same day, and the gates had been closed to all men attempting departure from the moment the death was discovered. How long an interval did that leave? Between the withdrawal of the brothers into the refectory and the finding of Gilbert dead, any man might have walked out by the gatehouse unquestioned. A matter of nearly two hours. That was one possibility.

The second possibility, thought Cadfael honestly, is that both cloth and pin are still here, somewhere within the enclave, but so well hidden that all our searching has not uncovered them.

And the third—he had been mulling it over in his mind all day, and repeatedly discarding it as a pointless aberration, but still it came back insistently, the one loophole. Yes, Hugh had put a guard on the gate from the moment the crime was known, but three people had been let out, all the same, the three who could not possibly have killed, since they had been in the abbot's company and Hugh's throughout. Einon ab Ithel and his two captains had ridden back to Owain Gwynedd. They had not taken any particle of guilt with them, yet they might unwittingly have taken evidence.

Three possibilities, and surely it might be worth examining even the third and most tenuous. He had lived with the other two for some days, and pursued them constantly, and all to no purpose. And for those countrymen of his penned in the castle, and for abbot and prior and brothers here, and for the dead man's family, there would be no true peace of mind until the truth was known.

Before Compline Cadfael took his trouble, as he had done many times before, to Abbot Radulfus.

'Either the cloth is still here among us, Father, but so well hidden that all our searching has failed to find it, or else it has been taken out of our walls by someone who left in the short time between the hour of dinner and the discovery of the sheriff's death, or by someone who left, openly and with sanction, after that discovery. From that time Hugh Beringar has had a watch kept on all who left the enclave. For those who may have passed through the gates before the death was known, I think they must be few indeed, for the time was short, and the porter did name three, all good folk of the Foregate on parish business, and all have been visited and are clearly blameless. That there may be others I do concede, but he has called no more to mind.'

'We know,' said the abbot thoughtfully, 'of three who left that same afternoon, to return to Wales, being by absolute proof clear of all blame. Also of one, the man Anion, who fled after being questioned. It is known to you, as it is to me, that for most men Anion's guilt is proven by his flight. It is not so to you?'

'No, Father, or at least not that mortal guilt. Something he surely knows, and fears, and perhaps has cause to fear. But not that. He has been in our infirmary for some weeks, his every possession is known to all those within – he has little enough, the list is soon ended – and if ever he had had in his hands such a cloth as I seek, it would have been noticed and questioned.'

Radulfus nodded agreement. 'You have not mentioned, though that also is missing, the gold pin from the lord Einon's cloak.'

'That,' said Cadfael, understanding the allusion, 'is possible. It would account for his flight. And he has been sought, and still is. But if he took the one thing, he did not bring the other. Unless he had in his hands such a cloth as I have shadowed for you, Father, then he is no murderer. And that little he had, many men here have seen and known. Nor, so far as ever we can discover, had this house ever such a weave within its store, to be pilfered and so misused.'

'Yet if this cloth came and went in that one day,' said Radulfus, 'are you saying it went hence with the Welsh lords? We know they did no wrong. If they had cause to think anything in their baggage, on returning, had to do with this matter, would they not have sent word?'

'They would have no such cause, Father, they would not know it had any importance to us. Only after they were gone did we recover those few frail threads I have shown you. How should they know we were seeking such a thing? Nor have we had any word from them, nothing but the message from Owain Gwynedd to Hugh Beringar. If Einon ab Ithel valued and has missed his jewel, he has not stopped to think he may have lost it here.'

'And you think,' asked the abbot, considering, 'that it might be well to speak with Einon and his officers, and examine these things?'

'At your will only,' said Cadfael. 'There is no knowing if it will lead to more knowledge than we have. Only, it *may*! And there are so many souls who need for their comfort to have this matter resolved. Even the guilty.'

'He most of all,' said Radulfus, and sat a while in silence. There in the parlour the light was only now beginning to fade. A cloudy day would have brought the dusk earlier. About this time, perhaps a little before, Hugh would have been waiting on the great dyke at Rhyd-y-Croesau by Oswestry for Owain Gwynedd. Unless, of course, Owain was like him in coming early to any meeting. Those two would understand each other without too many words. 'Let us go to Compline,' said the abbot, stirring, 'and pray for enlightenment. Tomorrow after Prime we will speak again.'

The Welsh of Powys had done very well out of their Lincoln venture, undertaken rather for plunder than out of any desire to support the earl of Chester, who was more often enemy than ally. Madog ap Meredith was quite willing to act in conjunction with Chester again, provided there was profit in it for Madog, and the news of Ranulf's probes into the borders of Gwynedd and Shropshire alerted him to pleasurable possibilities. It was some years since the men of Powys had captured and partially burned the castle of Caus, after the death of William Corbett and in the absence of his brother and heir, and they had held on to this advanced outpost ever since, a convenient base for further incursions. With Hugh Beringar gone north, and half the Shrewsbury garrison with him, the time seemed ripe for action.

The first thing that happened was a lightning raid from Caus along the valley towards Minsterley, the burning of an isolated farmstead and the driving off of a few cattle. The raiders drew off as rapidly as they had advanced, when the men of Minsterley mustered against them, and vanished into Caus and through the hills into Wales with their booty. But it was indication enough that they might be expected back and in greater strength, since this first assay had passed off so easily and without loss. Alan Herbard sweated, spared a few men to reinforce Minsterley, and waited for worse.

News of this tentative probe reached the abbey and the town next morning. The deceptive calm that followed was too good to be true, but the men of the borders, accustomed to insecurity as the commonplace of life, stolidly picked up the pieces and kept their billhooks and pitchforks ready to hand.

'It would seem, however,' said Abbot Radulfus, pondering the situation without surprise or alarm, but with concern for a shire threatened upon two fronts, 'that this conference in the north would be the better informed, on both parts, if they knew of this raid. There is a mutual interest. However short-lived it may prove,' he added drily, and smiled. A stranger to the Welsh, he had learned a great deal since his appointment in Shrewsbury. 'Gwynedd is close neighbour to Chester, as Powys is not, and their interests are very different. Moreover, it seems the one is to be trusted to be both honourable and sensible. The other – no, I would not say either wise or stable by our measure. I do not want these western people of ours harried and plundered, Cadfael. I have been thinking of what we said yesterday. If you return once again to Wales, to find these lords who visited us, you will also be close to where Hugh Beringar confers with the prince.'

'Certainly,' said Cadfael, 'for Einon ab Ithel is next in line to Owain Gwynedd's *penteulu*, the captain of his own guard. They will be together.'

'Then if I send you, as my envoy, to Einon, it would be well if you should also go to the castle, and make known to this young deputy there that you intend this journey, and can carry such messages as he may wish to Hugh Beringar. You know, I think,' said Radulfus with his dark smile, 'how to make such a contact discreetly. The young man is new to office.'

'I must, in any case, pass through the town,' said Cadfael mildly, 'and clearly I ought to report my errand to the authorities at the castle, and have their leave to pass. It is a good opportunity, where men are few and needed.'

'True,' said Radulfus, thinking how acutely men might shortly be needed down the border. 'Very well! Choose a horse to your liking. You have leave to deal as you think best. I want this death reconciled and purged, I want God's peace on my infirmary and within my walls, and the debt paid. Go, do what you can.'

There was no difficulty at the castle. Herbard needed only to be told that an envoy from the abbot was bound into Oswestry and beyond, and he added an embassage of his own to his sheriff. Raw and uneasy though he might be, he was braced and steeled to cope with whatever might come, but it was an additional snell of armour to have informed his chief. He was frightened but resolute; Cadfael thought he shaped well, and might be a useful man to Hugh, once blooded. And that might be no long way off.

'Let the lord Beringar know,' said Herbard, 'that I intend a close watch on the border by Caus. But I desire he should know the men of Powys are on the move. And if there are further raids, I will send word.'

'He shall know,' said Cadfael, and forthwith rode back a short spell through the town, down from the High Cross to the Welsh

117

bridge, and so north-west for Oswestry.

It was two days later that the next thrust came. Madog ap Meredith had been pleased with his first probe, and brought more men into the field before he launched his attack in force. Down the Rea valley to Minsterley they swarmed, burned and looted, wheeled both ways round Minsterley, and flowed on towards Pontesbury.

In Shrewsbury castle Welsh ears, as well as English, stretched and quivered to the bustle and fever of rumours.

'They are out!' said Elis, tense and sleepless beside his cousin in the night. 'Oh God, and Madog with this grudge to pay off! And *she* is there! Melicent is there at Godric's Ford. Oh, Eliud, if he should take it into his head to take revenge!'

'You're fretting for nothing,' Eliud insisted passionately. 'They know what they're doing here, they're on the watch, they'll not let any harm come to the nuns. Besides, Madog is not aiming there, but along the valley, where the pickings are best. And you saw yourself what the forest men can do. Why should he try that a second time? It wasn't his own nose was put out of joint there, either, you told me who led that raid. What plunder is there at Godric's Ford for such as Madog, compared with the fat farms in the Minsterley valley? No, surely she's safe there.'

'*Safe*! How can you say it? Where is there any safety? They should never have let her go.' Elis ground angry fists in the rustling straw of their palliasse, and heaved himself round in the bed. 'Oh, Eliud, if only I were out of here and free . . .'

'But you're not,' said Eliud, with the exasperated sharpness of one racked by the same pain, 'and neither am I. We're bound, and nothing we can do about it. For God's sake, do some justice to these English, they're neither fools nor cravens, they'll hold their city and their ground, and they'll take care of their women, without having to call on you or me. What right have you to doubt them? And you to talk so, who went raiding there yourself!'

Elis subsided with a defeated sigh and a drear smile. 'And got my come-uppance for it! Why did I ever go with Cadwaladr? God knows how often and how bitterly I've repented it since.'

'You would not be told,' said Eliud sadly, ashamed at having

118

salted the wound. 'But she will be safe, you'll see, no harm will come to her, no harm will come to the nuns. Trust these English to look after their own. You must! There's nothing else we can do.'

'If I were free,' Elis agonised helplessly, 'I'd fetch her away from there, take her somewhere out of all danger . . .'

'She would not go with you,' Eliud reminded him bleakly. 'You, of all people! Oh, God, how did we ever get into this quagmire, and how are we ever to get out of it?'

'If I could reach her, I could persuade her. In the end she would listen. She'll have remembered me better by now, she'll know she wrongs me. She'd go with me. If only I could reach her . . .'

'But you're pledged, as I am,' said Eliud flatly. 'We've given our word, and it was freely accepted. Neither you nor I can stir a foot out of the gates without being dishonoured.'

'No,' agreed Elis miserably, and fell silent and still, staring into the darkness of the shallow vault over them.

TEN

Brother Cadfael arrived in Oswestry by evening, to find town and castle alert and busy, but Hugh Beringar already departed. He had moved east after his meeting with Owain Gwynedd, they told him, to Whittington and Ellesmere, to see his whole northern border stiffened and call up fresh levies as far away as Whitchurch. While Owain had moved north on the border to meet the constable of Chirk and see that corner of the confederacy secure and well-manned. There had been some slight brushes with probing parties from Cheshire, but so tentative that it was plain Ranulf was feeling his way with caution, testing to see how well organised the opposition might prove to be. So far he had drawn off at the first encounter. He had made great gains at Lincoln and had no intention of endangering them now, but a very human desire to add to them if he found his opponents unprepared.

'Which he will not,' said the cheerful sergeant who received Cadfael into the castle and saw his horse stabled and the rider well entertained. 'The earl is no madman to shove his fist into a hornets' nest. Leave him one weak place he can gnaw wider and he'd be in, but we're leaving him none. He thought he might do well, knowing Prestcote was gone. He thought our lad would be green and easy. He's learning different! And if these Welsh of Powys have an ear pricked this way, they should also take the omens. But who's to reason what the Welsh will do? This Owain, now, he's a man on his own. Straw-gold like a Saxon, and big! What's such a one doing in Wales?'

'He came here?' asked Cadfael, feeling his Cambrian blood stir in welcome.

'Last night, to sup with Beringar, and rode for Chirk at dawn.

120

Welsh and English will man that fortress instead of fighting over it. There's a marvel!'

Cadfael pondered his errands and considered time. 'Where would Hugh Beringar be this night, do you suppose?'

'At Ellesmere, most like. And tomorrow at Whitchurch. The next day before we should look for him back here. He means to meet again with Owain, and make his way down the border after, if all goes well here.'

'And if Owain lies at Chirk tonight, where will he be bound tomorrow?'

'He has his camp still at Tregeiriog, with his friend Tudur ap Rhys. It's there he's called whatever new levies come in to his border service.'

So he must keep touch there always, in order to deploy his forces wherever they might be needed. And if he returned there the next night, so would Einon ab Ithel.

'I'll sleep the night here,' said Cadfael, 'and tomorrow I'll also make for Tregeiriog. I know the maenol and its lord. I'll wait for Owain there. And do you let Hugh Beringar know that the Welsh of Powys are in the field again, as I've told you. Small harm yet, and should there be worse, Herbard will send word here. But if this border holds fast, and bloodies Chester's nose wherever he ventures it, Madog ap Meredith will also learn sense.'

This extreme border castle of Oswestry, with its town, was the king's, but the manor of Maesbury, of which it had become the head, was Hugh's own native place, and there was no man here who did not hold with him and trust him. Cadfael felt the solid security of Hugh's name about him, and a garrison doubly loyal – to Stephen and to Hugh. It was a good feeling, all the more now that Owain Gwynedd spread the benign shadow of his hand over a border that belonged by location to Powys. Cadfael slept well after hearing Compline in the castle chapel, rose early, took food and drink, and crossed the great dyke into Wales.

He had all but ten miles to go to Tregeiriog, winding all the way through the enclosing hills, always with wooded slopes one side or the other or both, and in open glimpses the bald grass summits leaning to view, and a sky veiled and still and mild overhead. Not mountain country, not the steel-blue rocks of the north-west, but hill-country always, with limited vistas, leaning hangers of woodland, closed valleys that opened only at the last moment to permit another curtained view. Before he drew too close to Tregeiriog the expected pickets heaved out of the low brush, to challenge, recognise and admit him. His Welsh tongue was the first safe-conduct, and stood him in good stead.

All the colours had changed since last he rode down the steep hillside into Tregeiriog. Round the brown, timbered warmth of maenol and village beside the river, the trees had begun to soften their skeletal blackness with a delicate pale-green froth of buds, and on the lofty, rounded summits beyond the snow was gone, and the bleached pallor of last year's grass showed the same elusive tint of new life. Through the browned and rotting bracken the first fronds uncurled. Here it was already Spring.

At the gate of Tudur's maenol they knew him, and came readily to lead him in and take charge of his horse. Not Tudur himself, but his steward, came to welcome the guest and do the honours of the house. Tudur was with the prince, doubtless at this hour on his way back from Chirk. In the cleft of the tributary brook behind the maenol the turfed camp-fires of his border levies gave off blue wisps of smoke on the still air. By evening the hall would again be Owain's court, and all his chief captains in this border patrol mustered about his table.

Cadfael was shown to a small chamber within the house, and offered the ceremonial water to wash off the dust of travel from his feet. This time it was a maid-servant who waited upon him, but when he emerged into the court it was to see Cristina advancing upon him in a flurry of blown skirts and flying hair from the kitchens.

'Brother Cadfael . . . it *is* you! They told me,' she said, halting before him breathless and intent, 'there was a brother come from Shrewsbury, I hoped it might be you. You know them—you can tell me the truth . . . about Elis and Eliud . . .'

'What have they already told you?' asked Cadfael. 'Come within, where we can be quiet, and what I can tell you, that I will, for I know you must have been in bitter anxiety.' But for all that, he thought ruefully, as she turned willingly and led the way into the

122

hall, if he made that good, and told all he knew, it would be little to her comfort. Her betrothed, for whom she was contending so fiercely with so powerful a rival, was not only separated from her until proven innocent of murder, but disastrously in love with another girl as he had never been with her. What can you say to such a misused lady? Yet it would be infamous to lie to Cristina, just as surely as it would be cruel to bludgeon her with the blunt truth. Somewhere between the two he must pick his way.

She drew him with her into a corner of the hall, remote and shadowed at this hour when most of the men were out about their work, and there they sat down together against smoky tapestries, her black hair brushing his shoulder as she poured out what she knew and begged for what she needed to know.

'The English lord died, that I know, before ever Einon ab Ithel was ready to leave, and they are saying it was no simple death from his wounds, and all those who are not proven blameless must stay there as prisoners and suspect murderers, until the guilt is proven on some one man – English or Welsh, lay or brother, who knows? And here we must wait also. But what is being done to set them free? How are you to find the guilty one? Is all this true? I know Einon came back and spoke with Owain Gwynedd, and I know the prince will not receive his men back until they are cleared of all blame. He says he sent back a dead man, and a dead man cannot buy back one living. And moreover, that your dead man's ransom must be a life – the life of his murderer. Do *you* believe any man of ours owes that debt?'

'I dare not say there is any man who might not kill, given some monstrous, driving need,' said Cadfael honestly.

'Or any woman, either,' she said with a fierce, helpless sigh. 'But you have not fixed on any one man for this deed? No finger has been pointed? Not yet?'

No, of course she did not know. Einon had left before ever Melicent cried out both her love and her hatred, accusing Elis. No further news had yet reached these parts. Even if Hugh had now spoken of this matter with the prince, no such word had yet found its way back here to Tregeiriog. But surely it would, when Owain returned. In the end she would hear how her betrothed had fallen headlong in love with another woman, and been accused by her of her father's murder, murder for love that put an end to love. And where did that leave Cristina? Forgotten, eclipsed, but still in tenuous possession of a bridegroom who did not want her, and could not have the bride he did want! Such a tangled coil enmeshing all these four hapless children!

'Fingers have been pointed, more than one way,' said Cadfael, 'but there is no proof against one man more than another. No one is yet in danger of his life, and all are in health and well enough treated, even if they must be confined. There is no help for it but to wait and believe in justice.'

'Believing in justice is not always so easy,' she said tartly. 'You say they are well? And they are together, Elis and Eliud?'

'They are. They have that comfort. And within the castle wards they have their liberty. They have given their word not to try to escape, and it has been accepted. They are well enough, you may believe that.'

'But you can give me no hope, set me no period, when he will come home?' She sat confronting Cadfael with great, steady eyes, and in her lap her fingers were knotted so tightly that the knuckles shone white as naked bone. 'Even if he does come home, living and justified,' she said.

'That I can tell no more than you,' Cadfael owned wryly. 'But I will do what I can to shorten the time. This waiting is hard upon you, I know it.' But how much harder would the return be, if ever Elis came back vindicated, only to pursue his suit for Melicent Prestcote, and worm his way out of his Welsh betrothal. It might even be better if she had warning now, before the blow fell. Cadfael was pondering what he could best do for her, and with only half an ear tuned to what she was saying.

'At least I have purged my own soul,' she said, as much to herself as to him. 'I have always known how well he loves me, if only he did not love his cousin as well or better. Fosterlings are like that – you are Welsh, you know it. But if he could not bring himself to undo what was done so ill, I have done it for him now. I tired of silence. Why should we bleed without a cry? I have done what had to be done, I've spoken with my father and with his. In the end I shall have my way.'

She rose, giving him a pale but resolute smile. 'We shall be able to speak again, brother, before you leave us. I must go and see how things fare in the kitchen, they'll be home with the evening.'

He gave her an abstracted farewell, and watched her cross the hall with her free, boy's stride and straight, proud carriage. Not until she had reached the door did he realise the meaning of what she had said. 'Cristina!' he called in startled enlightenment; but the door had closed and she was gone.

There was no error, he had heard aright. *She knew how well he loved her, if only he did not love his cousin as well or better, in the way of fosterlings!* Yes, all that he had known before, he had seen it manifested in their warring exchanges, and misread it utterly. How a man can be deceived, where every word, every aspect, confirms him in his blindness! Not a single lie spoken or intended, yet the sum total a lie.

She had spoken with her father – *and with his!*

Cadfael heard in his mind's ear Elis ap Cynan's blithe voice accounting for himself when first he came to Shrewsbury. Owain Gwynedd was his overlord, and had overseen him in the fosterage where he had placed him when his father died . . .

'. . . with my uncle Griffith ap Meilyr, where I grew up with my cousin Eliud as brothers . . .'

Two young men, close as twins, far too close to make room for the bride destined for one of them. Yes, and she fighting hard for what she claimed as her rights, and knowing there was love deep enough and wild enough to match her love, *if only* . . . If only a mistaken bond made in infancy could be honourably dissolved. If only those two could be severed, that dual creature staring into a mirror, the left-handed image and the right-handed, and which of them the reality? How is a stranger to tell?

But now he knew. She had not used the word loosely, of the kinsman who had reared them both. No, she meant just what she had said. An uncle may also be a foster-father, but only a natural father is a father.

They came, as before, with the dusk. Cadfael was still in a daze when he heard them come, and stirred himself to go out and witness the torchlit bustle in the court, the glimmer on the coats of the horses, the jingle of harness, bit and spur, the cheerful and purposeful hum of entwining voices, the hissing and crooning of the grooms, the trampling of hooves and the very faint mist of warm breath in the chilling but frostless air. A grand, vigorous pattern of lights and shadows, and the open door of the hall glowing warmly for welcome.

Tudur ap Rhys was the first down from the saddle, and himself strode to hold his prince's stirrup. Owain Gwynedd's fair hair gleamed uncovered in the ruddy light of the torches as he sprang down, a head taller than his host. Man after man they came, chieftain after chieftain, the princelings of Gwynedd's nearer commoes, the neighbours of England. Cadfael stood to survey each one as he dismounted, and lingered until all were on foot, and their followers dispersed into the camps beyond the maenol. But he did not find among them Einon ab Ithel, whom he sought.

'Einon?' said Tudur, questioned. 'He's following, though he may come late to table. He had a visit to pay in Llansantffraid, he has a daughter married there, and his first grandson is come new into the world. Before the evening's out he'll be with us. You're heartily welcome to my roof again, brother, all the more if you bring news to please the prince's ear. It was an ill thing that happened there with you, he feels it as a sad stain on a clean acquaintance.'

'I'm rather seeking than bringing enlightenment,' Cadfael confessed. 'But I trust one man's ill deed cannot mar these meetings between your prince and our sheriff. Owain Gwynedd's goodwill is gold to us in Shropshire, all the more since Madog ap Meredith is showing his teeth again.'

'Do you tell me so? Owain will want to hear of it, but after supper will be the fitting time. I'll make you a place at the high table.'

Since he had in any case to wait for the arrival of Einon, Cadfael sat back to study and enjoy the gathering in Tudur's hall over supper, the warmth of the central fire, the torches, the wine, and the harping. A man of Tudur's status was privileged to possess a harp and maintain his own harper, in addition to his duty to be a generous patron to travelling minstrels. And with the prince here to praise and be praised, they had a rivalry of singers that lasted throughout the meal. There was still a deal of coming and going in the courtyard, late-comers riding in, officers from the camps patrolling their bounds and changing pickets, and the womenfolk fetching and carrying, and loitering to talk to the archers and men-at-arms. For the time being this was the court of Gwynedd, where petitioners, bringers of gifts, young men seeking office and favour, all must come.

The dishes had been removed, and the mead and wine were circulating freely, when Tudur's steward came into the hall and made for the high table.

'My lord, there's one here asks leave to present to you his natural son, whom he has acknowledged and admitted to his kinship only two days ago. Griffri ap Llywarch, from close by Meifod. Will you hear him?'

'Willingly,' said Owain, pricking up his fair head to stare down through the smoke and shadows of the hall with some curiosity. 'Let Griffri ap Llywarch come in and be welcome.'

Cadfael had not paid due attention to the name, and might not even have recognised it if he had, nor was he likely to recognise a man he had never seen before. The newcomer followed the steward into the hall, and up between the tables to the high place. A lean, sinewy man, perhaps fifty years old, balding and bearded, with a hillman's gait, and the weathered face and wrinkled, far-seeing eyes of the shepherd. His clothing was plain and brown, but good homespun. He came straight to the dais, and made the Welshman's brisk, unservile reverence to the prince.

'My lord Owain, I have brought you my son, that you may know and approve him. For the only son I had by my wife is two years and more dead, and I was without children, until this my son by another woman came to me declaring his birth and proving it. And I have acknowledged him mine and brought him into my kinship, and as mine he is accepted. Now I ask your countenance also.'

He stood proudly, glad of what he had to say and of the young man he had to present; and Cadfael would have had neither eyes nor ears for any other man present, if it had not been for the courteous silence that had followed him up the hall, and the one clear sound that carried in it. Shadows and smoke veiled the figure that followed respectfully at some yards distance, but the sound of its steps was plainly audible, and went haltingly, lighter and faster upon one foot. Cadfael's eyes were upon the son when he came hesitantly into the torchlight from the high table. This one he knew, though the black hair was trimmed and thrown proudly back from a face not now sullen and closed, but open, hopeful and eager, and there was no longer a crutch under the leaning armpit.

Cadfael looked back from Anion ap Griffri to Griffri ap Llywarch, to whose drear and childless middle age this unlooked-for son had suddenly supplied a warm heart of hope and content. The homespun cloak hanging loose upon Griffri's shoulders bore in its folds a long pin with a large, chased gold head secured with a thin gold chain. And that, too, Cadfael had seen before, and knew only too well.

So did another witness. Einon ab Ithel had come in, as one familiar with the household and desirous of making no inconvenient stir, by the high door from the private chamber, and emerged behind the prince's table unnoticed. The man who was holding all attention naturally drew his. The red of torchlight flashed from the ornament worn openly and proudly. Its owner had the best reason to know there could not be two such, not of that exact and massive size and ornamentation.

'God's breath!' swore Einon ab Ithel in a great bellow of astonishment and indignation. 'What manner of thief have we here, wearing my gold under my very eyes?'

Silence fell as ominously as thunder, and every head whirled from prince and petitioner to stare at this loud accuser. Einon came round the high table in a few long strides, dropped from the dais so close as to send Griffri lurching back in alarm, and stabbed a hard brown finger at the pin that glowed in the drab cloak.

'My lord, *this* – is mine! Gold out of my earth, I had it mined, I had it made for me, there is not another exactly like it in this or any land. When I came back from Shrewsbury, on that errand you know of, it was not in my collar, nor have I seen it since that day. I thought it fallen somewhere on the road, and made no ado about it. What is it to mourn for, gold! Now I see it again and marvel. My lord, it is in your hands. Demand of this man how he comes to be wearing what is mine.'

Half the hall was on its feet, and rumbling with menace, for theft, unmitigated by circumstances, was the worst crime they acknowledged, and the thief caught red-handed could be killed on sight by the wronged man. Griffri stood stricken dumb, staring in bewilderment. Anion flung himself with stretched arms and braced body between his father and Einon.

'My lord, my lord, I gave it, I brought it to my father. I did not steal . . . I took a price! Hold my father blameless, if there is blame it is mine only . . .'

He was sweating with terror, great sudden gouts that ran on his forehead and were snared in his thick brows. And if he knew a little Welsh, in this extremity it did not serve him, he had cried out in English. That gave them all a moment of surprise. And Owain swept a hand over the hall and brought silence.

'Sit, and keep closed mouths. This is my matter. I'll have quiet and all here shall have justice.'

They murmured, but they obeyed. In the ensuing hush Brother Cadfael rose unobtrusively to his feet and made his way round the table and down to the floor of the hall. His movements, however discreet, drew the prince's eye.

'My lord,' said Cadfael deprecatingly, 'I am of Shrewsbury, I know and am known to this man Anion ap Griffri. He was raised English, no fault of his. Should he need one to interpret, I can do that service, so that he may be understood by all here.'

'A fair offer,' said Owain, and eyed him thoughtfully. 'Are you also empowered, brother, to speak for Shrewsbury, since it seems this accusation goes back to that town, and the business of which we know? And if so, for shire and town or for abbey?'

'Here and now,' said Cadfael boldly, 'I will venture for both. And if any find fault hereafter, let it fall on me.'

'You are here, I fancy,' said Owain, considering, 'over this very matter.'

'I am. In part to look for this same jewel. For it vanished from Gilbert Prestcote's chamber in our infirmary on the day that he died. The cloak that had been added to the sick man's wrappings in the litter was handed back to Einon ab Ithel without it. Only after he had left did we remember and look for the brooch. And only now do I see it again.'

'From the room where a man died by murder,' said Einon.

129

'Brother, you have found more than the gold. You may send our men home.'

Anion stood fearful but steadfast between his father and the accusing stare of a hall full of eyes. He was white as ice, translucent, as though all the blood had left his veins. 'I did not kill,' he said hoarsely, and heaved hard to get breath enough to speak. 'My lord, I never knew . . . I thought the pin was his, Prestcote's. I took it from the cloak, yes—'

'After you had killed him,' said Einon harshly.

'No! I swear it! I never touched the man.' He turned in desperate appeal to Owain, who sat listening dispassionately at the table, his fingers easy round the stem of his wine-cup, but his eyes very bright and aware. 'My lord, only hear me! And hold my father clear of all, for all he knows is what I have told him, and the same I shall tell you, and as God sees me, I do not lie.'

'Hand up to me,' said Owain, 'that pin you wear.' And as Griffri hurried with trembling fingers to detach it, and reached up to lay it in the prince's hand: 'So! I have known this too long and seen it worn too often to be in any doubt whose it is. From you, brother, as from Einon here, I know how it came to be lying open to hand by the sheriff's bed. Now you may tell, Anion, how you came by it. English I can follow, you need not fear being misunderstood. And Brother Cadfael will put what you say into Welsh, so that all here may understand you.'

Anion gulped air and found a creaky voice that gathered body and passion as he used it. Shock and terror had contracted his throat, but the flow of words washed constraint away. 'My lord, until these last days I never saw my father, nor he me, but I had a brother, as he has said, and by chance I got to know him when he came into Shrewsbury with wool to sell. There was a year between us, and I am the elder. He was my kin, and I valued him. And once when he visited the town and I was not by, there was a fight, a man was killed and my brother was blamed for it. Gilbert Prestcote hanged him!'

Owain glanced aside at Cadfael, and waited until this speech had been translated for the Welshmen. Then he asked: 'You know of this case? Was it fairly done?'

'Who knows which hand did the killing?' said Cadfael. 'It was a street brawl, the young men were drunk. Gilbert Prestcote was hasty by nature, but just. But this is certain, here in Wales the young man would not have hanged. A blood-price would have paid it.'

'Go on,' said Owain.

'I carried that grudge on my heart from that day,' said Anion, gathering passion from old bitterness. 'But when did I ever come within reach of the sheriff? Never until your men brought him into Shrewsbury wounded and housed him in the infirmary. And I was there with this broken leg of mine all but healed, and that man only twenty paces from me, only a wall between us, my enemy at my mercy. While it was all still and the brothers at dinner, I went into the room where he was. He owed my house a life – even if I was mongrel, I felt Welsh then, and I meant to take my due revenge – I meant to kill! The only brother ever I had, and he was merry and good to look upon, and then to hang for an unlucky blow when he was full of ale! I went in there to kill. But I could not do it! When I saw my enemy brought down so low, so old and weary, hardly blood or breath in him . . . I stood by him and watched, and all I could feel was sadness. It seemed to me that there was no call there for vengeance, for all was already avenged. So I thought on another way. There was no court to set a blood-price or enforce payment, but there was the gold pin in the cloak beside him. I thought it was his. How could I know? So I took it as *galanas*, to clear the debt and the grudge. But by the end of that day I knew, we all knew, that Prestcote was dead and dead by murder, and when they began to question even me, I knew that if ever it came out what I had done it would be said I had also killed him. So I ran. I meant, in any case, to come and seek my father some day, and tell him my brother's death was paid for, but because I was afraid I had to run in haste.'

'And come to me he did,' said Griffri earnestly, his hand upon his son's shoulder, 'and showed me by way of warranty the yellow mountain stone I gave his mother long ago. But by his face I knew him, for he's like the brother he lost. And he gave me that thing you hold, my lord, and told me that young Griffri's death was requited, and this was the token price exacted, and the grudge buried, for our enemy was dead. I did not well understand him then, for I told him if he had slain Griffri's slayer, then he had no right to take a price as well. But he swore to me by most solemn oath that it was not he who had killed and I believe him. And judge if I am glad to have a son restored me in my middle years, to be the prop of my old age. For God's sake, my lord, do not take him from me now!'

In the dour, considering hush that followed Cadfael completed his translation of what Anion had said, and took his time about it to allow him to study the prince's impassive face. At the end of it the silence continued still for a long minute, since no one would speak until Owain made it possible. He, too, was in no hurry. He looked at father and son, pressed together there below the dais in apprehensive solidarity, he looked at Einon, whose face was as unrevealing as his own, and last at Cadfael.

'Brother, you know more of what has gone forward in Shrewsbury abbey than any of us here. You know this man. How do you say? Do you believe his story?'

'Yes,' said Cadfael, with grave and heartfelt gratitude, 'I do believe it. It fits with all I know. But I would ask Anion one question.'

'Ask it.'

'You stood beside the bed, Anion, and watched the sleeper. Are you sure that he was then alive?'

'Yes, surely,' said Anion wondering. 'He breathed, he moaned in his sleep. I saw and heard. I know.'

'My lord,' said Cadfael, watching Owain's enquiring eye, 'there was another heard to enter and leave that room, some little while later, someone who went not haltingly, as Anion did, but lightly. That one did not take anything, unless it was a life. Moreover, I believe what Anion has told us because there is yet another thing I have to find before I shall have found Gilbert Prestcote's murderer.'

Owain nodded comprehension, and mused for a while in silence. Then he picked up the gold pin with a brisk movement, and held it out to Einon. 'How say you? Was this theft?'

'I am content,' said Einon and laughed, releasing the tension in the hall. In the general stir and murmur of returning ease, the

132

prince turned to his host.

'Make a place below there, Tudur, for Griffri ap Llywarch, and his son Anion.'

ELEVEN

So there went Shrewsbury's prime suspect, the man gossip had already hanged and buried, down the hall on his father's heels, stumbling a little and dazed like a man in a dream, but beginning to shine as though a torch had been kindled within him; down to a place with his father at one of the tables, equal among equals. From a serving-maid's by-blow, without property or privilege, he was suddenly become a free man, with a rightful place of his own in a kindred, heir to a respected sire, accepted by his prince. The threat that had forced him to take to his heels had turned into the greatest blessing of his life and brought him to the one place that was his by right in Welsh law, true son to a father who acknowledged him proudly. Here Anion was no bastard.

Cadfael watched the pair of them to their places, and was glad that something good, at least, should have come out of the evil. Where would that young man have found the courage to seek out his father, distant, unknown, speaking another language, if fear had not forced his hand, and made it easy to leap across a frontier? The ending was well worth the terror that had gone before. He could forget Anion now. Anion's hands were clean.

'At least you've sent me one man,' observed Owain, watching thoughtfully as the pair reached their places, 'in return for my eight still in bond. Not a bad figure of a man, either. But no training in arms, I doubt.'

'An excellent cattle-man,' said Cadfael. 'He has an understanding with all animals. You may safely put your horses in his care.'

'And you lose, I gather, your chief contender for a halter. You have no after-thoughts concerning him?'

'None. I am sure he did as he says he did. He dreamed of

134

avenging himself on a strong and overbearing man, and found a broken wreck he could not choose but pity.'

'No bad ending,' said Owain. 'And now I think we might withdraw to some quieter place, and you shall tell us whatever you have to tell, and ask whatever you need to ask.'

In the prince's chamber they sat about the small, wire-guarded brazier, Owain, Tudur, Einon ab Ithel and Cadfael. Cadfael had brought with him the little box in which he had preserved the wisps of wool and gold thread. Those precise shades of deep blue and soft rose could not be carried accurately in the mind, but must continually be referred to the eye, and matched against whatever fabric came to light. He had the box in the scrip at his girdle, and was wary of opening it where there might be even the faintest draught, for fear the frail things within would be blown clean away. A breath from a loophole could whisk his ominous treasures out of reach in an instant.

He had debated within himself how much he should tell, but in the light of Cristina's revelation, and since her father was here in conference, he told all he knew, how Elis in his captivity had fallen haplessly in love with Prestcote's daughter, and how the pair of them had seen no possible hope of gaining the sheriff's approval for such a match, hence providing reason enough why Elis should attempt to disturb the invalid's rest – whether to remove by murder the obstacle to his love, as Melicent accused, or to plead his forlorn cause, as Elis himself protested.

'So that was the way of it,' said Owain, and exchanged a straight, hard look with Tudur, unsurprised, and forbearing from either sympathy or blame. Tudur was on close terms of personal friendship with his prince, and had surely spoken with him of Cristina's confidences. Here was the other side of the coin. 'And this was after Einon had left you?'

'It was. It came out that the boy had tried to speak with Gilbert, and been ordered out by Brother Edmund. When the girl heard of it, she turned on him for a murderer.'

'But you do not altogether accept that. Nor, it seems, has Beringar accepted it.'

'There is no more proof of it than that he was there, beside the

135

bed, when Edmund came and drove him out. It could as well have been for the boy's declared purpose as for anything worse. And then, you'll understand, there was the matter of the gold pin. We never realised it was missing, my lord, until you had ridden for home. But very certainly Elis neither had it on him, nor had had any opportunity to hide it elsewhere before he was searched. Therefore someone else had been in that room and taken it away.'

'But now that we know what befell my pin,' said Einon, 'and are satisfied Anion did not murder, does not that leave that boy again in danger of being branded for the killing of a sick and sleeping man? Though it sorts very poorly,' he added, 'with what I know of him.'

'Which of us,' said Owain sombrely, 'has never been guilty of some unworthiness that sorts very ill with what our friends know of us? Even with what we know, or think we know, of ourselves! I would not rule out any man from being capable once in his life of a gross infamy.' He looked up at Cadfael. 'Brother, I recall you said, within there, that there was yet one more thing you must find, before you would have found Prestcote's murderer. What is that thing?'

'It is the cloth that was used to smother Gilbert. By its traces it will be known, once found. For it was pressed down over his nose and mouth, and he breathed it into his nostrils and drew it into his teeth, and a thread or two of it we found in his beard. No ordinary cloth. Elis had neither that nor anything else in his hands when he came from the infirmary. Once I had found and preserved the filaments from it, we searched for it throughout the abbey precincts, for it could have been a hanging or an altar-cloth, but we have found nothing to match these fragments. Until we know what it was, and what became of it, we shall not know who killed Gilbert Prestcote.'

'This is certain?' asked Owain. 'You drew these threads from the dead man's nostrils and mouth? You think you will know, when you find it, the very cloth that was used to stifle him?'

'I do think so, for the colours are clear, and not common dyes. I have the box here. But open it with care. What's within is fine as cobweb.' Cadfael handed the little box across the brazier. 'But not here. The up-draught from the warmth could blow them away.'

136

Owain took the box aside, and held it low under one of the lamps, where the light would play into it. The minute threads quivered faintly, and again were still. 'Here's gold thread, that's plain, a twisted strand. The rest — I see it's wool, by the many hairs and the live texture. A darker colour and a lighter.' He studied them narrowly, but shook his head. 'I could not say what tints are here, only that the cloth had a good gold thread woven into it. And I fancy it would be thick, a heavy weave, by the way the wool curls and crimps. Many more such fine hairs went to make up this yarn.'

'Let me see,' said Einon, and narrowed his eyes over the box. 'I see the gold, but the colours . . . No, it means nothing to me.'

Tudur peered, and shook his head. 'We have not the light for this, my lord. By day these would show very differently.'

It was true, by the mellow light of these oil-lamps the prince's hair was deep harvest-gold, almost brown. By daylight it was the yellow of primroses. 'It might be better,' agreed Cadfael, 'to leave the matter until morning. Even had we better vision, what could be done at this hour?'

'This light foils the eye,' said Owain. He closed the lid over the airy fragments. 'Why did you think you might find what you seek here?'

'Because we have not found it within the pale of the abbey, so we must look outside, wherever men have dispersed from the abbey. The lord Einon and two captains beside had left us before ever we recovered these threads, it was a possibility, however frail, that unknowingly this cloth had gone with them. By daylight the colours will show for what they truly are. You may yet recall seeing such a weave.'

Cadfael took back the box. It had been a fragile hope at best, but the morrow remained. There was a man's life, a man's soul's health, snared in those few quivering hairs, and he was their custodian.

'Tomorrow,' said the prince emphatically, 'we will try what God's light can show us, since ours is too feeble.'

In the deep small hours of that same night Elis awoke in the dark cell in the outer ward of Shrewsbury castle, and lay with stretched ears, struggling up from the dullness of sleep and wondering what had shaken him out of so profound a slumber. He had grown used to all the daytime sounds native to this place, and to the normal unbroken silence of the night. This night was different, or he would not have been heaved so rudely out of the only refuge he had from his daytime miseries. Something was not as it should have been, someone was astir at a time when there was always silence and stillness. The air quivered with soft movements and distant voices.

They were not locked in, their word had been accepted without question, bond enough to hold them. Elis raised himself cautiously on an elbow, and leaned to listen to Eliud's breathing in the bed beside him. Deep asleep, if not altogether at peace. He twitched and turned without awaking, and the measure of his breathing changed uneasily, shortening and shallowing sometimes, then easing into a long rhythm that promised better rest. Elis did not want to disturb him. It was all due to him, to his pig-headed folly in joining Cadwaladr, that Eliud was here a prisoner beside him. He must not be drawn still deeper into question and danger, whatever happened to Elis.

There were certainly voices, at some small distance but muffled and made to sound infinitely more distant by the thick stone walls. And though at this remove there could not possibly be distinguishable words, yet there was an indefinable agitation about the exchanges, a quiver of panic on the air. Elis slid carefully from the bed, halted and held his breath a moment to make sure that Eliud had not stirred, and felt for his coat, thankful that he slept in shirt and hose, and need not fumble in the dark to dress. With all the grief and anxiety he carried about with him night and day, he must discover the reason of this added and unforeseen alarm. Every divergence from custom was a threat.

The door was heavy but well hung, and swung without a sound. Outside the night was moonless but clear, very faint starlight patterned the sky between the walls and towers that made a shell of total darkness. He drew the door closed after him, and eased the heavy latch into its socket gingerly. Now the murmur of voices had body and direction, it came from the guard-room within the gatehouse. And that crisp, brief clatter that struck a hidden spark on the ground was hooves on the cobbles. A rider at this hour?

He felt his way along the wall towards the sound, at every angle flattening himself against the stones to listen afresh. The horse shifted and blew. Shapes grew gradually out of the solid darkness, the twin turrets of the barbican showed their teeth against a faintly lighter sky, and the flat surface of the closed gate beneath had a tall, narrow slit of pallor carved through it, tall as a man on horseback, and wide enough for a horse to pass in haste. The rider's wicket was open. Open because someone had entered by it with urgent news only minutes since, and no one had yet thought to close it.

Elis crept nearer. The door of the guard-room was ajar, a long sliver of light from torches within quivered across the dark cobbles. The voices emerged by fits and starts, as they were raised and again lowered, but he caught words clearly here and there.

'. . . burned a farm west of Pontesbury,' reported a messenger, still breathless from his haste, 'and never withdrew . . . They're camped overnight . . . and another party skirting Minsterley to join them.'

Another voice, sharp and clear, most likely one of the experienced sergeants: 'What numbers?'

'In all . . . if they foregather . . . I was told it might be as many as a hundred and fifty . . .'

'Archers? Lancers? Foot or horse?' That was not the sergeant, that was a young voice, a shade higher than it should have been with alarm and strain. They had got Alan Herbard out of bed. This was grave matter.

'My lord, far the greater part on foot. Lancers and archers both. They may try to encircle Pontesbury . . . they know Hugh Beringar is in the north . . .'

'Halfway to Shrewsbury!' said Herbard's voice, taut and jealous for his first command.

'They'll not dare that,' said the sergeant. 'Plunder's the aim. Those valley farms . . . with new lambs . . .'

'Madog ap Meredith has a grudge to settle,' ventured the messenger, still short of breath, 'for that raid in February. They're close . . . but the pickings are smaller, there in the forest . . . I doubt . . .'

Halfway to Shrewsbury was more than halfway to the ford in the forest where that grudge had come to birth. And the pickings . . .

139

Elis turned his forehead into the chill of the stone against which he leaned and swallowed terror. A parcel of women! He was more than paid for that silly flaunt, who had a woman of his own there to sweat and bleed for, young, beautiful, fair as flax, tall like a willow. The square dark men of Powys would come to blows over her, kill one another for her, kill her when they were done.

He had started out of his shelter under the wall before he even knew what he intended. The patient, drooping horse might have given him away, but there was no groom holding it, and it stood its ground silently, unstartled, as he stole past, a hand raised to caress and beseech acceptance. He did not dare take it, the first clatter of hooves would have brought them out like hornets disturbed, but at least it let him pass unbetrayed. The big body steamed gently, he felt its heat. The tired head turned and nuzzled his hand. He drew his fingers away with stealthy gentleness, and slid past towards the elongated wicket that offered a way out into the night.

He was through, he had the descent to the castle Foregate on his right, and the way up into the town on his left. But he was out of the castle, he who had given his word not to pass the threshold, he who was forsworn from this moment, false to his word, outcast. Not even Eliud would speak for him when he knew.

The town gates would not open until dawn. Elis turned left, into the town, and groped his way by unknown lanes and passages to find some corner where he could hide until the morning. He was none too sure of his best way out, and did not stop to wonder if he would ever manage to pass unnoticed. All he knew was that he had to get to Godric's Ford before his countrymen reached it. He got his bearings by instinct, blundering blindly round towards the eastward gates. In Saint Mary's churchyard, though he did not know it for that, he shrank into the shelter of a porch from the chill of the wind. He had left his cloak behind in his dishonoured cell, he was half-naked to shame and the night, but he was free and on his way to deliver her. What was his honour, more than his life, compared with her safety?

The town woke early. Tradesmen and travellers rose and made their way down to the gates before full daylight, to be out and about their proper business betimes. So did Elis ap Cynan, going with them discreetly down the Wyle, cloakless, weaponless, desperate, heroic and absurd, to the rescue of his Melicent.

Eliud put out his hand, before he was fully awake, to feel for his cousin, and sat up in abrupt shock to find Elis's side of the bed empty and cold. But the dark red cloak was still draped over the foot of the bed, and Eliud's sense of loss was utterly irrational. Why should not Elis rise early and go out into the wards before his bedfellow was awake? Without his cloak he could not be far away. But for all that, and however brief the separation, it troubled Eliud like a physical pain. Here in their imprisonment they had hardly been a moment out of each other's company, as if for each of them faith in a final happy delivery depended upon the presence of the other.

Eliud rose and dressed, and went out to the trough by the well, to wash himself fully awake in the shock of the cold water. There was an unusual stir about the stables and the armoury, but he saw no sign of Elis anywhere in either place, nor was he brooding on the walls with his face towards Wales. The want of him began to ache like an amputation.

They took their meals in hall among their English peers, but on this clear morning Elis did not come to break his fast. And by this time others had remarked his absence.

One of the sergeants of the garrison stopped Eliud as he was leaving the hall. 'Where is your cousin? Is he sick?'

'I know no more than you,' said Eliud. 'I've been looking for him. He was out before I awoke, and I've seen nothing of him since.' And he added in jealous haste, seeing the man frown and give him the first hard stare of suspicion: 'But he can't be far. His cloak is still in the cell. There's so much stirring here, I thought he might have risen early to find out what was all the to-do.'

'He's pledged not to set foot out of the gates,' said the sergeant. 'But do you tell me he's given up eating? You must know more than you pretend.'

'No! But he's here within, he must be. He would not break his word, I promise you.'

The man eyed him hard, and turned abruptly on his heel to make for the gatehouse and question the guards. Eliud caught him entreatingly by the sleeve. 'What is it brewing here? Is there news?

Such activity in the armoury and the archers drawing arrows . . . What's happened overnight?'

'What's happened? Your countrymen are swarming in force along the Minsterley valley, if you want to know, burning farmsteads and moving in on Pontesbury. Three days ago it was a handful, it's past a hundred tribesmen now.' He swung back suddenly to demand: 'Did you hear aught in the night? Is that it? Has that cousin of yours run, broke out to join his ragamuffin kin and help in the killing? The sheriff was not enough for him?'

'No!' cried Eliud. 'He would not! It's impossible!'

'It's how we got him in the first place, a murdering, looting raid the like of these. It suited him then, it comes very timely for him now. His neck out of a noose and his friends close by to bring him off safely.'

'You cannot say so! You don't yet know but he's here within, true to his word.'

'No, but soon we shall,' said the sergeant grimly, and took Eliud firmly by the arm. 'Into your cell and wait. The lord Herbard must know of this.'

He flung away at speed and Eliud, in desolate obedience, trudged back to his cell and sat there upon the bed with only Elis's cloak for company. By then he was certain what the result of any search must be. Only an hour or two of daylight gone and there were endless places a man could be, if he felt no appetite either for food or for the company of his fellowmen, and yet the castle felt empty of Elis, as cold and alien as if he had never been there. And a courier had come in the night, it seemed, with news of stronger forces from Powys plundering closer to Shrewsbury, and closer still to the forest grange of the abbey of Polesworth at Godric's Ford. Where all this heavy burden had begun and where, perhaps, it must end. If Elis had heard that nocturnal arrival and gone out to discover the cause – yes, then he might in desperation forget oath and honour and all. Eliud waited wretchedly until Alan Herbard came, with two sergeants at his heels. A long wait it had been. They would have scoured the castle by now. By their grim faces it was clear they had not found Elis.

Eliud rose to his feet to face them. He would need all his powers and all his dignity now if he was to speak for Elis. This Alan

Herbard was surely no more than a year or two his senior, and being as harshly tested as he.

'If you know the manner of your cousin's flight,' said Herbard bluntly, 'you would be wise to speak. You shared this narrow space. If he rose in the night, surely you would know. For I tell you plainly, he is gone. He has run. In the night the wicket was opened for a man to enter. It's no secret now that it let out a man – renegade, forsworn, self-branded murderer. Why else should he so seize this chance?'

'No!' said Eliud. 'You wrong him and in the end it will be shown you wrong him. He is no murderer. If he has run, that is not the reason.'

'There is no *if*. He is gone. You know nothing of it? You slept through his flight?'

'I missed him when I awoke,' said Eliud. 'I know nothing of how he went or when. But I know *him*. If he rose in the night because he heard your man arriving and if he heard then – is it so? – that the Welsh of Powys are coming too close and in dangerous numbers, then I swear to you he has fled only out of dread for Gilbert Prestcote's daughter. She is there with the sisters at Godric's Ford and Elis loves her. Whether she has discarded him or no, he has not ceased to love her, and if she is in danger he will venture life, yes and his honour with it, to bring her to safety. And when that is done,' said Eliud passionately, 'he will return here, to suffer whatever fate may await him. He is no renegade! He has broken his oath only for Melicent's sake. He will come back and give himself up. I pledge my own honour for him! My own life!'

'I would remind you,' said Herbard grimly, 'you have already done so. Either one of you gave his word for both. At this moment you stand attainted as his surety for his treachery. I could hang you, and be fully justified.'

'Do so!' said Eliud, blanched to the lips, his eyes dilated into a blaze of green. 'Here am I, still his warranty. I tell you, this neck is yours to wring if Elis proves false. I give you leave freely. You are mustering to ride, I've seen it. You go against these Welsh of Powys. Take me with you! Give me a horse and a weapon, and I will fight for you, and you may have an archer at my back to strike me dead if I make a false step, and a halter about my neck ready for the nearest tree after the Powysmen are hammered, if Elis does not prove to you the truth of every word I say.'

He was shaking with fervour, strung taut like a bowstring. Herbard opened his eyes wide at such open passion, and studied him in wary surprise a long moment. 'So be it!' he said then abruptly, and turned to his men. 'See to it! Give him a horse and a sword, and a rope about his neck, and have your best shot follow him close and be ready to spit him if he plays false. He says he is a man of his word, that even this defaulting fellow of his is such. Very well, we'll take him at his word.'

He looked back from the doorway. Eliud had taken up Elis's red cloak and was holding it in his arms. 'If your cousin had been half the man you are,' said Herbard, 'your life would be safe enough.'

Eliud whirled, hugging the folded cloak to him as if applying balm to an unendurable ache. 'Have you not understood even yet? He is *better* than I, a thousand times better!'

TWELVE

In Tregeiriog, too, they were up with the first blush of light, barely two hours after Elis's flight through the wicket at Shrewsbury. For Hugh Beringar had ridden through half the night, and arrived with the dove-grey hush of pre-dawn. Sleepy grooms rose, blear-eyed, to take the horses of their English guests, a company of twenty men. The rest Hugh had left distributed across the north of the shire, well armed, well supplied, and so far proof against the few and tentative tests to which they had been subjected.

Brother Cadfael, as sensitive to nocturnal arrivals as Elis, had started out of sleep when he caught the quiver and murmur on the air. There was much to be said for the custom of sleeping in the full habit, apart from the scapular, a man could rise and go, barefoot or staying to reclaim his sandals, as complete and armed as in the middle of the day. No doubt the discipline had originated where monastic houses were located in permanently perilous places, and time had given it the blessing of tradition. Cadfael was out, and halfway to the stables, when he met Hugh coming thence in the pearly twilight, and Tudur equally wide awake and alert beside his guest.

'What brings you so early?' asked Cadfael. 'Is there fresh news?'

'Fresh to me, but for all I know stale already in Shrewsbury.' Hugh took him by the arm, and turned him back with them towards the hall. 'I must make my report to the prince, and then we're off down the border by the shortest way. Madog's castellan from Caus is pouring more men into the Minsterley valley. There was a messenger waiting for me when we rode into Oswestry or I'd meant to stay the night there.'

'Herbard sent the word from Shrewsbury?' asked Cadfael. 'It

was no more than a handful of raiders when I left, two days ago.'

'It's a war-party of a hundred or more now. They hadn't moved beyond Minsterley when Herbard got wind of the muster, but if they've brought out such a force as that, they mean worse mischief. And you know them better than I – they waste no time. They may be on the move this very dawn.'

'You'll be needing fresh horses,' said Tudur practically.

'We got some remounts at Oswestry, they'll be fit for the rest of the way. But I'll gladly borrow from you for the rest, and thank you heartily. I've left all quiet and every garrison on the alert across the north, and Ranulf seems to have pulled back his advance parties towards Wrexham. He made a feint at Whitchurch and got a bloody nose, and it's my belief he's drawn in his horns for this while. Whether or no, I must break off to attend to Madog.'

'You may make your mind easy about Chirk,' Tudur assured him. 'We'll see to that. Have your men in for a meal, at least, and give the horses a breather. I'll get the womenfolk out of their beds to see to the feeding of you, and have Einon rouse Owain, if he's not already up.'

'What do you intend?' Cadfael asked. 'Which way shall you head?'

'For Llansilin and down the border. We'll pass to east of the Breiddens, and down by Westbury to Minsterley, and cut them off, if we can, from getting back to their base in Caus. I tire of having men of Powys in that castle,' said Hugh, setting his jaw. 'We must have it back and make it habitable, and keep a garrison there.'

'You'll be few for such a muster as you report,' said Cadfael. 'Why not aim at getting to Shrewsbury first for more men, and westward to meet them from there?'

'The time's too short. And besides, I credit Alan Herbard with sense and stomach enough to field a good force of his own to mind the town. If we move fast enough we may take them between the two prongs and crack them like a nut.'

They had reached the hall. Word had gone before, the sleepers within were rolling out of the rushes in haste, servants were setting tables, and the maids ran with new loaves from the bakery, and great pitchers of ale.

'If I can finish my business here,' said Cadfael tempted, 'I'll ride with you, if you'll have me.'

'I will so and heartily welcome.'

'Then I'd best be seeing to what's left undone here, when Owain Gwynedd is free. While you're closeted with him, I'll see my own horse readied for the journey.'

He was so preoccupied with thoughts of the coming clash, and of what might already be happening in Shrewsbury, that he turned back towards the stables without at first noticing the light footsteps that came flying after him from the direction of the kitchens, until a hand clutched at his sleeve, and he turned to find Cristina confronting him and peering intently up into his face with dilated dark eyes.

'Brother Cadfael, is it true, what my father says? He says I need fret no longer, for Elis has found some girl in Shrewsbury, and wants nothing better now than to be rid of me. He says it can be ended with goodwill on both sides. That I'm free, and Eliud is free! Is it true?' She was grave, and yet she glowed. Elis's desertion was hope and help to her. The tangled knot could indeed be undone by consent, without grudges.

'It is true,' said Cadfael. 'But beware of building too high on his prospects as yet, for it's no way certain he'll get the lady he wants. Did Tudur also tell you it is she who accuses Elis of being her father's murderer? No very hopeful way to set up a marriage.'

'But he's in earnest? He loves the girl? Then he'll not turn back to me, whether he wins his way with her or no. He never wanted me. Oh, I would have done well enough for him,' she said, hoisting eloquent shoulders and curling a tolerant lip, 'as any girl his match in age and rank would have done, but all I ever was to him was a child he grew up with, and was fond of after a fashion. Now,' she said feelingly, 'he knows what it is to want. God knows I wish him his happiness as I hope for mine.'

'Walk with me down to the stables,' said Cadfael, 'and keep me company, these few minutes we have. For I'm away with Hugh Beringar as soon as his men have broken their fast and rested their horses, and I've had a word again with Owain Gwynedd and Einon ab Ithel. Come, and tell me plainly how things stand between you and Eliud, for once before when I saw you together I misread you utterly.'

147

She went with him gladly, her face clear and pure in the pearly light just flushing into rose. Her voice was tranquil as she said: 'I loved Eliud from before I knew what love was. All I knew was how much it hurt, that I could not endure to be away from him, that I followed and would be with him, and he would not see me, would not speak with me, put me roughly from his side as often as I clung. I was already promised to Elis, and Elis was more than half Eliud's world, and not for anything would he have touched or coveted anything that belonged to his foster-brother. I was too young then to know that the measure of his rejection of me was the measure of how much he wanted me. But when I came to understand what it was that tortured me, then I knew that Eliud went daily in the selfsame pain.'

'You are quite sure of him,' said Cadfael, stating, not doubting.

'I am sure. From the time I understood, I have tried to make him acknowledge what I know and he knows to be truth. The more I pursue and plead, the more he turns away and will not speak or listen. But ever the more he wants me. I tell you truth, when Elis went away, and was made prisoner, I began to believe I had almost won Eliud, almost brought him to admit to love and join with me to break this threatened marriage, and speak for me himself. Then he was sent to be surety for this unhappy exchange and all went for nothing. And now it's Elis who cuts the knot and frees us all.'

'Too early yet to speak of being free,' warned Cadfael seriously. 'Neither of those two is yet out of the wood – none of us is, until the matter of the sheriff's death is brought to a just end.'

'I can wait,' said Cristina.

Pointless, thought Cadfael, to attempt to cast any doubt over this new radiance of hers. She had lived in shadow far too long to be intimidated. What was a murder unsolved to her? He doubted if guilt or innocence would make any difference. She had but one aim, nothing would deflect her from it. No question but from childhood she had read her playfellows rightly, known the one who owned the right to her but valued it lightly, and the one who contained the gnawing grief of loving her and knowing her to be pledged to the foster-brother he loved only a little less. Perhaps no less at all, until he grew into the pain of manhood. Girl children are always years older than their brothers at the same age in years, and see more accurately and jealously.

'Since you are going back,' said Cristina, viewing the activity in the stables with a kindling eye, 'you will see him again. Tell him I am my own woman now, or soon shall be, and can give myself where I will. And I will give myself to no one but him.'

'I will tell him so,' said Cadfael.

The yard was alive with men and horses, harness and gear slung on every staple and trestle down the line of stalls. The morning light rose clear and pale over the timber buildings, and the greens of the valley forest were stippled with the pallor of new leaf-buds like delicate green veils among the darkness of fir. There was a small wind, enough to refresh without troubling. A good day for riding.

'Which of these horses is yours?' she asked.

Cadfael led him forth to be seen, and surrendered him to the groom who came at once to serve.

'And that great raw-boned grey beast? I never saw him before. He should go well, even under a man in armour.'

'That is Hugh Beringar's favourite,' said Cadfael, recognising the dapple with pleasure. 'And a very ill-conditioned brute towards any other rider. Hugh must have left him resting in Oswestry, or he would not be riding him now.'

'I see they're saddling up for Einon ab Ithel, too,' she said. 'I fancy he'll be going back to Chirk, to keep an eye on your Beringar's northern border while he's busy elsewhere.'

A groom had come out across their path with a draping of harness on one arm and a saddle-cloth over the other, and tossed them over a rail while he went back to lead out the horse that would wear them. A very handsome beast, a tall, bright bay that Cadfael remembered seeing in the great court at Shrewsbury. He watched its lively gait with pleasure as the groom hoisted the saddle-cloth and flung it over the broad, glossy back, so taken with the horse that he barely noticed the quality of its gear. Fringes to the soft leather bridle, and a tooled brow-band with tiny studs of gold. There was gold on Einon's land, he recalled. And the saddle-cloth itself . . .

He fixed and stared, motionless, for an instant holding his breath. A thick, soft fabric of dyed woollens, woven from heavy yarns in a pattern of twining, blossomy sprays, muted red roses, surely faded to that gentle shade, and deep blue irises. Through the centre of the flowers and round the border ran thick, crusted gold threads. It was not new, it had seen considerable wear, the wool had rubbed into tight balls here and there, some threads had frayed, leaving short, fine strands quivering.

No need even to bring out for comparison the little box in which he kept his captured threads. Now that he saw these tints at last he knew them past any doubt. He was looking at the very thing he had sought, too well known here, too often seen and too little regarded, to stir any man's memory.

He knew, moreover, instantly and infallibly, the meaning of what he saw.

He said never a word to Cristina of what he knew, as they walked back together. What could he say? Better by far keep all to himself until he could see his way ahead, and knew what he must do. Not one word to any, except to Owain Gwynedd, when he took his leave.

'My lord,' he said then, 'I have heard it reported of you that you have said, concerning the death of Gilbert Prestcote, that the only ransom for a murdered man is the life of the murderer. Is that truly reported? Must there be another death? Welsh law allows for the paying of a blood-price, to prevent the prolonged bloodshed of a feud. I do not believe you have forsaken Welsh for Norman law.'

'Gilbert Prestcote did not live by Welsh law,' said Owain, eyeing him very keenly. 'I cannot ask him to die by it. Of what value is a payment in goods or cattle to his widow and children?'

'Yet I think *galanas* can be paid in other mintage,' said Cadfael. 'In penitence, grief and shame, as high as the highest price judge ever set. What then?'

'I am not a priest,' said Owain, 'nor any man's confessor. Penance and absolution are not within my writ. Justice is,'

'And mercy also,' said Cadfael.

'God forbid I should order any death wantonly. Deaths atoned for, whether by goods or grief, pilgrimage or prison, are better far than deaths prolonged and multiplied. I would keep alive all such as have value to this world and to those who rub shoulders with them here in this world. Beyond that it is God's business.' The prince leaned forward, and the morning light through the embrasure shone on his flaxen head. 'Brother,' he said gently, 'had you not something we should have looked at again this morning by a better light? Last night we spoke of it.'

'That is of small importance now,' said Brother Cadfael, 'if you will consent to leave it in my hands some brief while. There shall be account rendered.'

'I will well!' said Owain Gwynedd, and suddenly smiled, and the small chamber was filled with the charm of his presence. 'Only, for my sake – and others, doubtless? – carry it carefully.'

THIRTEEN

Elis had more sense than to go rushing straight to the enclosure of the Benedictine sisters, all blown and mired as he was from his run, and with the dawn only just breaking. So few miles from Shrewsbury here, and yet so lonely and exposed! Why, he had wondered furiously as he ran, why had those women chosen to plant their little chapel and garden in so perilous a place? It was provocation! The abbess at Polesworth should be brought to realise her error and withdraw her threatened sisters. This present danger could be endlessly repeated, so near so turbulent a border.

He made rather for the mill on the brook, upstream, where he had been held prisoner, under guard by a muscular giant named John, during those few February days. He viewed the brook with dismay, it was so fallen and tamed, for all its gnarled and stony bed, no longer the flood he remembered. But if they came they would expect to wade across merrily where the bed opened out into a smooth passage, and would scarcely wet them above the knee. Those stretches, at least, could be pitted and sown with spikes or caltrops. And the wooded banks at least still offered good cover for archers.

John Miller, sharpening stakes in the mill-yard, dropped his hatchet and reached for his pitch-fork when the hasty, stumbling feet thudded on the boards. He whirled with astonishing speed and readiness for a big man, and gaped to see his sometime prisoner advancing upon him empty-handed and purposeful, and to be greeted in loud, demanding English by one who had professed total ignorance of that language only a few weeks previously.

'The Welsh of Powys – a war-party not two hours away! Do the women know of it? We could still get them away towards the town – they're surely mustering there, but *late* . . .'

'Easy, easy!' said the miller, letting his weapon fall, and scooping up his pile of murderous, pointed poles. 'You've found your tongue in a hurry, seemingly! And whose side may you be on this time, and who let you loose? Here, carry these, if you're come to make yourself useful.'

'The women must be got away,' persisted Elis feverishly. 'It's not too late, if they go at once . . . Get me leave to speak to them, surely they'll listen. If *they* were safe, we could stand off even a war-band. I came to warn them . . .'

'Ah, but they know. We've kept good watch since the last time. And the women won't budge, so you may spare your breath to make one man more, and welcome,' said the miller, 'if you're so minded. Mother Mariana holds it would be want of faith to shift an ell, and Sister Magdalen reckons she can be more use where she is, and most of the folks hereabouts would say that's no more than truth. Come on, let's get these planted – the ford's pitted already.'

Elis found himself running beside the big man, his arms full. The smoothest stretch of the brook flanked the chapel wall of the grange, and he realised as he fed out stakes at the miller's command that there was a certain amount of activity among the bushes and coppice-woods on both sides of the water. The men of the forest were well aware of the threat, and had made their own preparations, and by her previous showing, Sister Magdalen must also be making ready for battle. To have Mother Mariana's faith in divine protection is good, but even better if backed by the practical assistance heaven has a right to expect from sensible mortals. But a war-party of a hundred or more – and with one ignominious rout to avenge! Did they understand what they were facing?

'I need a weapon,' said Elis, standing aloft on the bank with feet solidly spread and black head reared towards the north-west, from which the menace must come. 'I can use sword, lance, bow, whatever's to spare . . . That hatchet of yours, on a long haft . . .' He had another chance weapon of his own, he had just realised it. If only he could get wind in time, and be the first to face them when they came, he had a loud Welsh tongue where they would be looking only for terrified English, he had the fluency of bardic stock, all the barbs of surprise, vituperation and scarifying

153

mockery, to loose in a flood against the cowardly paladins who came preying on holy women. A tongue like a whip-lash! Better still drunk, perhaps, to reach the true heights of scalding invective, but even in this state of desperate sobriety, it might still serve to unnerve and delay.

Elis waded into the water, and selected a place for one of his stakes, hidden among the water-weed with its point sharply inclined to impale anyone crossing in unwary haste. By the careful way John Miller was moving, the ford had been pitted well out in midstream. If the attackers were horsed, a step astray into one of those holes might at once lame the horse and toss the rider forward on to the pales. If they came afoot, at least some might fall foul of the pits, and bring down their fellows with them, in a tangle very vulnerable to archery.

The miller, knee-deep in midstream, stood to look on critically as Elis drove in his murderous stake, and bedded it firmly through the tenacious mattress of weed into the soil under the bank. 'Good lad!' he said with mild approval. 'We'll find you a pikel, or the foresters may have an axe to spare among them. You shan't go weaponless if your will's good.'

Sister Magdalen, like the rest of the household, had been up since dawn, marshalling all the linens, scissors, knives, lotions, ointments and stunning draughts that might be needed within a matter of hours, and speculating how many beds could be made available with decorum and where, if any of the men of her forest army should be too gravely hurt to be moved. Magdalen had given serious thought to sending away the two young postulants eastward to Beistan, but decided against it, convinced in the end that they were safer where they were. The attack might never come. If it did, at least here there was readiness, and enough stout-hearted forest folk to put up a good defence. But if the raiders moved instead towards Shrewsbury, and encountered a force they could not match, then they would double back and scatter to make their way home, and two girls hurrying through the woods eastward might fall foul of them at any moment on the way. No, better hold together here. In any case, one look at Melicent's roused and indignant face had given her due warning that that

154

one, at any rate, would not go even if she was ordered.

'I am not afraid,' said Melicent disdainfully.

'The more fool you,' said Sister Magdalen simply. 'Unless you're lying, of course. Which of us doesn't, once challenged with being afraid! Yet it's generations of being afraid, with good reason, that have caused us to think out these defences.'

She had already made all her dispositions within. She climbed the wooden steps into the tiny bell-turret and looked out over the exposed length of the brook and the rising bank beyond, thickly lined with bushes, and climbing into a slope once coppiced but now run to neglected growth. Countrymen who have to labour all the hours of daylight to get their living cannot, in addition, keep up a day-and-night vigil for long. Let them come today, if they're coming at all, thought Sister Magdalen, now that we're at the peak of resolution and readiness, can do no more, and can only grow stale if we must wait too long.

From the opposite bank she drew in her gaze to the brook itself, the deep-cut and rocky bed smoothing out under her walls to the broad stretch of the ford. And there John Miller was just wading warily ashore, the water turgid after his passage and someone else, a young fellow with a thatch of black curls, was bending over the last stake, vigorous arms and shoulders driving it home, low under the bank and screened by reeds. When he straightened up and showed a flushed face, she knew him.

She descended to the chapel very thoughtfully. Melicent was busy putting away, in a coffer clamped to the wall and strongly banded, the few valuable ornaments of the altar and the house. At least it should be made as difficult as possible to pillage this modest church.

'You have not looked out to see how the men progress?' said Sister Magdalen mildly. 'It seems we have one ally more than we knew. There's a young Welshman of your acquaintance and mine hard at work out there with John Miller. A change of allegiance for him, but by the look of him he relishes this cause more than when he came the last time.'

Melicent turned to stare, her eyes very wide and solemn. '*He?*' she said, in a voice brittle and low. 'He was prisoner in the castle. How can he be here?'

'Plainly he has slipped his collar. And been through a bog or two on his way here,' said Sister Magdalen placidly, 'by the state of his boots and hose, and I fancy fallen in at least one by his dirty face.'

'But why make this way? If he broke loose . . . what is he doing here?' demanded Melicent feverishly.

'By all the signs he's making ready to do battle with his own countrymen. And since I doubt if he remembers me warmly enough to break out of prison in order to fight for me,' said Sister Magdalen with a small, reminiscent smile, 'I take it he's concerned with *your* safety. But you may ask him by leaning over the fence.'

'No!' said Melicent in sharp recoil, and closed down the lid of the coffer with a clash. 'I have nothing to say to him.' And she folded her arms and hugged herself tightly as if cold, as if some traitor part of her might break away and scuttle furtively into the garden.

'Then if you'll give me leave,' said Sister Magdalen serenely, 'I think I have.' And out she went, between newly-dug beds and first salad sowings in the enclosed garden, to mount the stone block that made her tall enough to look over the fence. And suddenly there was Elis ap Cynan almost nose to nose with her, stretching up to peer anxiously within. Soiled and strung and desperately in earnest, he looked so young that she, who had never borne children, felt herself grandmotherly rather than merely maternal. The boy recoiled, startled, and blinked as he recognised her. He flushed beneath the greenish smear the marsh had left across his cheek and brow, and reached a pleading hand to the crest of the fence between them.

'Sister, is she – is Melicent within there?'

'She is, safe and well,' said Sister Magdalen, 'and with God's help and yours, and the help of all the other stout souls busy on our account like you, safe she'll remain. How you got here I won't enquire, boy, but whether let out or broken out you're very welcome.'

'I wish to God,' said Elis fervently, 'that she was back in Shrewsbury this minute.'

'So do I, but better here than astray in between. And besides, she won't go.'

'Does she know,' he asked humbly, 'that I am here?'

'She does, and what you're about, too.'

156

'Would she not – could you not persuade her? – to speak to me?'

'That she refuses to do. But she may think the more,' said Sister Magdalen encouragingly. 'If I were you, I'd let her alone to think the while. She knows you're here to fight for us – there's matter for thought there. Now you'd best go to ground soon and keep in cover. Go and sharpen whatever blade they've found for you and keep yourself whole. These flurries never take long,' she said, resigned and tolerant, 'but what comes after lasts a lifetime, yours and hers. You take care of Elis ap Cynan, and I'll take care of Melicent.'

Hugh and his twenty men had skirted the Breidden hills before the hour of Prime, and left those great, hunched outcrops on the right as they drove on towards Westbury. A few remounts they got there, not enough to relieve all the tired beasts. Hugh had held back to a bearable pace for that very reason, and allowed a halt to give men and horses time to breathe. It was the first opportunity there had been even to speak a word, and now that it came no man had much to say. Not until the business on which they rode was tackled and done would tongues move freely again. Even Hugh, lying flat on his back for ease beside Cadfael under the budding trees, did not question him concerning his business in Wales.

'I'll ride with you, if I can finish my business here,' Cadfael had said. Hugh had asked him nothing then, and did not ask him now. Perhaps because his mind was wholly engrossed in what had to be done to drive the Welsh of Powys back into Caus and beyond. Perhaps because he considered this other matter to be very much Cadfael's business, and was willing to wait for enlightenment until it was offered, as at the right time it would be.

Cadfael braced his aching back against the bole of an oak just forming its tight leaf-buds, eased his chafed feet in his boots, and felt his sixty-one years. He felt all the older because all these troubled creatures pulled here and there through this tangle of love and guilt and anguish were so young and vulnerable. All but the victim, Gilbert Prestcote, dead in his helpless weakness – for whom Hugh would, because he must, take vengeance. There could be no clemency, there was no room for it. Hugh's lord had been done to death, and Hugh would exact payment. In iron duty, he had no choice.

'Up!' said Hugh, standing over him, smiling the abstracted but affectionate smile that flashed like a reflection from the surface of his mind when his entire concern was elsewhere. 'Get your eyes open! We're off again.' And he reached a hand to grip Cadfael's wrist and hoist him to his feet, so smoothly and carefully that Cadfael was minded to take offence. He was not so old as all that, nor so stiff! But he forgot his mild grievance when Hugh said: 'A shepherd from Pontesbury brought word. They're up from their night camp and making ready to move.'

Cadfael was wide awake instantly. 'What will you do?'

'Hit the road between them and Shrewsbury and turn them back. Alan will be up and alert, we may meet him along the way.'

'Dare they attempt the town?' wondered Cadfael, astonished.

'Who knows? They're blown up with success, and I'm thought to be far off. And our man says they've avoided Minsterley but brought men round it by night. It seems they may mean a foray into the suburbs, at least, even if they draw off after. Town pickings would please them. But we'll be faster, we'll make for Hanwood or thereabouts and be between.'

Hugh made a gentle joke of hoisting Cadfael into the saddle, but for all that, Cadfael set the pace for the next mile, ruffled at being humoured and considered like an old man. Sixty-one was not old, only perhaps a little past a man's prime. He had, after all, done a great deal of hard riding these last few days, he had a right to be stiff and sore.

They came over a hillock into view of the Shrewsbury road, and beheld, thin and languid in the air above the distant trees beyond, a faint column of smoke rising. 'From their douted fires,' said Hugh, reining in to gaze. 'And I smell older burning than that. Somewhere near the rim of the forest, someone's barns have gone up in flames.'

'More than a day old and the smoke gone,' said Cadfael, sniffing the air. 'Better make straight for them, while we know where they are, for there's no telling which way they'll strike next.'

Hugh led his party down to the road and across it, where they could deploy in the fringes of woodland, going fast but quietly in thick turf. For a while they kept within view of the road, but saw no sign of the Welsh raiders. It began to seem that their present thrust

158

was not aimed at the town after all, or even the suburbs, and Hugh led his force deeper into the woodland, striking straight at the deserted night camp. Beyond that trampled spot there were traces enough for eyes accustomed to reading the bushes and grass. A considerable number of men had passed through here on foot, and not so long ago, with a few ponies among them to leave droppings and brush off budding twigs from the tender branches. The ashen, blackened ruin of a cottage and its clustering sheds showed where their last victim had lost home, living and all, if not his life, and there was blood dried into the soil where a pig had been slaughtered. They spurred fast along the trail the Welsh had left, sure now where they were bound, for the way led deeper into the northern uplands of the Long Forest, and it could not be two miles now to the cell at Godric's Ford.

That ignominious rout at the hands of Sister Magdalen and her rustic army had indeed rankled. The men of Caus were not averse to driving off a few cattle and burning a farm or two by the way, but what they wanted above all, what they had come out to get, was revenge.

Hugh set spurs to his horse and began to thread the open woodland at a gallop, and after him his company spurred in haste. They had gone perhaps a mile more when they heard before them, distant and elusive, a voice raised high and bellowing defiance.

It was almost the hour of High Mass when Alan Herbard got his muster moving out of the castle wards. He was hampered by having no clear lead as to which way the raiders planned to move, and there was small gain in careering aimlessly about the western border hunting for them. For want of knowledge he had to stake on his reasoning. When the company rode out of the town they aimed towards Pontesbury itself, prepared to swerve either northward, to cut across between the raiders and Shrewsbury, or south-west towards Godric's Ford, according as they got word on the way from scouts sent out before daylight. And this first mile they took at speed, until a breathless countryman started out of the bushes to arrest their passage, when they were scarcely past the hamlet of Beistan.

'My lord, they've turned away from the road. From Pontesbury

159

they're making eastward into the forest towards the high commons. They've turned their backs on the town for other game. Bear south at the fork.'

'How many?' demanded Herbard, already wheeling his horse in haste.

'A hundred at least. They're holding all together, no rogue stragglers left loose behind. They expect a fight.'

'They shall have one!' promised Herbard and led his men south down the track, at a gallop wherever the going was fairly open.

Eliud rode among the foremost, and found even that pace too slow. He had in full all the marks of suspicion and shame he had invited, the rope to hang him coiled about his neck for all to see, the archer to shoot him down if he attempted escape close at his back, but also he had a borrowed sword at his hip, a horse under him and was on the move. He fretted and burned, even in the chill of the March morning. Here Elis had at least the advantage of having ridden these paths and penetrated these woodlands once before. Eliud had never been south of Shrewsbury, and though the speed they were making seemed to his anxious heart miserably inadequate, he could gain nothing by breaking away, for he did not know exactly where Godric's Ford lay. The archer who followed him, however good a shot he might be, was no very great horseman, it might be possible to put on speed, make a dash for it and elude him, but what good would it do? Whatever time he saved he would inevitably waste by losing himself in these woods. He had no choice but to let them bring him there, or at least near enough to the place to judge his direction by ear or eye. There would be signs. He strained for any betraying sound as he rode, but there was nothing but the swaying and cracking of brushed branches, and the thudding rumble of their hooves in the deep turf, and now and again the call of a bird, undisturbed by this rough invasion, and startlingly clear.

The distance could not be far now. They were threading rolling uplands of heath, to drop lower again into thick woodland and moist glades. All this way Elis must have run afoot in the night hours, splashing through these hollows of stagnant green and breasting the sudden rises of heather and scrub and outcrop rock.

Herbard checked abruptly in open heath, waving them all to

stillness. 'Listen! Ahead on our right – men on the move.'

They sat straining their ears and holding their breath. Only the softest and most continuous whisper of sounds, compounded of the swishing and brushing of twigs, the rustle of last autumn's leaves under many feet, the snap of a dead stick, the brief and soft exchange of voices, a startled bird rising from underfoot in shrill alarm and indignation. Signs enough of a large body of men moving through woods almost stealthily, without noise or haste.

'Across the brook and very near the ford,' said Herbard sharply. And he shook his bridle, spurred and was away, his men hard on his heels. Before them a narrow ride opened between well-grown trees, a long vista with a glimpse of low timber buildings, weathered dark brown, distant at the end of it, and a sudden lacework of daylight beyond, between the trees, where the channel of the brook crossed.

They were halfway down the ride when the boiling murmur of excited men breaking out of cover eddied up from the invisible waterside, and then, soaring loudly above, a single voice shouting defiance, and even more strangely, an instant's absolute hush after the sound.

The challenge had meant nothing to Herbard. It meant everything to Eliud. For the words were Welsh, and the voice was the voice of Elis, high and imperious, honed sharp by desperation, bidding his fellow-countrymen: 'Stand and turn! For shame on your fathers, to come whetting your teeth on holy women! Go back where you came from and find a fight that does you some credit!' And higher and more peremptorily: 'The first man ashore I spit on this pikel, Welsh or no, he's no kinsman of mine!'

This to a war-band roused and happy and geared for killing!

'Elis!' cried Eliud in a great howl of anger and dismay, and he lay forward over his horse's neck and drove in his heels, shaking the bridle wild. He heard the archer at his back shout an order to halt, heard and felt the quivering thrum of the shaft as it skimmed his right shoulder, tore away a shred of cloth, and buried itself vibrating in the turf beyond. He paid no heed, but plunged madly ahead, down the steep green ride and out on to the bank of the brook.

*   *   *

161

They had come by way of the thicker cover a little downstream, to come at the grange and the ford before they were detected, and leave aimless and out of range any defenders who might be stationed at the mill, where there was a better field for archery. The little footbridge had not yet been repaired, but with a stream so fallen from its winter spate there was no need of a bridge. From stone to stone the water could be leaped in two or three places, but the attackers favoured the ford, because so many could cross there shoulder to shoulder and bring a battering-ram of lances in one sweep to drive along the near bank. The forest bowmen lay in reeds and bushes, dispersed along the brink, but such a spearhead, with men and weight enough behind it, could cleave through and past them and be into the precinct within moments.

They were deceived if they thought the forest men had not detected their approach, but there was no sign of movement as the attackers threaded their way quietly between the trees to mass and sweep across the brook. Perhaps twenty cottars, woodsmen and hewers of laborious assarts from the forests lay in cover against more than a hundred Welsh, and every man of the twenty braced himself, and knew only too well how great a threat he faced. They knew how to keep still until the proper moment to move. But as the lurkers in the trees signalled along their half-seen ranks and closed all together in a sudden surge into the open at the edge of the ford, one man rose out of the bushes opposite and bestrode the grassy shelf of the shore, brandishing a long, two-tined pikel lashed to a six-foot pole, and sweeping the ford with it at breast-height.

That was enough to give them an instant's pause out of sheer surprise. But what stopped them in mid-stride and set them back on their heels was the indignant Welsh trumpet blaring: 'Stand and turn! For shame on your fathers, to come whetting your teeth on holy women!'

He had not done, there was more, rolling off the inspired tongue in dread of a pause, or in such flight as to be unable to pause. 'Cowards of Powys, afraid to come north and meddle with men! They'll sing you in Gwynedd for this noble venture, how you jumped a brook and showed yourselves heroes against women older than your mothers, and a world more honest. Even your drabs of dams will disown you for this. You and your mongrel pedigrees shall be known for ever by the songs we'll make . . .'

They had begun to stir out of their astonishment, to scowl and to grin. And still the hidden bowmen in the bushes held their hands, willing to wait the event, though their shafts were fitted and their bows partly drawn, ready to brace and loose. If by some miracle this peril might dissolve in withdrawal and conciliation, why lose arrows or blunt blades?

'*You*, is it?' shouted a Welshman scornfully. 'Cynan's pup, that we left spewing water and being pumped dry by the nuns. He, to halt us! A lickspit of the English now!'

'A match for you and better!' flashed Elis, and swung the pikel towards the voice. 'And with grace enough to let the sisters here alone, and to be grateful to them, too, for a life they could as well have let go down the stream, for all they owed me. What are you looking for here? What plunder is there, here among the willing poor? And for God's sake and your Welsh fathers' sake, what glory?'

He had done all he could, perhaps provided a few minutes of time, but he could do little more, and it was not enough. He knew it. He even saw the archer in the fringe of the trees opposite fit his shaft without haste, and draw very steadily and deliberately. He saw it out of the corner of his eye, while he continued to confront the lances levelled against him, but there was nothing he could do to deflect or elude, he was forced to stand and hold them as long as he could, shifting neither foot nor eye.

Behind him there was a rush of hooves, stamping deep into the turf, and someone flung himself sobbing out of the saddle in one vaulting bound, and along the shelf of grass above the water, just as the forest bowmen drew and loosed their first shafts, every man for himself, and the archer on the opposite shore completed his easy draw, and loosed full at Elis's breast, Welsh of Powys striking coldly at Welsh of Gwynedd. Eliud vented a scream of anger and defiance, and hurled himself between, embracing Elis breast to breast and covering him with his own body, sending them both reeling a pace backwards into the turf, to crash against a corner of the sisters' garden fence. The pikel with its long handle was jerked out of Elis's hand, and slashed into the stream in a great fan of water. The Welshman's arrow jutted from under Eliud's right shoulder-blade, transfixing his body and piercing through the under-flesh of Elis's upper arm, pinning the two together inseparably. They slid down the fence and lay in the grass locked in each other's arms, and their blood mingled and made one, closer even than fostering.

And then the Welsh were over and ashore, floundering in the pits of the ford, ripped on the stakes among the reeds, trampling the two fallen bodies, and battle was joined along the banks of the brook.

Almost at the same moment, Alan Herbard deployed his men along the eastern bank and waded into the fighting, and Hugh Beringar swept through the trees on the western bank, and drove the Welsh outposts into the churned and muddied ford.

The clang of hammer on anvil, with themselves cracked between, demoralised the Welsh of Powys, and the battle of Godric's Ford did not last long. The din and fury was out of proportion to the damage done, when once they had leisure to assess it. The Welsh were ashore when their enemies struck from both sides, and had to fight viciously and hard to get out of the trap and melt away man by man into cover, like the small forest predators whose kinship with the earth and close understanding of it they shared. Beringar, once he had shattered the rear of the raiders, herded them like sheep but held his hand from unnecessary killing as soon as they fled into cover and made for home. Alan Herbard, younger and less experienced, gritted his teeth and thrust in with all his weight, absolute to make a success of his first command, and perhaps did more execution than was heedful out of pure anxiety.

However it was, within half an hour it was over.

What Brother Cadfael most keenly remembered, out of all that clash, was the apparition of a tall girl surging out of the fenced enclosure of the grange, her black habit kilted in both hands, the wimple torn from her head and her fair hair streaming silvery in sudden sunlight, a long, fighting scream of defiance trailing like a bannerole from her drawn-back lips, as she evaded a greedy Welsh hand grasping at her, and flung herself on her knees beside the trampled, bruised, bleeding bodies of Elis and Eliud, still clamped in each other's arms against the bloodied fence.

FOURTEEN

It was done, they were gone, vanishing very rapidly and quietly, leaving only the rustling of bushes behind them on the near side of the brook, to make for some distant place where they could cross unseen and unpursued. On the further side, where the bulk of their numbers fled, the din of their flight subsided gradually into the depths of the neglected coppices, seeking thicker cover into which they could scatter and be lost. Hugh was in no haste, he let them salvage their wounded and hustle them away with them, several among them who might, indeed, be dead. There would be cuts and grazes and wounds enough among the defenders, by all means let the Welsh tend their own and bury their own. But he deployed his men, and a dozen or so of Herbard's party, like beaters after game, to herd the Welshmen back methodically into their own country. He had no wish to start a determined blood-feud with Madog ap Meredith, provided this lesson was duly learned.

The defenders of the grange came out of hiding, and the nuns out of their chapel, all a little dazed, as much by the sudden hush as by the violence that had gone before. Those who had escaped hurt dropped their bows and forks and axes, and turned to help those who were wounded. And Brother Cadfael turned his back on the muddy ford and the bloodied stakes, and knelt beside Melicent in the grass.

'I was in the bell-turret,' she said in a dry whisper. 'I saw how splendid . . . He for us and his friend for him. They will live, they *must* live, both . . . we can't lose them. Tell me what I must do.'

She had done well already, no tears, no shaking, no outcry after that first scream that had carried her through the ranks of the Welsh like the passage of a lance. She had slid an arm carefully

165

under Elis's shoulders to raise him, and prevent the weight of the two of them from falling on the head of the arrow that had pinned them together. That spared them at least the worst agony and aggravated damage of being impaled. And she had wrapped the linen of her wimple round the shaft beneath Elis's arm to stem the bleeding as best she could.

'The iron is clean through,' she said. 'I can raise them more, if you can reach the shaft.'

Sister Magdalen was at Cadfael's shoulder by then, as sturdy and practical as ever, but having taken a shrewd look at Melicent's intent and resolute face she left the girl the place she had chosen, and went off placidly to salve others. Folly to disturb either Melicent or the two young men she nursed on her arm and her braced knee, when shifting them would only be worse pain. She went, instead, to fetch a small saw and the keenest knife to be found, and linen enough to stem the first bursts of bleeding when the shaft should be withdrawn. It was Melicent who cradled Elis and Eliud as Cadfael felt his way about the head of the shaft, sawed deeply into the wood, and then braced both hands to snap off the head with the least movement. He brought it out, barely dinted from its passage through flesh and bone, and dropped it aside in the grass.

'Lay them down now – so! Let them lie a moment.' The solid slope, cushioned by turf, received the weight gently as Melicent lowered her burden. 'That was well done,' said Cadfael. She had bunched the blood-stained wimple and held it under the wound as she drew aside, freeing a cramped and aching arm. 'Now do you rest, too. The one of these is shorn through the flesh of his arm, and has let blood enough, but his body is sound, and his life safe. The other – no blinking it, his case is grave.'

'I know it,' she said, staring down at the tangled embrace that bound the pair of them fast. 'He made his body a shield,' she said softly, marvelling. 'So much he loved him!'

And so much *she* loved him, Cadfael thought, that she had blazed forth out of shelter in much the same way, shrieking defiance and rage. To the defence of her father's murderer? Or had she long since discarded that belief, no matter how heavily circumstances might tell against him? Or had she simply forgotten everything else, when she heard Elis yelling his solitary challenge? Everything but his invited peril and her anguish for him?

No need for her to have to see and hear the worst moment of all. 'Go fetch my scrip from the saddle yonder,' said Cadfael, 'and bring more cloth, padding and wrapping both, we shall need plenty.'

She was gone long enough for him to lay firm hold on the impaling shaft, rid now of its head, and draw it fast and forcefully out from the wound, with a steadying hand spread against Eliud's back. Even so it fetched a sharp, whining moan of agony, that subsided mercifully as the shaft came free. The spurt of blood that followed soon slowed; the wound was neat, a mere slit, and healthy flesh closes freely over narrow lesions, but there was no certainty what damage had been done within. Cadfael lifted Eliud's body carefully aside, to let both breathe more freely, though the entwined arms relinquished their hold very reluctantly. He enlarged the slit the arrow had made in the boy's clothing, wadded a clean cloth against the wound, and turned him gently on his back. By that time Melicent was back with all that he had asked; a wild, soiled figure with a blanched and resolute face. There was blood drying on her hands and wrists, the skirts of her habit at the knee were stiffening into a hard, dark crust, and her wimple lay on the grass, a stained ball of red. It hardly mattered. She was never going to wear that or any other in earnest.

'Now we'd best get these two indoors, where I can strip and cleanse their injuries properly,' said Cadfael, when he was assured the worst of the bleeding was checked. 'Go and ask Sister Magdalen where we may lay them, while I find some stout men to help me carry them in.'

Sister Magdalen had made provision for more than one cell to be emptied within the grange, and Mother Mariana and the nuns of the house were ready to fetch and carry, heat water and bandage minor injuries with very good will, relieved now of the fear of outrage. They carried Elis and Eliud within and lodged them in neighbouring cells, for the space was too small to allow free movement to Cadfael and those helping him, if both cots were placed together. All the more since John Miller, who had escaped without a scratch from the mêlée, was one of the party. The gentle giant could not only heft sturdy young men as lightly as babies, he also had a deft and reassuring hand with injuries.

Between the two of them they stripped Eliud, slitting the clothes from him to avoid racking him with worse pain, washed and dressed the wounds in back and breast, and laid him in the cot with his right arm padded and cradled to lie still. He had been trampled in the rush of the Welshmen crossing to shore, bruises were blackening on him, but he had no other wound, and it seemed the tramping feet had broken no bones. The arrowhead had emerged well to the right, through his shoulder, to pierce the flesh of Elis's upper arm. Cadfael considered the line the shot had taken, and shook his head doubtfully but not quite hopelessly over the chances of life and death. With this one he would stay, sit with him the evening through – the night if need be – wait the return of sense and wit. There were things they had to say to each other, whether the boy was to live or die.

Elis was another matter. He would live, his arm would heal, his honour would be vindicated, his name cleared, and for all Cadfael could see, there was no reason in the world why he should not get his Melicent. No father to deny him, no overlord at liberty to assert his rights in the girl's marriage, and Lady Prestcote would be no bar at all. And if Melicent had flown to his side before ever the shadow was lifted from him, how much more joyfully would she accept him when he emerged sunlit from head to foot. Happy innocent, with nothing left to trouble him but a painful arm, some weakness from loss of blood, a wrenched knee that gave him pain at an incautious movement, and a broken rib from being trampled. Troubles that might keep him from riding for some time, but small grievances indeed, now he had opened dazed dark eyes on the unexpected vision of a pale, bright face stooped close to his, and heard a remembered voice, once hard and cold as ice, saying very softly and tenderly: 'Elis . . . Hush, lie still! I'm here, I won't leave you.'

It was another hour and more before Eliud opened his eyes, unfocussed and feverish, glittering greenly in the light of the lamp beside his bed, for the cell was very dim. Even then he roused to

168

such distress that Cadfael eased him out of it again with a draught of poppy syrup, and watched the drawn lines of pain gradually smooth out from the thin, intense face, and the large eyelids close again over the distracted gleam. No point in adding further trouble to one so troubled in body and soul. When he revived so far as to draw the garment of his own dignity about him, then his time would come.

Others came in to look down at him for a moment, and as quietly depart. Sister Magdalen came to bring Cadfael food and ale, and stood a while in silence watching the shallow, painful heave and fall of Eliud's breast, and the pinched flutter of his nostrils on whistling breath. All her volunteer army of defenders had dispersed about its own family business, every hurt tended, the stakes uprooted from the ford, the pitted bed raked smooth again, a day's work very well done. If she was tired, she gave no sign of it. Tomorrow there would be a number of the injured to visit again, but there had been few serious hurts, and no deaths. Not yet! Not unless this boy slipped through their fingers.

Hugh came back towards evening, and sought out Cadfael in the silent cell. 'I'm off back to the town now,' he said in Cadfael's ear. 'We've shepherded them more than halfway home, you'll see no more of them here. You'll be staying?'

Cadfael nodded towards the bed.

'Yes – a great pity! I'll leave you a couple of men, send by them for whatever you need. And after this,' said Hugh grimly, 'we'll have them out of Caus. They shall know whether there's still a sheriff in the shire.' He turned to the bedside and stood looking down sombrely at the sleeper. 'I saw what he did. Yes, a pity . . .' Eliud's soiled and dismembered clothing had been removed; he retained nothing but the body in which he had been born into the world, and the means by which he had demanded to be ushered out of it, if Elis proved false to his word. The rope was coiled and hung over the bracket that held the lamp. 'What is this?' asked Hugh, as his eye lit upon it, and as quickly understood. 'Ah! Alan told me. This I'll take away, let him read it for a sign. This will never be needed. When he wakes, tell him so.'

'I pray God!' said Cadfael, so low that not even Hugh heard.

*   *   *

And Melicent came, from the cell where Elis lay sore with trampling, but filled and overfilled with unexpected bliss. She came at his wish, but most willingly, saw Cadfael to all appearances drowsing on his stool against the wall, signed Eliud's oblivious body solemnly with the cross, and stooped suddenly to kiss his furrowed forehead and hollow cheek, before stealing silently away to her own chosen vigil.

Brother Cadfael opened one considerate eye to watch her draw the door to softly after her, and could not take great comfort. But with all his heart he hoped and prayed that God was watching with him.

In the pallid first light before dawn Eliud stirred and quivered, and his eyelids began to flutter stressfully as though he laboured hard to open them and confront the day, but had not yet the strength. Cadfael drew his stool close, leaning to wipe the seamed brow and working lips, and having an eye to the ewer he had ready to hand for when the tormented body needed it. But that was not the unease that quickened Eliud now, rousing out of his night's respite. His eyes opened wide, staring into the wooden roof of the cell and beyond, and shortened their range only when Cadfael leaned down to him braced to speak, seeing desperate intelligence in the hazel stare, and having something ripe within him that must inevitably be said.

He never needed to say it. It was taken out of his mouth.

'I have got my death,' said the thread of a voice that issued from Eliud's dry lips, 'get me a priest. I have sinned – I must deliver all those others who suffer doubt . . .'

Not his own deliverance, not that first, only the deliverance of all who laboured under the same suspicion.

Cadfael stooped closer. The gold-green eyes were straining too far, they had not recognised him. They did so now and lingered, wondering. 'You are the brother who came to Tregeiriog. Welsh?' Something like a sorrowful smile mellowed the desperation of his face. 'I do remember. It was you brought word of him . . . Brother, I have my death in my mouth, whether he take me now of this grief or leave me for worse . . . A debt . . . I pledged it . . .' He essayed, briefly, to raise his right hand, being strongly right-handed, and gave up the attempt with a whining intake of breath at the pain it cost him and shifted, pitiless, to the left, feeling at his neck where the coiled rope should have been. Cadfael laid a hand to the lifted wrist, and eased it back into the covers of the bed.

'Hush, lie still! I am here to command, there's no haste. Rest, take thought, ask of me what you will, bid me whatever you will. I'm here, I shan't leave you.'

He was believed. The slight body under the brychans seemed to sink and slacken in one great sigh. There was a small silence. The hazel eyes hung upon him with a great weight of trust and sorrow, but without fear. Cadfael offered a drop of wine laced with honey, but the braced head turned aside. 'I want confession,' said Eliud faintly but clearly, 'of my mortal sin. Hear me!'

'I am no priest,' said Cadfael. 'Wait, he shall be brought to you.'

'I cannot wait. Do I know my time? If I live,' he said simply, 'I will tell it again and again – as long as there's need – I am done with all conceal.'

They had neither of them observed the door of the cell slowly opening, it was done so softly and shyly, by one troubled with dawn voices, but as hesitant to disturb those who might wish to be private as unwilling to neglect those who might be in need. In her own as yet unreasoned and unquestioned happiness Melicent moved as one led by angelic inspiration, exalted and humbled, requiring to serve. Her bloodied habit was shed, she had a plain woollen gown on her. She hung in the half-open doorway, afraid to advance or withdraw, frozen into stillness and silence because the voice from the bed was so urgent and uncomforted.

'I have killed,' said Eliud clearly. 'God knows I am sorry! I had ridden with him, cared for him, watched him founder and urged his rest . . . And if ever he came home alive, then Elis was free . . . to go back to Cristina, to marry . . .' A great shudder went through him head to foot, and fetched a moan of pain out of him. 'Cristina . . . I loved her always . . . from when we were children, but I did not, I did not speak of it, never, never . . . She was promised to him before ever I knew her, in her cradle. How could I touch, how could I covet what was his?'

'She also loved,' said Cadfael, nursing him along the way. 'She let you know of it . . .'

'I would not hear, I dared not, I had no right . . . And all the while she was so dear, I could not bear it. And when they came back without Elis, and we thought him lost . . . Oh, God, can you conceive such trouble as was mine, half-praying for his safe return, half wishing him dead, for all I loved him, so that at last I might speak out without dishonour, and ask for my love . . . And then— you know it, it was you brought word . . . and I was sent here, my mouth stopped just when it was so full of words . . . And all that way I thought, I could not stop thinking, the old man is so sick, so frail, if he dies there'll be none to exchange for Elis . . . If he dies I can return and Elis must stay . . . Even a little time and I could still speak . . . All I needed was a little time, now I was resolved. And that last day when he foundered . . . I did all I could, I kept him man alive, and all the time, all the time it was clamouring in me, let him die! I did not do it, we brought him still living . . .'

He lay still for a minute to draw breath, and Cadfael wiped the corners of the lips that laboured against exhaustion to heave the worst burden from heart and conscience. 'Rest a little. You try yourself too hard.'

'No, let me end it. Elis . . . I loved him, but I loved Cristina more. And he would have wed her, and been content, but she . . . He did not know the burning we knew. He knows it now. I never willed it . . . it was not planned, what I did. All I did was to remember the lord Einon's cloak and I went, just as I was, to fetch it. I had his saddle-cloth on my arm—' He closed his eyes against what he remembered all too clearly, and tears welled out from under the bruised lids and ran down on either cheek. 'He was so still, hardly breathing at all—so like death. And in an hour Elis would have been on his way home and I left behind in his place. So short a step to go! I did the thing I wish to God I had cut off my hands rather than do, I held the saddle-cloth over his face. There has not been a waking moment since when I have not wished it undone,' whispered Eliud, 'but to undo is not so easy as to do. As soon as I understood my own evil I snatched my hands away, but he was gone. And I was cowardly afraid and left the cloak lying, for if I'd taken it, it would have been known I'd been there. And that was the quiet hour and no one saw me, going or coming.'

Again he waited, gathering strength with a terrible, earnest

172

patience to continue to the end. 'And all for nothing – for nothing! I made myself a murderer for nothing. For Elis came and told me how he loved the lord Gilbert's daughter and willed to be released from his bond with Cristina, as bitterly as she willed it, and I also. And he would go to make himself known to her father . . . I tried to stop him . . . I needed someone to go there and find my dead man, and cry it aloud, but not Elis, oh, not Elis! But he would go. And even then they still thought the lord Gilbert alive, only sleeping. So I had to fetch the cloak, if no one else would cry him dead – but not alone . . . a witness, to make the discovery. I still thought Elis would be held and I should go home. He longed to stay and I to go . . . This knot some devil tied,' sighed Eliud, 'and only I have deserved it. All they three suffer because of me. And you, brother, I did foully by you . . .'

'In choosing me to be your witness?' said Cadfael gently. 'And you had to knock over the stool to make me look closely enough, even then. Your devil still had you by the hand, for if you had chosen another there might never have been the cry of murder that kept you both prisoners.'

'It was my angel, then, no devil. For I am glad to be rid of all lies and known for what I am. I would never have let it fall on Elis – nor on any other man. But I am human and fearful,' he said inflexibly, 'and I hoped to go free. Now that is solved. One way or another, I shall give a life for a life. I would not have let Elis bear it . . . Tell her so!'

There was no need, she already knew. But the head of the cot was towards the door, and Eliud had seen nothing but the rough vault of the cell, and Cadfael's stooping face. The lamp had not wavered, and did not waver now, as Melicent withdrew from the threshold very softly and carefully, drawing the door to by inches after her.

'They have taken away my halter,' said Eliud, his eyes wandering languidly over the bare little room. 'They'll have to find me another one now.'

When it was all told he lay drained, very weak and utterly biddable, eased of hope and grateful for contrition. He let himself be handled for healing, though with a drear smile that said Cadfael wasted his pains on a dead man. He did his best to help the handling, and bore pain without a murmur when his wounds were probed and cleansed and dressed afresh. He tried to swallow the draughts that were held to his lips, and offered thanks for even the smallest service. When he drifted into an uneasy sleep, Cadfael went to find the two men Hugh had left to run his errands, and sent one of them riding to Shrewsbury with the news that would bring Hugh back again in haste. When he returned into the precinct, Melicent was waiting for him in the doorway. She read in his face the mixture of dismay and resignation he felt at having to tell over again what had been ordeal enough to listen to in the first place, and offered instant and firm reassurance.

'I know. I heard. I heard you talking, and his voice . . . I thought you might need someone to fetch and carry for you, so I came to ask. I heard what Eliud said. What is to be done now?' For all her calm, she was bewildered and lost between father killed and lover saved, and the knowledge of the fierce affection those two foster-brothers had for each other, and every way was damage and every escape was barred. 'I have told Elis,' she said. 'Better we should all know what we are about. God knows I am so confused now, I doubt if I know right from wrong. Will you come to Elis? He's fretting for Eliud.'

Cadfael went with her in perplexity as great as hers. Murder is murder, but if a life can pay the debt for a life, there was Elis to level the account. Was yet another life demanded? Another death justifiable? He sat down with her beside the bed, confronted by an Elis wide awake and in full possession of his senses, for all he hesitated on the near edge of fever.

'Melicent has told me,' said Elis, clutching agitatedly at Cadfael's sleeve. '*But is it true?* You don't know him as I do! Are you sure he is not making up this story, because he fears I may yet be charged? May he not even believe I did it? It would be like him to shoulder all to cover me. So he has done in old times when we were children, so he might even now. You saw, you saw what he has already done for me! Should I be here alive now but for Eliud? I can't believe so easily . . .'

Cadfael went about hushing him the most practical way, by examining the dressing on his arm and finding it dry, unstained

174

and causing him no pain, let well alone for the time being. The tight binding round his damaged rib had caused him some discomfort and shortness of breath, and might be slightly slackened to ease him. And whatever dose was offered him he swallowed almost absently, his eyes never shifting from Cadfael's face, demanding answers to desperate questions. And there would be small comfort for him in the naked truth.

'Son,' said Cadfael, 'there's no virtue in fending off truth. The tale Eliud has told fits in every particular and it is truth. Sorry I am to say it, but true it is. Put all doubts out of your head.'

They received that with the same white calm and made no further protest. After a long silence Melicent said: 'I think you knew it before.'

'I did know it, from the moment I set eyes on Einon ab Ithel's brocaded saddle-cloth. That, and nothing else, could have killed Gilbert, and it was Eliud whose duty it was to care for Einon's horse and harness. Yes, I knew. But he made his confession willingly, eagerly, before I could question or accuse him. That must count to him for virtue, and speak on his side.'

'God knows,' said Melicent, shutting her pale face hard between her hands, as if to hold her wits together, 'on what side I dare speak, who am so torn. All I know is that Eliud cannot, does not carry all the guilt. In this matter, which of us is innocent?'

'*You* are!' said Elis fiercely. 'How did you fail? But if I had taken a little thought to see how things were with him and with Cristina . . . I was too easy, too light, too much in love with myself to take heed. I'd never dreamed of such a love, I didn't know . . . I had all to learn.' It had been no easy lesson for him, but he had it by heart now.

'If only I had had more faith in myself and my father,' said Melicent, 'we could have sent word honestly into Wales, to Owain Gwynedd and to my father, that we two loved and entreated leave to marry . . .'

'If only I had been as quick to see what ailed Eliud as he always was to put trouble away from me . . .'

'If none of us ever fell short, or put a foot astray,' said Cadfael sadly, 'everything would be good in this great world, but we stumble and fall, every one. We must deal with what we have. He did it, and all we must share the gall.'

Out of a drear hush Elis asked: 'What will become of him? Will there be mercy? Surely he need not die?'

'It rests with the law, and with the law I have no weight.'

'Melicent relented to me,' said Elis, 'before ever she knew I was clean of her father's blood . . .'

'Ah, but I did know!' she said quickly. 'I was sick in mind that ever I doubted.'

'And I love her the more for it. And Eliud has made confession when no man was accusing, and that must count for virtue to him, as you said, and speak on his side.'

'That and all else that speaks for him,' promised Cadfael fervently, 'shall be urged in his defence. I will see to that.'

'But you are not hopeful,' said Elis bleakly, watching his face with eyes all too sharp.

He would have liked to deny it, but to what end, when Eliud himself had accepted and embraced, with resignation and humility, the inevitable death? Cadfael made what comfort he could, short of lying, and left them together. The last glimpse, as he closed the door, was of two braced, wary faces following his going with a steady, veiled stare, their minds shuttered and secret. Only the fierce alliance of hand clasping hand on the brychan betrayed them.

Hugh Beringar came next day in a hurry, listened in dour silence as Eliud laboured with desolate patience through the story yet again, as he had already done for the old priest who said Mass for the sisters. As Eliud's soul faced humbly toward withdrawal from the world, Cadfael noted his misused body began to heal and find ease, very slowly, but past any doubt. His mind consented to dying, his body resolved to live. The wounds were clean, his excellent youth and health fought hard, whether for or against him who could say?

'Well, I am listening,' said Hugh somewhat wearily, pacing the bank of the brook with Cadfael at his side. 'Say what you have to say.' But Cadfael had never seen his face grimmer.

'He made full and free confession,' said Cadfael, 'before ever a finger was pointed at him, as soon as he felt he might die. He was in desperate haste to do justice to all, not merely Elis, who might lie under the shadow of suspicion because of him. You know me, I know you. I have said honestly, I was about to tell him that I knew he had killed. I swear to you he took that word clean out of my mouth. He wanted confession, penance, absolution. Most of all he wanted to lift the threat from Elis and any other who might be overcast.'

'I take your word absolutely,' said Hugh, 'and it is something. But enough? This was no hot-blood squall blown up in a moment before he could think, it was an old man, wounded and sick, sleeping in his bed.'

'It was not planned. He went to reclaim his lord's cloak. That I am sure is true. But if you think the blood was cold, dear God, how wrong you are! The boy was half-mad with the long bleeding of hopeless love, and had just come to the point of rebellion, and the thread of a life – one he had been nursing in duty! – cut him off from the respite his sudden courage needed. God forgive him, he had hoped Gilbert would die! He has said so honestly. Chance showed him a thread so thin it could be severed by a breath, and before ever he took thought, he blew! He says he has repented of it every moment that has passed since that moment, and I believe it. Did you never, Hugh, do one unworthy thing on impulse, that grieved and shamed you ever after?'

'Not to the length of killing an old man in his bed,' said Hugh mercilessly.

'No! Nor nothing to match it,' said Cadfael with a deep sigh and briefer smile. 'Pardon me, Hugh! I am Welsh and you are English. We Welsh recognise degrees. Theft, theft absolute, without excuse, is our most mortal offence, and therefore we hedge it about with degrees, things which are not theft absolute – taking openly by force, taking in ignorance, taking without leave, providing the offender owns to it, and taking to stay alive, where a beggar has starved three days – no man hangs in Wales for these. Even in dying, even in killing, we acknowledge degrees. We make a distinction between homicide and murder, and even the worst may sometimes be compounded for a lesser price than hanging.'

'So might I make distinctions,' said Hugh, brooding over the placid ford. 'But this was my lord, into whose boots I step, for want of my king to give orders. He was no close friend of mine, but he was fair to me always, he had an ear to listen, if I was none too happy with some of his more austere judgments. He was an honourable man and did his duty by this shire of mine as he best knew, and his death fetters me.'

Cadfael was silent and respectful. It was a discipline removed now from his, but once there had been such a tie, such a fealty, and he remembered it, and they were none so far apart.

'God forbid,' said Hugh, 'that I should hurl out of the world any but such as are too vile to be let live in it. And this is no such monster. One mortal error, one single vileness, and a creature barely – what's his age? Twenty-one? And driven hard, but which of us is not? He shall have his trial and I shall do what I must,' said Hugh hardly. 'But I would to God it was taken out of my hands!'

FIFTEEN

Before he left that evening he made his will clear for the others. 'Owain may be pressed, if Chester moves again, he wants his men. I have sent to say that all who are clear now shall leave here the day after tomorrow. I have six good men-at-arms belonging to him in Shrewsbury. They are free, and I shall equip them for their journey home. The day after tomorrow as early as may be, around dawn, they will be here to take Elis ap Cynan with them, back to Tregeiriog.'

'Impossible,' said Cadfael flatly. 'He cannot yet ride. He has a twisted knee and a cracked rib, besides the arm wound, though that progresses well. He will not ride in comfort for three or four weeks. He will not ride hard or into combat for longer.'

'He need not,' said Hugh shortly. 'You forget we have horses borrowed from Tudur ap Rhys, rested and ready for work now, and Elis can as well ride in a litter as could Gilbert in far worse condition. I want all the men of Gwynedd safely out of here before I move against Powys, as I mean to. Let's have one trouble finished and put by before we face another.'

So that was settled and no appeal. Cadfael had expected the order to be received with consternation by Elis, both on Eliud's account and his own, but after a brief outcry of dismay, suddenly checked, there was a longer pause for thought, while Elis put the matter of his own departure aside, not without a .hard, considering look, and turned only to confirm that there was no chance of Eliud escaping trial for murder and very little of any sentence but death being passed upon him. It was a hard thing to accept, but in the end it seemed Elis had no choice but to accept it. A strange, embattled calm had taken possession of the lovers, they had a way of looking at each other as though they shared thoughts that needed no words to be communicated, but were exchanged in a silent code no one else could read. Unless, perhaps, Sister Magdalen understood the language. She herself went about in thoughtful silence and with a shrewd eye upon them both.

'So I am to be fetched away early, the day after tomorrow,' said Elis. He cast one brief glance at Melicent and she at him. 'Well, I can and will send in proper form from Gwynedd, it's as well the thing should be done openly and honestly when I pay my suit to Melicent. And there will be things to set right at Tregeiriog before I shall be free.' He did not speak of Cristina, but the thought of her was there, desolate and oppressive in the room with them. To win her battle, only to see the victory turn to ash and drift through her fingers. 'I'm a sound sleeper,' said Elis with a sombre smile, 'they may have to roll me in my blankets and carry me out snoring, if they come too early.' And he ended with abrupt gravity: 'Will you ask Hugh Beringar if I may have my bed moved into the cell with Eliud these last two nights? It is not a great thing to ask of him.'

'I will,' said Cadfael, after a brief pause to get the drift of that, for it made sense more ways than one. And he went at once to proffer the request. Hugh was already preparing to mount and ride back to the town, and Sister Magdalen was in the yard to see him go. No doubt she had been deploying for him, in her own way, all the arguments for mercy which Cadfael had already used, and perhaps others of which he had not thought. Doubtful if there would be any harvest even from her well-planted seed, but if you never sow you will certainly never reap.

'Let them be together by all means,' said Hugh, shrugging morosely, 'if it can give them any comfort. As soon as the other one is fit to be moved I'll take him off your hands, but until then let him rest. Who knows, that Welsh arrow may yet do the solving for us, if God's kind to him.'

Sister Magdalen stood looking after him until the last of the escort had vanished up the forested ride.

'At least,' she said then, 'it gives him no pleasure. A pity to proceed where nobody's the gainer and every man suffers.'

180

'A great pity! He said himself,' reported Cadfael, equally thoughtfully, 'he wished to God it could be taken out of his hands.' And he looked along his shoulder at Sister Magdalen, and found her looking just as guilelessly at him. He suffered a small, astonished illusion that they were even beginning to resemble each other, and to exchange glances in silence as eloquently as did Elis and Melicent.

'Did he so?' said Sister Magdalen in innocent sympathy. 'That might be worth praying for. I'll have a word said in chapel at every office tomorrow. If you ask for nothing, you deserve nothing.'

They went in together, and so strong was this sense of an agreed understanding between them, though one that had better not be acknowledged in words, that he went so far as to ask her advice on a point which was troubling him. In the turmoil of the fighting and the stress of tending the wounded he had had no chance to deliver the message with which Cristina had entrusted him, and after Eliud's confession he was divided in mind as to whether it would be a kindness to do so now, or the most cruel blow he could strike.

'This girl of his in Tregeiriog—the one for whom he was driving himself mad—she charged me with a message to him and I promised her he should be told. But now, with this hanging over him . . . Is it well to give him everything to live for, when there may be no life for him? Should we make the world, if he's to leave it, a thousand times more desirable? What sort of kindness would that be?'

He told her, word for word, what the message was. She pondered, but not long.

'Small choice if you promised the girl. And truth should never be feared as harm. But besides—from all I see, he is willing himself to die, though his body is determined on life, and without every spur he may win the fight over his body, turn his face to the wall, and slip away. As well, perhaps, if the only other way is the gallows. But if—I say *if*!—the times relent and let him live, then pity not to give him every armour and every weapon to survive to hear the good news.' She turned her head and looked at him again with the deep, calculating glance he had observed before, and then she smiled. 'It is worth a wager,' she said.

'I begin to think so, too,' said Cadfael and went in to see the wager laid.

They had not yet moved Elis and his cot into the neighbouring cell; Eliud still lay alone. Sometimes, marking the path the arrow had taken clean through his right shoulder, but a little low, Cadfael doubted if he would ever draw bow again, even if at some future time he could handle a sword. That was the least of his threatened harms now. Let him be offered as counter-balance the greatest promised good.

Cadfael sat down beside the bed, and told how Elis had asked leave to join him and been granted what he asked. That brought a strange, forlorn brightness to Eliud's thin, vulnerable face. Cadfael refrained from saying a word about Elis's imminent departure, however, and wondered briefly why he kept silent on that matter, only to realise hurriedly that it was better not even to wonder, much less question. Innocence is an infinitely fragile thing and thought can sometimes injure, even destroy it.

'And there is also a word I promised to bring you and have had no quiet occasion until now. From Cristina when I left Tregeiriog.' Her name caused all the lines of Eliud's face to contract into a tight, wary pallor, and his eyes to dilate in sudden bright green like stormy sunlight through June leaves. 'Cristina sends to tell you, by me, that she has spoken with her father and with yours and soon, by consent, she will be her own woman to give herself where she will. And she will give herself to none but you.'

An abrupt and blinding flood drowned the green and sent the sunlight sparkling in sudden fountains, and Eliud's good left hand groped lamely after anything human he might hold by for comfort, closed hungrily on the hand Cadfael offered, and drew it down against his quivering face, and lower into the bed, against his frantically beating heart. Cadfael let him alone thus for some moments, until the storm passed. When the boy was still again, he withdrew his hand gently.

'But she does not know,' whispered Eliud wretchedly, 'what I am . . . what I have done . . .'

182

'What she knows of you is all she needs to know, that she loves you as you love her, and there is not nor ever could be any other. I do not believe that guilt or innocence, good or evil can change Cristina towards you. Child, by the common expectation of man you have some thirty years at least of your life to live, which is room for marriage, children, fame, atonement, sainthood. What is done matters, but what is yet to do matters far more. Cristina has that truth in her. When she does know all, she will be grieved, but she will not be changed.'

'My expectation,' said Eliud faintly through the covers that hid his ravaged face, 'is in weeks, months at most, not thirty years.'

'It is God fixes the term,' said Cadfael, 'not men, not kings, not judges. A man must be prepared to face life, as well as death, there's no escape from either. Who knows the length of the penance, or the magnitude of the reparation, that may be required of you?'

He rose from his place then, because John Miller and a couple of other neighbours, nursing the small scars of the late battle, carried in Elis, cot and all, from the next cell and set him down beside Eliud's couch. It was a good time to break off, the boy had the spark of the future already alive in him, however strongly resignation prompted him to quench it, and now this reunion with the other half of his being came very aptly. Cadfael stood by to see them settled and watch John Miller strip down the covers from Eliud and lift and replace him bodily, as lightly as an infant and as deftly as if handled by a mother. John had been closeted with Elis and Melicent, and was grown fond of Elis as of a bold and promising small boy from among his kin. A useful man, with his huge and balanced strength, able to pick up a sick man from his sleep – provided he cared enough for the man! – and carry him hence without disturbing his rest. And devoted to Sister Magdalen, whose writ ran here firm as any king's.

Yes, a useful ally.

Well . . .

The next day passed in a kind of deliberate hush, as if every man and every woman walked delicately, with bated breath, and kept the ritual of the house with particular awe and reverence.

warding off all mischance. Never had the horarium of the order been more scrupulously observed at Godric's Ford. Mother Mariana, small, wizened and old, presided over a sisterhood of such model devotion as to disarm fate. And her enforced guests in their twin cots in one cell were quiet and private together, and even Melicent, now a lay guest of the house and no postulant, went about the business of the day with a pure, still face, and left the two young men to their own measures.

Brother Cadfael observed the offices, made some fervent prayers of his own, and went out to help Sister Magdalen tend the few injuries still in need of supervision among the neighbours.

'You're worn out,' said Sister Magdalen solicitously, when they returned for a late bite of supper and Compline. 'Tomorrow you should sleep until Prime, you've had no real rest for three nights now. Say your farewell to Elis tonight, for they'll be here at first light in the morning. And now I think of it,' she said, 'I could do with another flask of that syrup you brew from poppies, for I've emptied my bottle, and I have one patient to see tomorrow who gets little sleep from pain. Will you refill the flask if I bring it?'

'Willingly,' said Cadfael, and went to fetch the jar he had had sent from Brother Oswin in Shrewsbury after the battle. She brought a large green glass flask, and he filled it to the brim without comment.

Nor did he rise early in the morning, though he was awake in good time; he was as good at interpreting a nudge in the ribs as the next man. He heard the horsemen when they came, and the voice of the portress and other voices, Welsh and English both, and among them, surely, the voice of John Miller. But he did not rise and go out to speed them on their way.

When he came forth for Prime, the travellers, he reckoned, must be two hours gone on their way into Wales, armed with Hugh's safe-conduct to cover the near end of the journey, well mounted and provided. The portress had conducted them to the cell where their charge, Elis ap Cynan, would be found in the nearer bed, and John Miller had carried him out in his arms, warmly swathed, and bestowed him in the litter sent to bear him home. Mother Mariana herself had risen to witness and bless their going.

After Prime Cadfael went to tend his remaining patient. As well to continue just as in the previous days. Two clear hours should be ample start, and someone had to be the first to go in—no, not the first, for certainly Melicent was there before him, but the first of the others, the potential enemy, the uninitiated.

He opened the door of the cell, and halted just within the threshold. In the dim light two roused, pale faces confronted him, almost cheek to cheek. Melicent sat on the edge of the bed, supporting the occupant in her arm, for he had raised himself to sit upright, with a cloak draped round his naked shoulders, to meet this moment erect. The bandage swathing his cracked rib heaved to a quickened and apprehensive heartbeat, and the eyes that fixed steadily upon Cadfael were not greenish hazel, but almost as dark as the tangle of black curls.

'Will you let the lord Beringar know,' said Elis ap Cynan, 'that I have sent away my foster-brother out of his hands, and am here to answer for all that may be held against him. He put his neck in a noose for me, so do I now for him. Whatever the law wills can be done to me in his place.'

It was said. He drew a deep breath, and winced at the stab it cost him, but the sharp expectancy of his face eased and warmed now the first step was taken, and there was no more need of any concealment.

'I am sorry I had to deceive Mother Mariana,' he said. 'Say I entreat her forgiveness, but there was no other way in fairness to all here. I would not have any other blamed for what I have done.' And he added with sudden impulsive simplicity: 'I'm glad it was you who came. Send to the town quickly, I shall be glad to have this over. And Eliud will be safe now.'

'I'll do your errand,' said Cadfael gravely, 'both your errands. And ask no questions.' Not even whether Eliud had been in the plot, for he already knew the answer. From all those who had found it necessary to turn a blind eye and a deaf ear, Eliud stood apart in his despairing innocence and lamentable guilt. Someone among those bearers of his on the road to Wales might have a frantically distressed invalid on his hands when the long, deep sleep drew to a close. But at the end of the enforced flight, whatever measures Owain Gwynedd took in the matter, there was Cristina waiting.

'I have provided as well as I could,' said Elis earnestly. 'They'll send word ahead, she'll come to meet him. It will be a hard enough furrow, but it will be life.'

A deal of growing up seemed to have been done since Elis ap Cynan first came raiding to Godric's Ford. This was not the boy who had avenged his nervous fears in captivity by tossing Welsh insults at his captors with an innocent face, nor the girl who had cherished dreamy notions of taking the veil before ever she knew what marriage or vocation meant.

'The affair seems to have been well managed,' said Cadfael judicially. 'Very well, I'll go and make it known – here and in Shrewsbury.'

He had the door half-closed behind him when Elis called: 'And then will you come and help me do on my clothes? I would like to meet Hugh Beringar decent and on my feet.'

And that was what he did, when Hugh came in the afternoon, grim-faced and black-browed, to probe the loss of his felon. In Mother Mariana's tiny parlour, dark-timbered and bare, Elis and Melicent stood side by side to face him. Cadfael had got the boy into his hose and shirt and coat, and Melicent had combed out the tangles from his hair, since he could not do it himself without pain. Sister Magdalen, after one measuring glance as he took his first unsteady steps, had provided him a staff to reinforce his treacherous knee, which would not go fairly under him as yet, but threatened to double all ways to let him fall. When he was ready he looked very young, neat and solemn, and understandably afraid. He stood twisted a little sideways, favouring the knitting rib that shortened his breath. Melicent kept a hand ready, close to his arm, but held off from touching.

'I have sent Eliud back to Wales in my place,' said Elis, stiff as much with apprehension as with resolve, 'since I owe him a life. But here am I, at your will and disposal, to do with as you see fit. Whatever you hold due to him, visit upon me.'

'For God's sake sit down,' said Hugh shortly and disconcertingly. 'I object to being made the target of your self-inflicted suffering. If you're offering me your neck, that's enough, I have no need of your present pains. Sit and take ease. I am not interested in heroes.'

Elis flushed, winced and sat obediently, but he did not take his eyes from Hugh's grim countenance.

'Who helped you?' demanded Hugh with chilling quietness.

'No one. I alone made this plan. Owain's men did as they were ordered by me.' That could be said boldly, they were well away in their own country.

'*We* made the plan,' said Melicent firmly.

Hugh ignored her, or seemed to. 'Who helped you?' he repeated forcibly.

'No one. Melicent knew, but she took no part. The sole blame is mine. Deal with me!'

'So alone you moved your cousin into the other bed. That was marvel enough, for a man crippled himself and unable to walk, let alone lift another man's weight. And as I hear, a certain miller of these parts carried Eliud ap Griffith to the litter.'

'It was dark within, and barely light without,' said Elis steadily, 'and I . . .'

'*We*,' said Melicent.

'. . . I had already wrapped Eliud well, there was little of him to see. John did nothing but lend his strong arms in kindness to me.'

'Was Eliud party to this exchange?'

'*No!*' they said together, loudly and fiercely.

'No!' repeated Elis, his voice shaking with the fervour of his denial. 'He knew nothing. I gave him in his last drink a great draught of the poppy syrup that Brother Cadfael used on us to dull the pain, that first day. It brings on deep sleep. Eliud slept through all. He never knew! He never would have consented.'

'And how did you, bed-held as you were, come by that syrup?'

'*I* stole the flask from Sister Magdalen,' said Melicent. 'Ask her! She will tell you what a great dose has been taken from it.' So she would, with all gravity and concern. Hugh never doubted it, nor did he mean to put her to the necessity of answering. Nor Cadfael either. Both had considerately absented themselves from this trial, judge and culprits held the whole matter in their hands.

There was a brief, heavy silence that weighed distressfully on Elis, while Hugh eyed the pair of them from under knitted brows, and fastened at last with frowning attention upon Melicent.

'You of all people,' he said, 'had the greatest right to require payment from Eliud. Have you so soon forgiven him? Then who else dare gainsay?'

'I am not even sure,' said Melicent slowly, 'that I know what forgiveness is. Only it seems a sad waste that all a man's good should not be able to outweigh one evil, however great. That is the world's loss. And I wanted no more deaths. One was grief enough, the second would not heal it.'

Another silence, longer than the first. Elis burned and shivered, wanting to hear his penalty, whatever it might be, and know the best and the worst. He quaked when Hugh rose abruptly from his seat.

'Elis ap Cynan, I have no charge to make in law against you. I want no exaction from you. You had best rest here a while yet. Your horse is still in the abbey stables. When you are fit to ride, you may follow your foster-brother home.' And before they had breath to speak, he was out of the room, and the door closing after him.

Brother Cadfael walked a short way beside his friend when Hugh rode back to Shrewsbury in the early evening. The last days had been mild, and in the long green ride the branches of the trees wore the first green veil of the spring budding. The singing of the birds, likewise, had begun to throb with the yearly excitement and unrest before mating and nesting and rearing the young. A time for all manner of births and beginnings, and for putting death out of mind.

'What else could I have done?' said Hugh. 'This one has done no murder, never owed me that very comely neck he insists on offering me. And if I had hanged him I should have been hanging both, for God alone knows how even so resolute a girl as Melicent—or the one you spoke of in Tregeiriog for that matter— is ever going to part the two halves of that pair. Two lives for one is no fair bargain.' He looked down from the saddle of the raw-boned grey which was his favourite mount, and smiled at

188

Cadfael, and it was the first time for some days that he had been seen to smile utterly without irony or reserve. 'How much did you know?'

'Nothing,' said Cadfael simply. 'I guessed at much, but I can fairly say I knew nothing and never lifted finger.' In silence and deafness and blindness he had connived, but no need to say that, Hugh would know it, Hugh, who could not have connived. Nor was there any need for Hugh ever to say with what secret gratitude he relinquished the judgement he would never have laid down of his own will.

'What will become of them all?' Hugh wondered. 'Elis will go home as soon as he's well enough, I suppose, and send formally to ask for his girl. There's no man of her kin to ask but her own mother's brother, and he's far off with the queen in Kent and out of reach. I fancy Sister Magdalen will advise the girl to go back to her step-mother for the waiting time, and have all done in proper form, and she has sense enough to listen to advice, and the patience to wait for what she wants, now she's assured of getting it in the end. But what of the other pair?'

Eliud and his companions would be well into Wales by this time and need not hurry, to tire the invalid too much. The draught of forgetfulness they had given him might dull his senses for a while even when he awoke, and his fellows would do their best to ease his remorse and grief, and his fear for Elis. But that troubled and passionate spirit would never be quite at rest.

'What will Owain do with him?'

'Neither destroy nor waste him,' said Cadfael, 'provided you cede your rights in him. He'll live, he'll marry his Cristina – there'll be no peace for prince or priest or parent until she gets her way. As for his penance, he has it within him, he'll carry it lifelong. There is nothing but death itself you or any man could lay upon him that he will not lay upon himself. But God willing, he will not have to carry it alone. There is no crime and no failure can drive Cristina from him.'

They parted at the head of the ride. It was premature dusk under the trees, but still the birds sang with the extreme and violent joy that seemed loud enough to shake such fragile instruments into dust or burst the hearts in their breasts. There were windflowers quivering in the grass.

'I go lighter than I came,' said Hugh, reining in for a moment before he took the homeward road.

'As soon as I see that lad walking upright and breathing deep, I shall follow. And glad to be going home.' Cadfael looked back at the low timber roofs of Mother Mariana's grange, where the silvery light through gossamer branches reflected the ceaseless quivering of the brook. 'I hope we have made, between us all, the best of a great ill, and who could do more? Once, I remember, Father Abbot said that our purpose is justice, and with God lies the privilege of mercy. But even God, when he intends mercy, needs tools to his hand '

All Futura Books are available at your bookshop or newsagent, or can be ordered from the following address:
Futura Books, Cash Sales Department.
P.O. Box 11, Falmouth, Cornwall.

Please send cheque or postal order (no currency), and allow 55p for postage and packing for the first book plus 22p for the second book and 14p for each additional book ordered up to a maximum charge of £1.75 in U.K.

Customers in Eire and B.F.P.O. please allow 55p for the first book, 22p for the second book plus 14p per copy for the next 7 books, thereafter 8p per book.

Overseas customers please allow £1 for postage and packing for the first book and 25p per copy for each additional book.